A HATE LIKE THIS

WHITNEY DINEEN

MELANIE SUMMERS

For all those brave souls working in the service industry these last couple of years,
We hope you know how much joy you bring, in helping make the world feel slightly more normal for the rest of us.
XO Whitney and Melanie

Books by Whitney Dineen
and Melanie Summers

The Accidentally in Love Series

Text Me on Tuesday
The Text God
Text Wars
Text in Show
Mistle Text
Text and Confused

A Gamble on Love Mom-Com Series

No Ordinary Hate
A Hate Like This
Hate, Rinse, Repeat (Coming soon)

Also by Whitney Dineen

Romantic Comedies

The Mimi Chronicles

The Reinvention of Mimi Finnegan

Mimi Plus Two

Kindred Spirits

Relatively Series

Relatively Normal

Relatively Sane

Relatively Happy

Creek Water Series

The Event

The Move

The Plan

The Dream

Seven Brides for Seven Mothers Series

Love is a Battlefield

Ain't She Sweet

It's My Party

You're So Vain

Head Over Feet

Queen of Hearts (Coming Soon)

She Sins at Midnight

Going Up?

Love for Sale

Conspiracy Thriller

See No More

Non-Fiction Humor

Motherhood, Martyrdom & Costco Runs

Middle Reader

Wilhelmina and the Willamette Wig Factory

Who the Heck is Harvey Stingle?

Children's Books

The Friendship Bench

Also by Melanie Summers

ROMANTIC COMEDIES

The Crown Jewels Series

The Royal Treatment

The Royal Wedding

The Royal Delivery

Paradise Bay Series

The Honeymooner

Whisked Away

The Suite Life

Resting Beach Face

Pride and Piña Coladas (Coming Soon)

Crazy Royal Love Series

Royally Crushed

Royally Wild

Royally Tied

Stand-Alone Books

Even Better Than the Real Thing

WOMEN'S FICTION

The After Wife

Chapter 1

Moira

My mornings are complete chaos. Actually, my whole life is a bit of a circus. Being a single mom of three boys has me scrambling around like a house elf on crack. You'd think it would be easier now that the kids are old enough to do things for themselves. And it would be, except for my compulsory need to prove that I can be mom, dad, and sole provider—all with a carefree smile on my face. A smile that probably looks like I'm fighting—and losing—a battle against constipation.

Brushing back my overgrown dark bangs, I sigh while mentally trying to schedule some time for a big, fat cry. Can I make it 'til Thursday?

My husband, Everett, died seven years ago while I was pregnant with our twins, Colton and Ash. His crabbing boat was hit by a freak storm. Normally, a storm wouldn't have been a problem, but Everett's penchant for deferring maintenance on his boat was the deal breaker. The motor conked out before he could make it to shore.

According to his crew, Bob and Fareek, after dropping anchor to ride out the squall, my husband was washed overboard by a monster wave. My guess is there was some drinking going on.

While very much in love when we got married, Everett and I were not in the best place when he died. We'd just bought a house in need of major repairs, we had a toddler who refused to sleep and was into everything, and I was pregnant with twins. Life had started to feel like we were competitors in the Hunger Games instead of husband and wife.

Grabbing ahold of a scorching hot, cast-iron skillet, I yell, "Son of a …"

My oldest, Wyatt, walks through the door and completes my sentence for me. "Bitch!"

"Butterfly," I correct him sharply, rushing to the sink to cool off burn number three this week. Note to self: hot pads are your friend.

"Yeah, son of a butterfly," he laughs. "Good one, Mom." He pulls out a creaky wooden chair from the table before plopping down and filling his plate with pancakes. "You know, we could just come with you and eat at the diner. You don't have to make us breakfast at home."

"You eat too many meals there, especially in the summer." After the twins were weaned, and I'd made peace with my new lot in life, my brother, Digger, and our Grandpa Jack gave me the money I needed for the down payment on the only diner in Gamble, Alaska.

With the help of my grandmother's extensive recipe collection, and Lloyd, my amazing and reliable cook, I've built a business that will allow me to raise my kids in relative comfort. Meaning I keep a roof over their heads, food in their stomachs, and shoes on their feet. There are precious few extras as Everett and I didn't have any life insurance. No one ever thinks they'll die young.

"Moooooooooom, Colton stole my Spider-Man T-shirt and won't give it back!" The twins come tearing into the kitchen like their britches are on fire.

"Sit down and eat your breakfast," I tell them. "Colton, you wore yours yesterday which means you'll have to wait until wash day. You can't just take your brother's."

"But he's wearing my Hulk Underoos!" Colton whines.

I purse my lips at the absurdity of this conversation. "Really?"

Shrugging, he says, "Yeah, but it's not like anyone will see them."

What difference does that make? Nope. Not asking. I do not have time for kid logic right now. "If you're wearing his Underoos, he can wear your shirt. But after today, you both wear your own clothes. And I mean it. Now, eat up. Mrs. Turner will be over in a minute to keep you from killing each other."

"Geesh, Mom, we don't need a babysitter anymore. You treat us like little kids," Ash complains.

"I treat you like three boys who nearly burned down the shed last month." I shoot him my fiercest "mom" glare.

"How did I know there were leftover firecrackers in that box?" Colton demands. Then he turns to his twin and nudges his arm. "That was the coolest, wasn't it?" Ash nods his head vigorously.

"You're only seven," I tell them.

"Wyatt's ten," Ash reminds me.

"Wyatt's the one who thought it was a good idea to catch field mice and raise them in his room without a cage." I didn't find out about it until there were mouse droppings all over the house. It took months and a very expensive exterminator to finally get rid of their extensive progeny.

"You're gonna have to trust us some time," Wyatt says while shoveling an enormous forkful of pancakes into his mouth.

"Hopefully, by the time you're eighteen I'll be able to leave you alone." I'm only semi-teasing.

I untie my apron and grab my purse before reminding them, "We're having supper with Uncle Digger, Harper and the kids tonight. I'll meet you up at the lodge after closing." Or, you know, after I go home and have a hot bath and a glass of wine in an empty house.

The house erupts into boy cheers as the front door slams behind me. I say a quick prayer that they don't do any real damage until our neighbor arrives. Edna Turner has been a lifesaver. When Everett died, she practically moved in with me to help me adjust to my new lot. Her husband, Ed, comes over any time I need something fixed, plunged, or WD-40'd.

After shutting the door to my Jeep, I crank an old Soundgarden CD and inhale deeply. A memory of more carefree times washes over me as Edna appears on her front step, dressed in a bright green pantsuit à la 1976. She waves to me as I pull out onto the road.

Unrolling the window, I call out, "They're just finishing breakfast."

She gives me a thumbs up. "I'm going to teach them how to play blackjack today."

I would much rather the kids work on their math skills than learn to gamble, but you've got to choose your battles. As summer vacation just started, math will have to wait. "Have fun!"

"Oh, I will," she yells with a twinkle in her eye. "The only wagers we're going to place are on who does what chores."

Driving to the diner, I wonder what my life would have been like had I left Gamble for greener pastures after high school. I could have gone to college or culinary school. I might have married someone who didn't die on me. I might even own my own upscale restaurant featured in *Food & Wine*—I know magazines are the dinosaurs of the publishing world, but I still subscribe to a couple. I can take them into the bath with me and dream until my skin resembles a prune.

Yet if I'd followed the yellow brick road to Oz, I wouldn't have my boys. And as much as they make me crazy, I wouldn't trade them for the world.

I'm beyond grateful that summer has returned to the Northern Hemisphere, bringing with it much-anticipated sunshine. I'm starting to think I have seasonal affective disorder. In the winter months, I act like a bear preparing for hibernation. As in, I love to eat, and have no interest in going for a jog in the dark to burn off the extra calories. In the summer, I can't seem to stop moving.

Spotting my diner, aptly named The Diner, makes my heart rate pick up speed. I'm lucky to have my own business, and while I dream of re-covering the fabric on the booths and updating the counter stools, it's still all mine— an accomplishment I'm very proud of.

The door is unlocked, and the lights are on, so Lloyd must already be in the kitchen. The smell of fresh coffee and the muffled strains of the Violent Femmes confirms my suspicion. Lloyd is a fifty-year-old Gamble native who I lucked into hiring six years ago when I opened shop. Not only has he never called in sick, but he's often willing to work late when someone else is out with whatever ailment is running through town.

"Lloyd!" I call out. "I'm here!"

The music instantly lowers as my right hand pushes open the door from the kitchen. "Hey, boss lady, what's shaking?"

Lloyd is well over six feet tall and looks more like a lumberjack than a cook. I long ago gave him the choice of shaving his beard or wearing a hairnet on his face—you only let a customer complain of finding a red curly hair in their eggs once. He chose to shave.

Pulling a recipe out of my purse, I hand it to him. "Grandma Adele's homestyle meatloaf. I thought we'd do grilled meatloaf sandwiches on sourdough with caramelized onions and Swiss cheese for today's special."

"Yum!" He grabs the card and I leave the kitchen to stock the coffee cups and refill the sugar containers. I'm so in the zone topping off salt and pepper shakers and marrying the ketchups, I almost ignore my phone when it rings. A vision of a burning shed changes my mind.

"Hello."

"Hey, little sister," Digger says. "Harper was wondering if you wanted us to pick up the kids early and keep them overnight so you can have a free evening. You know, hit the pub, maybe meet yourself a nice guy."

"Yes to the kids, and no to the nice guy," I grumble. I'm fairly certain every man in Gamble—nice or not— is already married with a wife who would, at the very least, ram me with her cart in the supermarket if she ever caught me making eyes at her husband.

"I thought we'd made ourselves a little bet last year." He pauses like I might actually help him dig my own grave. When I don't, he prompts, "You know, something along the lines of you giving love another shot if I did?

May I remind you that my wedding is only a few months away?"

"Yeah, but at the time, I had no idea Harper Kennedy would run from the paparazzi and hide out in Gamble, Alaska." I sound irritated but I'm not. Harper and her kids are the best thing that's ever happened to my grisly, perpetual-bachelor brother. Also, having a movie star living up at the lodge has done wonders for business.

"What does that have to do with it?"

"There's got to be some sort of clause when it comes to events as unlikely as getting struck by lightning in a snowstorm."

"There were no conditions to our deal," Digger reminds me. "You said if I got married, you'd put yourself out there again. It's time to pay up."

"Fine, pick up the kids whenever you want, and I'll go man shopping tonight." I'll do no such thing, but if it will get my brother off my back and get me a night alone, I have no problem lying to him.

"I may have to stop in to see that you're holding up your end of the bargain," he threatens.

"It's your time to waste," I tell him.

"Hmmm."

Before he can comment further, I say, "Remind Harper that she's coming by today to discuss wedding cakes." I'm making their wedding cake as my gift.

"She can't wait," he assures me. "I love you, Moira, and I know you're lying about going out tonight. But just so you know, I'm not giving up on you finding your own happily-ever-after."

"Which does not in any way require me getting married," I tell him. It could, however, involve a cleaning lady, and an occasional vacation. Before he can protest, I hurriedly add, "I have to go."

Hanging up, I wonder at the magic that has turned my brother from a commitment-phobe into a full-on fan of matrimony. I silently offer a prayer to the heavens, "God save me from well-meaning family members."

Chapter 2

Ethan

"No, Mom, I didn't quit. I'm taking a sabbatical," I say into the speakerphone. I'm currently packing up my desk in my corner office at HCI Entertainment Law. After fifteen years representing Hollywood's elite, I'm about to have six glorious months off. I'm going to write a book, and sleep without being woken up at two a.m. by some coked-up actor needing to be bailed out of jail. It's going to be heaven.

"A sabbatical? Who takes a sabbatical?" my mom asks. "You're in the prime of your career. You can't just walk away."

"Yes, I can. I've been wanting to write a novel since I was a kid. I would have thought you'd be happy for me to pursue one of my dreams."

"But all that money we spent on law school ..." she moans. My mom is one of the hardest working people I've ever known. Not that she *had* to work. My dad certainly made enough money as a talent agent with one of the biggest agencies in LA, but it wasn't in my mom's nature to sit around and watch kids finger paint. She took a grand total of three weeks off work after giving birth to me and my sister before going back to being the most respected and feared casting agent in Hollywood.

"Again, not quitting, Mom. Just taking a break." I walk over to the wall of windows and stare out at the Century City skyline through the smog. "I'd say in the fifteen years I've been practicing law, I've definitely gotten your money's worth out of my law degree."

"You're too young to retire," she says. "I only retired last year and *I'm* too young." She lowers her voice as though not wanting to be overheard. "Your dad and I were not meant to be home alone together, day in and day out. He's driving me crazy."

"Most people would say that sixty-eight is the perfect age to stop working," I tell her, hoping to put an end to her complaints. "Maybe you and Dad should travel, you know, see the world, do the things you've never made time for."

"The last time Isaac and I went on vacation, he forgot his sunscreen and instead of buying a new tube, he decided to fry. There's a reason he got that patch of skin cancer on his nose." She stops talking long enough to juice her celery for her morning cleanse. "How will you pay your bills while you're off pretending not to be a lawyer?"

"I've put a lot aside, Mom. Plus, I'll still make my base salary while I'm away."

"Away? You're not writing your book in LA? Where in the world are you going?"

"I'm heading up to Alaska," I tell her, feeling slightly sheepish at hearing the words out loud. "I'm thinking of basing my psychological thriller there."

"So, you're really serious?" Before I can answer, she

demands, "You know who writes books? People who went to school to write books."

"I'm a good writer, Mom."

"If you say so."

"Thanks a lot." I make a mental note to tell Harper about this conversation when I get to Alaska. Somehow, laughing with my best friend about this kind of stuff makes it so much more bearable. As her parents never understood her career path either, Harper gets it.

"I still don't understand why you can't just work on your little book during your free time. It's not like you've got a family to look after."

And we're onto her second favorite topic. The "you need a wife and kids right away" bullet point presentation … which will bring us to the end of this conversation. I've been hoping she'd pick up the pattern and stop, but so far, no luck.

"Sorry, Mom, I've got to run. I have a meeting in a couple of minutes on the other side of the building."

"Okay." But her tone says that: a) it is not okay, and b) she doesn't believe me about the meeting.

"Love you. I'll call you on Sunday."

"Love you, too."

I hang up and turn back to my desk as a jolt of excitement shoots through me. After today, I won't be sitting here for a very long time. If ever again. I don't want to give my parents simultaneous heart attacks, but the truth is, I've wanted out of this line of work for a very long time. I lost my passion for representing spoiled, entitled rich people years ago.

I knew the exact moment it was over for me, too. It was mid-December, four years ago. I was about to get on a flight to Cancun to spend the holidays with my family when I got a call from a particularly problematic client. He was an actor-turned-MMA fighter—what could go wrong, huh?

Heinrich had just been caught in a hotel room with not one, but *three* teenage girls. My gut reaction was to tell him to rot in prison and die, but as his attorney, I did what I had to do. I left the airport and bailed him out of jail. Then I babysat him while Prisha Choudree—Harper's and my other close friend, not to mention the top PR person in town—tried to work her magic and mitigate the damage.

A knock at my door interrupts my thoughts. Speak of the devil, Prisha strides in. She slides her hands into the pockets of her wide-leg slacks and glances at the boxes on my desk. "So, you're really doing this."

"Yes, and I couldn't be happier."

"You do remember what it's like in Alaska, right? The dusty roads, the mosquitos, the starving bears just waiting for their chance to eat you alive."

Chuckling, I tell her, "I remember the quiet rustle of the leaves in the wind, the sounds of ocean waves lapping against the shore, air so clean, you can see for miles." Pointing behind me, I say, "No smog."

"Clean air is overrated. I like a little texture in my oxygen." Flopping onto one of the armchairs facing my desk, she sighs heavily. "First Harper, now you. You'll probably meet the woman of your dreams and stay up in the Last Frontier, abandoning me forever."

"I assure you, Prisha, that's not going to happen." I open my middle drawer and unceremoniously start to empty it into a box.

"Sure, it is. You'll find some outdoorsy gal who will teach you how to gut a fish or turn bear poops into ... I don't know ... pottery. You'll grow a beard, start wearing flannel, and never come back."

"Again, not happening. Definitely not the relationship

anyway." I glance up at the ceiling. "Maybe the beard, but I promise that will be temporary because I'll get rid of it when I come back in six months." If I let Prisha know I may not come back, she'll tackle me to the ground and perform a house arrest to keep me from getting on the plane. It's not like I'm going to move to Alaska, but I might try my hand at Bali next, or New Zealand.

It's unlikely I'll become the next John Grisham, but even so, I'm almost eighty percent sure I'm through with Hollywood. If I do have to continue making my living as a lawyer, I'm definitely going to change my specialty. Maybe I'll move to St. Lucia and practice real estate law from a shack on the beach.

"I'm not going to follow you, you know. Sheila and I are not wilderness people," Prisha warns. "We're not giving up vegan restaurants and hot yoga classes just because you and Harper have lost your minds."

"Nobody's asking you to follow us," I tell her.

"Harper is," she says defensively.

"Really?"

"Well, not in so many words, but she's constantly talking about how happy she is up there in the godforsaken North Pole. She won't shut up about how great small-town life is. Not only that, but she's always asking when I'm coming to visit."

"Sounds awful." I roll my eyes.

"It's a lot of pressure, and I don't need it from you, too, mister," she says in a warning tone.

"I'm going to miss you, Prish."

"Well, I'm not going to miss you." She starts to sputter as she jabs her pointer finger in my direction. "You're … you're … you're just some nut who cuts and runs off to the woods to pretend he's Ernest Hemingway."

"Is that what you came to tell me?"

"No," she says with a shrug. "I wanted to know if you'd like to go for lunch. Since it is your last chance for edible food and all."

Yeah, because Alaska isn't known for some of the best and freshest seafood in the world. But there's no way I'm going to poke the bear. Grinning, I grab my phone off my desk and pocket it. "Ban Thai?"

"Obviously."

"Let's go."

Once we're on the elevator, she looks over at me. "Do you need a ride to the airport tomorrow?"

"My flight's at seven a.m. I'll take an Uber."

She shakes her head vigorously, causing her curtain of thick black hair to dance around. "Forget it. I'll take you."

"You sure?"

"Yeah. I'll be up anyway, feeling sad about another friend abandoning me." She drops her chin like she's about to start bawling.

Wrapping my arm around her shoulder, I pull her in for a side hug, then drop a kiss on her forehead. "I love you, too, Prish. I promise I'll be back before you know it."

"Liar," she hisses, but she doesn't pull out of my embrace.

Chapter 3

Moira

Lunch is always the busiest time of day at the diner. Every table is full, and there's regularly a line out the door. As Abigail and I run around like chickens with our tail feathers on fire, I overhear Sissy Sinclair tell her husband, "I don't know why you wanted to eat *here*. I could have made you a sandwich at home."

"Which is exactly what I wanted to avoid. I'm sick to death of your tuna fish surprise. Guess what, Sissy? After all these years, pickle relish isn't all that surprising."

Travis Sinclair was my husband's nemesis at school, so it's no wonder his wife hates my guts and their kid, Hunter, hates Wyatt. They're a family of malcontents.

After wiping down a table in the corner, I call out, "Sissy, Travis, over here." Then I slam down two waters and turn around to take another table's order. Sissy makes sure to knock into me as she walks by.

When I turn around to take the Sinclairs' order, Sissy is

tapping her fingers on the tabletop like she's been waiting for a month. "Finally," she announces loudly.

"We're doing grilled meatloaf sandwiches for our special today," I say, ignoring her snide comment. "What can I get for you?" I'm careful not to make eye contact. Sissy is much like a wild bear in temperament. One false move, and her claws will rip me to shreds.

"I'll have the meatloaf." Travis eyes me up and down like I *am* the meatloaf. *Gross, Travis. Never gonna happen.*

Sissy's gaze darts between us as though trying to solve an advanced calculus equation. "Are you …"—she turns to her husband before standing up and yelling—"banging this trollop?"

"What? No!" he hisses. "God, Sissy, just because a man wants meatloaf instead of tuna doesn't mean he's cheating on you. Quit making a scene."

Her gaze travels around what has become a very quiet dining room. When she finally plops back down into her chair, she says, "I'll have the tuna."

A full body shiver overtakes me as I wonder if Everett and I would have turned out like these two.

I bustle around all morning. Things don't start to settle down until after one, and by that time, I'm more than ready to get off my feet for a few minutes. "Lloyd, I'll have a meatloaf sandwich," I call through the window to the kitchen, as saliva starts to form in my mouth. I've been serving those things all day and it's been all I could do not to take a bite out of each one before handing it off.

"No dice, boss lady. We sold out. How about a nice, juicy patty melt?"

"Fine," I say with more than a hint of disappointment. Then I turn to Abigail. "I'm gonna be in the back corner in case Harper comes in."

The wide-set, almost black eyes of my best server pop

open like she's been jabbed with a live cattle prod. "I'm not sure I'll ever get used to Harper Kennedy living in Gamble. It's plain surreal."

I used to feel the same way until I got to know her. "Harper is nothing like *People* magazine would have you believe," I tell Abigail.

"She was still voted the most gorgeous woman alive— twice! Gamble is not prepared for that kind of glamour." She's still shaking her head as she walks off to bus tables.

Too bad being the most gorgeous woman alive doesn't afford you perks like having a faithful husband. Harper came to Alaska to hide from the press while her lying scumbag of a spouse carried on with their nanny in the most public way possible—he took her on vacation to Hawaii. Luckily, Brett Kennedy's philandering didn't put Harper off men. She and my wonderful—not to mention loyal—brother are perfect for each other.

Halfway through my patty melt, my soon-to-be sister-in-law walks through the front door. I know this even though my back is facing the entrance, as the hive of busy chatter takes on a whole new level of excitement.

Harper sits down across from me, looking nothing like her movie star roots would lead you to think she'd look. She's wearing jean shorts, an old band T-shirt of my brother's, and Jesus sandals. Her hair is in a ponytail and if I'm not mistaken, there are a fair number of twigs tangled in it.

"Rolling around in the woods before stopping by?" I ask jokingly.

Her hand immediately goes to her head. She starts to pull out leaves while explaining, "I was working on the garden up at our new house site. Turns out it's a more daunting task than I thought it would be."

"Why didn't you just hire someone to do it?" I ask.

Heck, if I were in her shoes, I'd hire practically everything out.

"No way. If I'm going to live in Gamble, I'm going to behave like a native."

"You're going to learn how to do taxidermy and let your leg hair grow out?" I point at the uneaten half of my patty melt in offering.

Pulling the plate across the table, Harper says, "You know it. I'm hoping it'll be long enough to braid by winter."

While she eats, I ask, "So what kind of cake are you thinking of?"

Tipping her head from side to side, she swallows. "My favorite is chocolate, but Digger likes carrot, and the kids want a white cake. It's going to be hard to make everyone happy."

"Not if we do a cupcake tower," I tell her. "I know those things are probably out of style for the rest of the world, but luckily Gamble doesn't care about trends. If we did, you wouldn't see so many Members Only jackets around here."

Harper laughs loudly. "That's one of the best parts of living here."

"The Members Only jackets?"

"The complete lack of caring about what's in fashion," she tells me. "A person can feel free to be who she is and not who everyone expects her to be."

"I suppose." I don't sound like I'm selling it. Harper shoots me a questioning look, so I explain, "I go around just being myself all the time and I still have idiots like Sissy Sinclair thinking that I'm sleeping with her husband."

"Ew. Not that Travis is particularly gross or anything, but you're no cheat."

"Word on the street is that I'm looking for a new husband, and apparently, I'm not opposed to poaching him out from under someone else. Sometimes I *hate* small town life."

"Have you *ever* considered getting married again?" She's trying to act all innocent as she purposely avoids eye contact

"You're starting to sound like Digger."

"I just want you to have someone to share your life with." Clearing her throat, she adds, "Did I mention that my friend Ethan is arriving today?"

"About forty-seven times," I tell her grumpily.

"You two seemed to hit it off last year when he and Prisha rented rooms at your house."

"You're as subtle as a sledgehammer, Harper. I barely spoke to the guy, and let's not forget that he lives in California. I'm not about to get involved in a long-distance relationship. I barely have time to floss these days. There's no way I'm going to fly across the country for a booty call."

"He'll be in town for six months. He's renting the place right up the hill." Happy couples have got to learn how to reel it in a bit. Her eyes are sparkling like she just got hit with a glitter bomb.

"And then he's going home," I tell her. "No, thank you." I take a long sip of my iced tea. "Just because you and Digger are over the moon in love doesn't mean everyone has to be."

She sighs. "I was in an unhappy marriage for years. But if I could find love again, so can you." She wipes her mouth with a paper napkin before adding, "I also know what it's like for people to be up in my business like an intestinal worm, so I won't say another thing about it."

"Thank you. I'm not saying I'll never date again, but it's going to be a long time before I have any interest in that kind of thing. Currently, I'm more invested in finding someone to teach the boys how to mow the lawn. Between the three of them, they're always leaving big hairy patches behind."

Harper laughs. "Speaking of your boys, how about if I go get them now? Lily and Liam want to show them a new fishing spot they found."

"They would love that more than anything. And thanks for taking them off my hands tonight. I've got a book with my name on it." I don't mention that it's a spicy romance novel. No sense stirring the pot.

Chapter 4

Ethan

I pull into Gamble just after two in the afternoon, which is impressive considering how far I've come since I woke up this morning. I feel like Tom Cruise in that old movie *Jerry Maguire*—the part when he's in his car singing "Free Fallin'." For the first time in my adult life, I'm truly free. My time is my own, and I'm going to make the most of it.

Grinning, I slow down and take in the familiar sights of Gamble's "downtown." All four-square blocks of it. The SUV I rented is already covered in a thick layer of dust, which I'm guessing makes washing it superfluous. In LA, I have my car cleaned every week to keep it shiny. *Clearly I think I'm a Kardashian or something.*

I'm as hungry as my mom on the third day of a juice cleanse. After pulling into The Diner, I get out and stretch my legs while the warm Alaska sun beats down on my skin. Taking a deep breath, I inhale the fresh, clean air. Gamble is close enough to the ocean to be scented with salt water, but there's also a hint of pine. Where I'm standing, the delectable aroma of real home-cooked diner food mixes in. My stomach growls loudly in response.

The bell rings when I open the door. After stepping inside, my eyes land directly on Moira Bishop, the owner and operator of The Diner. Moira is also a single mom to three rowdy boys, and a slew of pets that she regularly threatens with rehoming. She put Prisha and me up at her house for a few nights last year when we were here to help Harper navigate her nasty break-up with Brett (aka worst human being in Hollywood—which is really saying something).

I thought I would hate staying there, but it turned out to be a lot more fun than I expected. I even played touch football with Moira's boys in their backyard a couple of times, which made me feel like a kid again.

The aforementioned diner owner's back is currently toward me as she scrubs something off an empty booth. She calls out, "Come on in!" I can't help but stare as her hips shift with the force of her work. If I were a different sort of guy, I'd try to make something happen with her. But I'm no Brett Kennedy. I have morals, one of which is you don't take advantage of a single mom, no matter how pretty her smile is, or how good you think her body might feel against yours. The last thing she needs is some jerk who's hoping to love her and leave her.

When she turns around and sees me, her face lights up. "Ethan! Harper told me you were arriving today. I didn't think I'd see you so soon."

"The smell of whatever you're cooking caused me to pull over on the spot." I forgot how blue her eyes are. They're like the Pacific on a clear day.

"Today's special was grilled meatloaf sandwiches, but

sadly, we're all sold out. Might I suggest a classic bacon cheeseburger with fries?"

"You had me at bacon."

Chuckling, Moira says, "Sit wherever you'd like. I'll holler at Lloyd to rustle you up a burger. What can I get you to drink?"

"I'd love an ice water, thank you."

"You betcha." She disappears into the kitchen.

I look around the half-full dining room before sitting in a booth near the window. This way, I can do some people-watching while I eat. Observing the locals sounds like something a real writer would do.

A minute later, Moira appears with my water. "Are you heading to the lodge later?"

I nod. "I told Harper I'd come by tonight after I settle into my rental. Are you and the boys going to be there?" I hope they will be.

"The boys are already there, but I'm taking a much-needed night off from being a mom."

"And well-deserved, I'm sure," I say, totally under-standing her need for peace.

"Between work, Wyatt's baseball games, and the twins' swim meets, I'm pretty much never alone."

"Wyatt plays baseball? I'd love to come watch him sometime."

"Really? Why?" she asks, looking surprised.

I take a sip of my water before answering, "I love baseball."

"I'm sure Wyatt would love having another person cheering him on. His next game is on Friday at six o'clock, but I won't tell him you're coming, in case you change your mind."

"I won't change my mind," I tell her. "It's not like I have a full social calendar."

She smiles her million-dollar smile before rushing off to seat a small group of whom I'm guessing are tourists. *Stop with the tube socks and sandals, people! Is it any wonder Americans are the butt of so many travel jokes?*

A few minutes later, another waitress drops my burger in front of me. After my first bite, I'm ready to declare it the most delicious thing I've ever eaten.

Three bites in, my phone pings with a message from Harper:

Harper: *You're here already?*

Me: *How in the world did you know that?*

Harper: *Please, this is Gamble. Everybody knows everything.*

Me: *Moira texted you, didn't she?*

Harper: *She thought I'd like to know you arrived safely and are now ruining your appetite.*

Me: *Don't worry. I'm sure I'll be hungry for whatever Digger's cooking. What can I bring? Some wine, maybe?*

Harper: *Nope, just yourself. The kids are SO excited to see you.*

Me: *Same here. I need to meet the landlord at the cabin in a bit, then grab a few groceries. I'll be up right afterward.*

Harper: *See you soon, my friend!*

I make short work of my lunch, hoping Moira will make it back over to talk to me, but she doesn't. When I finish, I leave a twenty on the table and sneak out, not wanting to bother her. Just as I pull the door open, she calls to me, "See you Friday!"

I turn and grin. "I'm sure you'll see me before then. The food here is better than anything I could make myself."

Her cheeks brighten and I leave with a warm feeling in my bones. Eating out here is the complete opposite of dining out in LA. LaLa Land eateries involve being seated by a snooty hostess who thinks she's holding the keys to heaven, then being waited on by a slew of young wannabe actors who don't know the first thing about service— they're too busy giving you smoldering looks in case you're someone who can discover them and launch their careers. Finally, you're offered Lilliputian portions of whatever is the "in" thing to eat. The coup de grâce is a bill King Midas would cringe at. I'm *so* not going to miss that.

A quick trip up Main Street takes me to the turnoff for Birch Road, where I'll be staying. When I pull up in front of number three, I see an older woman in jeans and a plaid flannel shirt standing on the porch. The house is a large two-story log cabin with enormous windows that overlook the lake. It's the perfect spot to pen my first novel. Quiet and relaxed with a breathtaking view. I get out and wave hello to her.

"Are you Ethan?"

"I am," I tell her, hurrying up the flagstone path to the front steps.

"I'm Julia. I'm here to show you around." She pushes the front door open and walks in ahead of me. She's clearly a no-nonsense kind of person, very unlike the realtors you see on Selling Sunset. Laughter bubbles up inside me at the thought of one of those gals in their five-inch stilettos and mile-long hair extensions trying to sell houses here.

As we walk over the threshold, I'm greeted by the scent of cedar, and the sight of a wall of windows that meets up with the vaulted, wood-plank ceiling. There's an expansive view of the calm, crystal clear lake. It's so bright outside, it takes my eyes a second to adjust to the dimmer lighting in the large room.

The large kitchen is to my right. It has a big L-shaped island with stools facing the window. I'll probably set up my laptop there. To my left is an airy living room with a long, brown, leather couch and two matching armchairs. A flat screen TV adorns the far wall and is surrounded by bookshelves filled with paperback novels, board games, and some Indigenous wood carvings.

"So? What do you think?" Julia asks.

"It's perfect." Seriously, if someone asked me to describe my ultimate writing lair, this place would be it.

"Good. Your payment cleared, so you're good to go. No parties. No smoking. No pets of any kind."

"No problem," I say in a light tone.

Narrowing her eyes, she asks, "I'm not going to have trouble with you, am I?"

Yikes. Apparently there's no joking around either. "I'm just here to do some writing."

"Writing," she scoffs. "That's what they all say, then I find cigarette butts in the garbage, sheets are missing, and the carpets are so soaked with beer they have to be professionally cleaned."

"I don't smoke, I promise if I drink the odd beer while I'm here, it'll go directly down my throat and not on the floor, and I have no intention of stealing your sheets." This lady is a total character.

"Don't get wise with me, young man," she says while glaring at me like I've just come up from the bowels of hell to pillage her property.

"Sorry, ma'am," I find myself saying while trying to keep my voice from cracking with humor.

"I'll leave you to it then," she sniffs. "But if I find out there's been any funny business, you'll be out on your ass so fast you won't have time to put your pants on."

My suppressed laughter emerges as a bark.

"You think I'm joking? Do I look like a clown to you?"

Oh, no. She's Alaska's answer to Joe Pesci in *Goodfellas*. "Not at all."

Julia glares at me for a second, then yanks open the front door. She gives the "I'll be watching you" gesture as she points first at her eyes and then mine. She finally walks out, letting the screen door slam behind her.

"Welcome to Alaska," I mutter.

"Uncle Ethan!" Lily screams as soon as she sees me walk through the front door of the lodge.

"Lily!" I crouch down in preparation of her launching herself into my arms. When she does, I swoop her up and give her a big hug while she squishes my cheek with hers. "How's my favorite girl?"

"I'm great. Alaska's the best. We had a moose and her calf in our yard the other day. In our *yard*, Uncle Ethan. Can you believe it?" She doesn't wait for an answer, but just keeps talking. "Thank goodness kindergarten is over. I'm worn out from all that learning. Now I can finally relax."

I set her down and ruffle her hair. "I bet."

Snapping her fingers, she says, "Nuts. I forgot it's my turn to feed Otis. I'll be right back."

Just as she rushes off, her brother, Liam, walks into the

lodge. He's carrying an enormous rainbow trout on a chain. "Hey, Uncle Ethan! Look what I caught."

"Wow. Is that for our supper?"

He shrugs, looking awfully nonchalant for a nine-year-old. "I've just gotta gut it and hand it off to Digger so he can grill it up."

"Gut it, huh? I bet that's something you never thought you'd be doing?"

"That's how we do it up here." He sounds like a local already.

Harper appears from the office behind the front desk and runs at me full force as Liam jumps out of her way. "I've missed you so much!" she exclaims while throwing herself into my arms.

When she pulls back, she's got tears in her eyes, and I find myself choking up. "I've missed you, too." Needing to change the subject, I use my thumb to point in the direction of the kitchen where Liam has gone. "He's quite the outdoorsman these days."

She grins. "Tell me about it."

"How is it that your son was born an old man?" Ever since Liam could walk, he's preferred to wear socks with his sandals and he'd rather watch documentaries than cartoons. He and my dad have a lot in common.

"He's acting a lot more like a kid now that we live up here," she says, looping her arm through mine. "Let's go find Digger."

My smile turns into a cringe. Digger and I didn't exactly see eye-to-eye on things when I was here last year. We were both trying to protect Harper in our own way, which turned out to be completely opposite of each other. My friend has said more than once that it was like having two bulls in the same pen.

I follow Harper out the back door where Digger is

firing up the grill. As soon as he sees us, he offers a genuine-looking smile as he holds his hand out. "Ethan, how was the trip?"

"Uneventful, which is exactly what I was hoping for," I tell him. Glancing around at the forest behind the lodge, I smile. "I'm so glad to be out of LA."

"Can I get you a beer?" he offers.

"Only if you're having one."

He flips open the cooler next to the grill and takes out two cans of Bud. He offers one to Harper, and then one to me before going back in for his. Harper holds up her can. "To old friends and fresh starts."

"Here, here," I say, as we clink the cans together.

After we all take a celebratory sip, Digger asks, "So, did you meet Julia?"

"I met her all right."

He and Harper burst out laughing before Harper asks, "Did she accuse you of wanting to steal her sheets?"

"Among other things," I laugh. "Why didn't you tell me I was renting a place from an old-school gangster?"

"I told you we should have warned him," Digger tells Harper.

She shakes her head. "It's more fun this way."

"So, I spend fifteen years taking care of you, and you just throw me to the wolves the first chance you get," I say with a grin to let her know I'm kidding. "If I wake up with a horse head in bed with me, we're gonna have words."

She shrugs. "Hey, this is the Last Frontier. You've got to be tough to make it up here."

The evening passes far too quickly as I catch Harper up on the latest Hollywood gossip and she fills me in on her and Digger's wedding plans. By ten o'clock, I'm yawning from the long day. "I think it's time I head home and find out why those sheets are so special."

"I'll let you have tomorrow to get settled, but after that, I'm going to expect you up here for regular visits. I need to get my Ethan fix before you leave me again."

"First of all," I tell her, "you left me and Prisha. Secondly, I'm here for six months, so we'll have plenty of time together."

Digger and Harper walk me around to the front of the lodge. Digger wraps an arm over Harper's shoulder before saying, "You'd better watch out. If Harper has her way, you'll be moving up here next. She's hoping you'll fall in love with a local and decide to stay."

I roll my eyes at the notion. "Just because you're getting married again, Harper, doesn't mean I've changed my mind about the institution. Tried it once, hated how it ended."

Tilting her face towards her fiancé, Harper says, "Ethan's letting one bad apple spoil the bunch."

"Hey, Paige wasn't just a bad apple. She was poison."

"Paige was three years ago, Ethan. And she doesn't represent the entire female population on the planet."

"I didn't know you were married before," Digger says.

I shake my head, my gut tightening. "I only got as far as the proposal. Instead of yes, she said she didn't love me and wasn't sure she ever had."

"Ouch, I can see why that would put a guy off marriage," Digger says.

Turning to Harper, I say, "See? Digger gets it."

"Digger doesn't know you like I do. You always wanted to get married, and you're letting one bad experience change the entire trajectory of your life."

"Trust me when I say I don't want that anymore. I'm happy on my own. Really, I am. I don't need you to set me up with anyone or try to talk me into getting back on that horse. I promise you I am doing fine on foot."

Harper opens her mouth, but I hold up one finger. "Seriously, I'm good."

After we say our goodbyes, I walk out into the sunlit evening and I take a deep breath. The mention of Paige's name doesn't bother me like it used to. She's a distant, if bad, memory now. A cautionary tale, and nothing more.

I feel a shift in the breeze as I stroll down the path toward the parking lot. I have the same sense of rightness I did when I first arrived in town. I don't know what's going to happen while I'm here, but I have a feeling this place is going to change me.

Chapter 5

Moira

It turns out I don't know how to have a night to myself. My brain doesn't seem interested in making my dream of taking a bubble bath while drinking wine and reading a romance novel become a reality. I get as far as pouring a glass of chardonnay and getting into the tub. Then I begin to obsess over the crappy condition of my bathroom.

Not only is the clawfoot tub in desperate need of reglazing, but the linoleum tiles are peeling and there appears to be mold growing on the far wall. Mold! How have I not noticed that before?

Closing my eyes, I take a deep breath and try to remember the last time I was home alone. It was last summer when Digger and Harper took the kids up the mountain to camp for a few days. I spent whatever free time I had sanding down and repainting the back steps. At this rate, I should have all my house repairs done by the time I'm three hundred and sixty. Good times.

My gaze shoots over to my book sitting on the toilet lid. *His Willing Captive* looked promising online, but here in my house it looks ridiculous. I'm already captive to three little men who take up every free moment of my life. I don't need to read about being some Victorian sea captain's sex slave. Who's got the energy?

Trying to empty my head of all thoughts, I focus on the soothing sensation of hot water inching up toward my shoulders. I'm about ready to turn off the faucet when the shower head starts shooting out icy rain. What the ... I shriek as I jump out of the tub. My wet feet hit the floor, and I fly across the room like I've just rounded third base and am intent on sliding into home.

Throwing towels down to wipe up the puddles left in my wake, I briefly wonder if the house is haunted. That would be so much more interesting than the reality of the situation— the whole place is in the process of falling down around me.

Everett was never much of a DIY kind of guy, but he certainly knew his way around tools better than I do. I wonder if I should get Julia Simms out here to give me an idea of what this place is worth. I don't have the energy, time, or money to fix it up myself and Ed Turner is getting too old to keep coming to my aid. Maybe I should sell and buy something smaller that's in better shape. We'd lose some land, but as far as I'm concerned that would just mean less maintenance.

The only reason Everett and I bought this house was because it was the cheapest we could afford. There was already a load of deferred maintenance on it even back then. The amount has easily tripled.

Turning off the water, I climb back into the tub and add "check the water heater and shower head" to the growing inventory of things I need to take care of. An overwhelming sense of futility starts to pour out of my tear ducts. Twenty minutes later my eyes are puffy, and my head is full of snot.

The bath water is only just starting to cool—score one point for cast iron tubs—as I hurry to wash up before pulling the plug on the drain. After towel drying my hair and putting on a summer nightgown, I trod down to the kitchen to pour another glass of wine. There, I'm met with chipped kitchen cabinets, stained countertops, and appliances so old I can barely stand the sight of them. You've got to hand it to the seventies: while their color choices left a lot to be desired—I'm talking to you, Harvest Gold—those buggers were meant to last.

Opening the fridge, I stare inside and try to decide what to have for supper. I have no interest in cooking, so I opt for cheese and crackers with a side of dill pickles and capers. I'm eyeing a Toaster Strudel for dessert.

After my first few crackers, the phone rings. "Hello."

"Hey, Sis." It's Digger. "How about I keep the boys for the night? That way you can stay out a little longer." Making it clear he knows I'm home, he adds, "The pub sounds quiet tonight."

"Yeah, well, Tuesday nights in Gamble are pretty tame."

"So, yes to my keeping the kids?" I hate the sound of concern in his tone.

"That's fine, thanks." Then I tell him, "I'm thinking about asking Julia to come out."

"You want to sell?" Why does he sound so surprised? He's over here enough to know what a mess this place is.

"I want less to take care of," I tell him.

"Yeah, but the boys have so much land there to play and explore."

I burst into tears for the second time tonight. "It's just too much, Digger. I can't stay on top of everything."

"I'll come by and look at your list. I'll get started on it as soon as I can." You've got to love big brothers who want to solve all your problems.

"You're in the middle of building your own house, planning a wedding, and doing everything you do around the lodge. Don't you dare take on my burdens."

"Moira," Digger says gently, "you've got a lot on your plate. Let me stop by and see if there's anything I can do. Please."

"Well, if you insist. I'd appreciate your opinion on my hot water heater. It's been acting up lately."

"I'll see you in the morning." Before he hangs up, he says, "I love you. You've got this."

I'm suddenly too tired to heat up a Toaster Strudel. Dragging myself up the stairs, I realize that I'm tired of my whole life. While I love my kids and I'm appreciative for all that I have, I hate the amount of responsibility that comes with it. I hate feeling tired and overwhelmed. I hate the small-minded bitches, like Sissy Sinclair, who cast aspersions on my character. I hate this house.

I could go on hating for hours, but as I crawl between the crisp cotton sheets of my bed, I force the litany to end. I remember my grandmother telling me, "For everything you hate, you have to like two things, or you're gonna slide into the pit of despair, girl."

Starting a new list, I announce to the empty room, "I love my boys. I love the color green. I love chocolate. I love summer evenings. I love Digger and Grandpa Jack. I love …" Shoot, that's all I can come up with. I'm either going to have to learn how to love more, or I'm going to have to give up hating so much. At this point, I'm not sure which would be easier.

An image of Ethan Caplan pops into my mind. Tall, handsome, polite, interested in baseball ... *What am I doing?* I am not going to let myself start pining for some unattainable man. That's no way to make my life better.

As I doze off to sleep, I dream that I made different choices. I fantasize that I told Everett that I couldn't marry him because I'd decided to go to culinary school. I dream that I packed up and moved to some big city like New York or Los Angeles, to live a life full of adventure and excitement.

My imaginings go on for hours and I love every one of them. From opening my own fine dining establishment, to vacationing in exotic locations, which include riding horses on a beach in Cancun; I travel the world and go out dancing nightly. I relish the choices I could have made but didn't. But then I hear one word in the back of my reverie, and it wakes me with a start. *Mom.*

I know why I didn't leave Gamble when I had the opportunity, and that reason is my mother. Bethany McKenzie was never satisfied with life in a small town. So much so, she packed up and left me, Digger, and our dad here while she moved to Hollywood to follow her dream of becoming a movie star.

She didn't call us; she didn't visit us; she just walked away like we were nothing to her. For her troubles, she wound up hooked on drugs and was found dead in an alley before we could make our peace with her.

I remind myself that I *chose* to stay in Gamble. I had something to prove to the universe—I was nothing like my mom. I wasn't a malcontent who always needed more. I convinced myself that I was happy with my lot, and I was going to raise children the way I wish I'd been raised.

An icy sweat starts to form on my neck as I continue to reassure myself that I am nothing like the woman who gave me life. I love my kids and I'll do everything I can to make sure they have the lives they deserve. I need to quit pining for more. I have enough, and come hell or high water, I'm going to focus on what really matters.

My stomach lets out a loud groan. Those three crackers have given up the ghost and I'm starving. The thought of Grandma Adele's raspberry coffee cake makes me drool. Looking at the clock, I see it's already four in the morning—only an hour before I usually get up.

Throwing off the top sheet, I slide out of bed, intent on making a coffee cake before going into work. Even though my boys aren't here to enjoy it, I remind myself that good mothers put their kids' needs above their own. I'll drop some off at Digger's before going into work because *that's* what a good mother would do.

Chapter 6

Ethan

I sleep like a rock for the first time since I was a kid, and I don't wake up until after ten. I would have probably stayed in bed longer, but my stomach lets out a roar like a monster truck gearing up for destruction. Popping open my eyes, I stare up at the vaulted ceiling and smile. Day one of my new life has begun. I'm going to go for a long run every day, and maybe throw in a few push-ups and core exercises, then I'll spend the rest of my days writing. But first, breakfast.

I mentally run over the meager things I usually eat at home and decide that Moira's cook can probably do a lot better. The thought of a farmer's omelet, or a stack of fluffy pancakes catapults me out of bed.

After a quick shower, I throw on some jeans and a T-shirt and make my way down the road to the diner. I love the feel of the terrain here. It's lush and rugged, almost like I've driven through a time portal to an ancient land. *Look at me flexing my descriptive muscles like a real author.*

Getting out of my rental car, I realize that I'm more than a little excited about the meal to come. As I walk through the door, the bell rings, announcing my arrival. There is only a smattering of customers seated around the dining room, making me think the breakfast rush comes earlier around here. Moira is carrying a coffee pot as she hurries from table-to-table, topping people up. She briefly makes eye contact and offers a small smile, but I'm not buying it. There's something about her energy that's off.

Making my way over to the table I sat at yesterday, I pluck the laminated menu off the wire rack that also holds the napkins, ketchup bottle, and salt and pepper shakers. A few seconds later, Moira appears with an empty mug in one hand and a carafe in the other. "Coffee?"

"Absolutely, thank you." Noticing the dark circles under her eyes, I ask, "How's your morning going?"

"I've had better," she says while filling my cup.

"Anything I can help with?"

"Do you have a time machine?"

"That bad, huh?"

She purses her lips tightly. "Some days the whole single mom, running a diner, living in a house falling down around your ears thing gets to be a bit much. There's never enough time in the day to do what needs doing." She stops, as though she realizes she's said more than she'd probably planned to. "Anyway, I'll be back in a minute to take your order, unless you already know what you want."

"I'll have the woodsman's breakfast and whole wheat toast, please. Dry."

"You want that with three eggs or five?"

"Five eggs?" My mouth hangs open. "Who eats five eggs for breakfast?"

She points across the dining room to a guy that bears more than a passing resemblance to Grizzly Adams. "He does."

"Yeah, well, he looks like he probably has a very physical job. You know, like picking up houses with his bare hands."

She lets out a startled laugh. "He's a fisherman. But, yeah, it's definitely a physically demanding job." She glances down at her pad before looking back at me. "How do you feel about hash browns and bacon?"

"I like them both, but if I eat all that, I don't think I'll be able to move."

"Movement is overrated." As she turns around, she adds, "Sit tight, and I'll be right back with your food."

Moira Bishop is something of a conundrum. On the surface she looks like a go-getting live wire, but beneath that façade she appears to be experiencing her own struggles. Being a parent has never been a driving force in my life, so I don't spend much time imagining what it's like. Yet I can certainly see that being a single parent to three boys is an exhausting endeavor. Add her job at the diner, and she probably doesn't have a minute for herself.

Moira goes over to a youngish couple sitting at a table on the other side of the dining room. The woman openly scowls at her before demanding a coffee refill. I wonder if they had some sort of argument before I got here. Or maybe the hostile customer is just a horrible person. She has a hard look about her. I pull my phone out of my pocket and open the notes tab—I might be staring at the villain in my novel. I hurry and type out a description of her.

A few minutes later, Moira sets my meal in front of me. "I brought hash browns and bacon to help fuel your day.

But only three eggs, so you won't get weighed down." Her eyes sparkle with humor.

"You realize the amount of food on this plate could feed a family of six in Beverly Hills for a month."

She giggles loudly. "I doubt most families in Beverly Hills would eat much of what we serve here."

"Priorities are definitely a bit skewed there. So are portion sizes."

"Remind me never to move to Beverly Hills," she says sardonically.

"You can see why it was imperative I got away," I tell her. "I've been slowly starving for years."

As she walks back to the counter, I look down at my plate and dig in with gusto. While I stuff my face, I watch as Moira zips around refilling cups and dropping off bills. By the time I've eaten every bite, I'm so full I wish I'd ordered a bowl of Special K.

Moira returns to my table. Staring at my empty plate, she says, "Oh, dear, what would the good folks from Beverly Hills say?"

"They'd either get busy planning an intervention or they'd pool their resources and find me a surgeon to perform an emergency gastric bypass." I look around the now-empty diner before indicating the seat across from me. "Care to join me?"

"Sure." She sits down on the banquette across from me and groans. "Oh, that's nice." Her trainer-clad feet suddenly appear on the bench next to me. "It's still early, but my dogs are already barking. What's up?"

I stare at her for a second, trying to decide if I should say anything or not, but my desire to flesh out the villain in my book nudges me onward. "I know it's none of my business, but I couldn't help but notice some tension between you and that woman with the red hair," I say. "She seemed like a real ... delight."

Moira nods her head slowly. "You know that saying 'the way to a man's heart is through his stomach?'"

"I've heard."

Her cheeks turn pink as she matter-of-factly intones, "It seems a lot of women in town believe that. They see me as a threat."

"Shouldn't they be threatened by Lloyd then?" I ask her.

She chuckles. "Surprisingly, they're not as worried about him."

Even though she's trying to act like it doesn't bother her, I can see in her eyes that it does. "Well, I think I might be falling in love with Lloyd. Don't tell him yet, because I want to make sure before I propose."

She performs a comical double take as though trying to ascertain my sexual preference. "I was just kidding," I tell her. "I'm a devout heterosexual."

"Good thing," she snorts. "I wouldn't want you to come to blows with Lloyd's wife. She's pretty fond of him, and no offense, but I think she could take you."

"Ouch."

"Helena is six feet and she's better built than Lloyd." She raises her eyebrows to add emphasis to her statement.

"Note to self, do not make Helena mad." Getting back to the topic at hand, I tell her, "I'm sorry there are petty women in this town who take out their shortcomings on you. It doesn't seem fair."

"It's fine. I really don't care what they think." She blinks rapid-fire and quickly amends that to, "I've had a long time to get used to it and I've got far bigger fish to fry."

"I'd have thought that in a small town like this, the

other women would have rallied around you when you lost your husband."

"You'd think so," she says. "But luckily, I've got my family, and now I've got Harper. She's terrific, and at the end of the day, one true friend is all you really need."

"Harper's the best, and she's got nothing but wonderful things to say about you."

I want to say more, but the door opens, setting off the bell again. Moira slides out of the booth. "Back to it for me. Thanks for the chat."

She leaves me alone with my thoughts and I start wondering what I can possibly do to help make Moira's life a little easier. I'm not talking about becoming her sugar daddy or anything, but there has to be something.

Chapter 7

Moira

After the lunch rush, I take off my apron and tell Abigail, "Shelly and Barb will be in at four for the dinner rush. You can take off when they get here."

"About that ..." She leans against the counter, resting her full-figured bottom against the ledge. "Shelly called earlier and she's not coming in tonight."

"Is she sick?" I ask.

"Sick in love," Abigail tells me. "Toby Quinn just came home for summer break and Shelly made plans with him. She's hoping she can talk him into taking that logging job with her dad's company, so he won't go back to college."

I roll my eyes so hard I feel like I pull a muscle. "What's wrong with that girl? If she's determined to have a future with Toby, she should follow him to college and get herself an education. That way she won't be stuck working here for the rest of her life." I hurriedly add, "No offense, Abigail."

She waves her hand in front of her face. "None taken." Given that she's only a couple years older than me—making her thirty-four—that might mean she could be here for another thirty years or so.

"Don't you ever wonder what it would be like to live someplace else?" I ask her. "Do something else?" I sound like I'm trying to talk my best server into leaving me, but I really want to know.

"Moira …" Abigail shifts so her weight is on her heels. Crossing one foot over the other, she says, "My family has lived on this land for thousands of years. My spirit is rooted so deeply that moving away would probably kill me."

"I love how the Sugpiaq culture respects their ancestry. All I know about mine is that there's some Scots, Irish, English, and Dutch. I don't feel a connection to any of it."

"You might if your people had stayed on their land for as long as mine have. But no matter, I'll hang out and cover Shelly's shift. I remember what it was like to be young and in love." Abigail married her high school sweetheart, and all signs point to it being a wonderful marriage.

"You're the best," I tell her. "Close early if you're not busy. No sense standing around for nothing." As I walk out the door, I have an insane urge to run away. I don't know where I'd run to, but I'm not sure it matters. I just want to go.

When I get in the truck, I immediately open the windows to let some air in. I spot Wyatt's baseball photo taped to the dashboard. Alas, no running for me. After turning the ignition, I back out without looking and nearly get my back end hit by a logging truck. Pulling forward again, I shift into park and try to force my heart rate to slow down. I'm so distracted lately; I'm becoming a liability.

When I finally get home, I spot Digger out front playing baseball with my boys. I cut the engine in time to hear him yell, "That's right, Ash, swing like you're trying to hit the moon!"

"I'll give you the moon," Colton adds before turning around and dropping his shorts, so his startling white bottom is front and center.

Opening the driver's side door, I yell, "Pull your pants up, Colton!"

All three of my sons turn and run toward me. Before I can bend my knees to center my gravity for impact, they're on top of me like a puppy pile. My initial response is to push them off so I can get up, but I suddenly want nothing more than to have my babies in my arms. I roll over, pulling them with me, and then I start tickling them like I did when they were little.

"Mom, stop!" Wyatt convulses in giggles. "You're gonna make me pee!"

"I already peed!" Ash nudges his older brother.

Digger walks over and looms above us with his hands on his hips and a smile on his face. "Now this is a sight," he says. "Remember how Grandpa Jack used to tickle us?"

"Of course," I tell him as I roll over on my back to catch my breath. Staring up at him, I say, "We had a pretty good childhood, didn't we?"

He nods his head. "I'd say that we made the best out of a less-than-ideal situation. As in, we'd both have preferred our mother was a different person, and that our father hadn't turned to bourbon after she left, but we didn't have it so bad."

"Grandpa Jack and Grandma Adele were awesome though." I look over at my boys who are once again rolling around in a ball of youthful excitement. A feeling of peace comes over me. I've spent so much time feeling angry about the things that have gone wrong in my life, I don't think I've felt nearly enough gratitude for the things that have gone right.

"You want the good news or the bad news first?" Digger asks.

"Always the bad," I tell him.

He reaches out his hand to help me up and when I'm solidly on my feet, he says, "Your water heater is toast."

"No surprise there. It must be twenty years old. What's the good news? It'll only cost me a thousand bucks to get a new one?" Sarcasm is my go-to in times of distress.

Shaking his head, he tells me, "We're upgrading at the lodge, so I can give you a used one that's in decent shape."

I eye him skeptically. "Why are you upgrading if yours are in good shape?"

"We're switching over to on-demand water heaters. Danny Etok said he'd give us a deal if we upgraded all of them. I figured it made sense to do it all in one fell swoop rather than piecemeal."

"That's a lot of money, Digger." Like he doesn't already know that.

"Yeah, well, business has been booming this year. Also, Harper wants to invest. Far be it from me to tell my soon-to-be wife that her money is no good here." He puts his hands in his pockets. "I'll give you the best of the lot and it should last you another three to five years."

Leading the way into the house, I confess, "I'm not too proud to say no. In fact, thank you very much. You're really saving my bacon."

"What else can I help with? You sounded so upset last night."

I walk over to the fridge and pull out two beers. Handing him one, I gesture around the room. "I have no idea where to start. Everywhere I look, there's something that needs doing."

"What room bothers you the most?" he asks.

"The kitchen." I plop down at the table. "I can't stand being in here."

"How about if the boys and I get busy sanding down the cabinets? A nice coat of paint ought to perk the place up."

"Don't you have a job?" I ask him jokingly.

"I do, but we've hired some new help recently, so I'm not always on the go. In fact …" He walks across the room and opens the screen door and calls out, "Boys, get into my truck, we're going to the hardware store!"

I hear their whoops of excitement. Shaking my head, I ask, "Why are you taking my kids to the hardware store?"

"We're gonna get some sandpaper and supplies. I'll bring some paint chips so you can start getting a feel for what color you want."

"Just like that? I've wanted to paint this room for years and haven't gotten around to it, and you're just going to do it?"

"Call me Santa Claus," he says with a huge grin on his face. "I figure with the kids helping, we can get the cabinets finished by Sunday. Then we can decide what's to be done about the floor and counters."

"The floor and counters might have to wait a bit," I tell him. Like maybe five years. But instead of interjecting negativity, I tell him, "I'll bake a batch of cookies and put some fish fillets on the grill." Before he walks away, I add, "Thanks, Digger. You're the best."

"It's true," he says with a twinkle in his eye. "Plus, if I help out here, that'll give you some time to put yourself out there and maybe find a nice guy."

"Is that a condition?" I ask.

"No, ma'am. That's just your supremely wise and all-knowing older brother giving you his two cents."

As he walks out the door, I briefly let myself wonder what it would be like to have a husband around again. I'm surprised when an image of Ethan Caplan pops into my head and it takes more effort than it should to move it out. No, if I ever do consider dating again, I'm going to have to find someone who lives right here in Gamble. Good luck to me.

Chapter 8

Ethan

"It turns out that writing fiction is a lot harder than writing entertainment contracts," I tell Harper. After hours of sitting in front of a blank Word document on my laptop, I decided to pop in on her and complain.

I'm currently following her around while she tends to the many indoor plants around the lodge. Glancing up from her work, she asks, "What have you got so far?"

"Chapter one."

"You wrote the first chapter already? What are you complaining about? That's great!"

"No, I only wrote the words 'chapter' and 'one.' That's it." I hand her the tiny set of shears she's been using to clip back dead leaves. "I was so sure the cabin was going to be the ultimate place to write—quiet, comfortable, beautiful view—but so far ..." I shake my head in disgust. "Nada."

"It's only been three days," she says. "I'm sure it takes a while to warm up."

Lifting the watering can to give the fern a big drink, I tell her, "Back at the office, I'd get interrupted constantly. I always used to think that if I could only just sit somewhere quiet, I'd be able to get so much more done in a day. But now that I've got that, I can't seem to focus."

"Maybe it's *too* quiet," Harper suggests. "Maybe you're the type of writer who needs to sit somewhere noisy."

"I don't think the middle of Main Street is even noisy here."

"How about the diner?" Her eyebrows ascend in question.

She might be right. "Actually, the one time this week I did have an idea was when I was there. There was this nasty redhead who kept glaring at Moira. I made a bunch of notes about her for my villain."

"Big hoop earrings and a low-cut top?" she asks.

"That's the one. Who is she?"

"Just some girl Moira went to high school with. I gather she's the jealous type and she takes her insecurities out on Moira. She'd make a great villain, for sure." We cross the dining room and Harper sets her bucket of tools down in front of a tall palm.

"Do you think Moira would mind my taking up a table at the diner? I don't want her to lose any business."

"Why not rent it, then?" Harper says, misting the plant's broad leaves. "You can ask her tonight."

Tonight is Wyatt's Little League game. Harper, Digger, and Jack will all be there, along with the kids. I've been finding myself looking forward to it a lot more than I should, and I'm starting to think it has less to do with baseball than one of the players' mothers.

∾

The sun shines brightly overhead as the baseball players warm up. It's hot out, but there's a nice breeze making its way to the field from the ocean nearby. I'm sitting in the stands next to Harper. Digger is on her other side, and his grandpa, Jack, is next to him. Ash, Colton, Liam, and Lily are seated on the bench in front of us. Moira is in the dugout, handing out bottled water to the team. I watch her for a minute, glad I'm wearing sunglasses so no one else will notice that I'm staring at her.

Moira Bishop intrigues me. It's not only that she's extraordinarily beautiful with her thick, shiny, dark brown hair and intense blue eyes. She's strong and in charge; she's nurturing and fearless. She's the whole package, really. If I were interested in settling down, I'd definitely be asking her out.

Digger leans forward so he can see me. "So, Ethan, how's your novel coming along?"

"Not great." I tear my eyes away from his sister, who's now climbing the metal bleacher steps toward us. "I'm having a little trouble getting started."

"Getting started is probably the hardest part," he says.

"Getting started on what?" Moira asks, settling down next to me.

"His novel," Digger tells her.

Releasing a groan, she says, "I couldn't write a book if my life depended on it. I'm impressed you're even trying."

"I appreciate that," I tell her. "But I think we all have a book in us somewhere. I bet you could do it if you put your mind to it."

She smirks. "Let me rephrase that. I have no desire to figure out if I could write a book. If I had that kind of time, I'd take up something more relaxing, like napping."

A chuckle escapes me. "My biggest problem seems to be that my house is too quiet. Apparently, my brain needs more stimulation to be creative. Harper thinks I need to work in a place with a lot of background noise." Then I drop the bomb. "You know, like the diner ..."

She stares at me as her mouth opens and closes several times without any response. Before I can backpedal out of my suggestion, Harper interjects, "I suggested he rent a table from you."

"You'd really want to rent a table in a noisy diner?" Moira asks.

"If it wouldn't put you out too much."

"I wouldn't even know where to begin thinking of a fee for something like that."

"If I were in LA, I'd pay at least a thousand dollars a month for one of those shared office spaces," I tell her. "So, how about that?"

"That seems a bit steep." She sounds unsure, making me wish I'd never brought it up.

"How about if you throw in unlimited coffee?" I ask. "I drink a lot of coffee."

She nods her head slowly while saying, "I guess that would be okay."

Trying to release the tension a bit, Harper says, "Your diner could be like that bar Ernest Hemingway wrote at in Havana."

Moira suddenly laughs. "I could put a sign up over the booth. Maybe a picture of Ethan tapping away on his laptop."

I love to see Moira laugh. I haven't seen her do it often, and the sight of it makes me want more. I turn to Digger. "I can't tell if they're making plans for me or making fun of me."

He grins and raises a brow. "Most of the time, I just assume I'm the butt of their jokes. You get used to it."

The first pitch is thrown, and the batter smacks it with

an abundance of enthusiasm. Wyatt, who's playing short-stop, launches himself into the air, but comes up just shy of catching the ball. The batter takes off for first and the cheering begins as the center fielder rushes to pick up what is now a grounder bouncing its way through the grass. They finally manage to stop the runner at third. Wyatt starts a series of arm stretches in preparation for the next pitch.

Moira makes a little grunting sound. "He won't be happy about that."

"The only thing he could have done on that play would have been growing a few inches before it was made," I tell her.

She nods her head. "I'll have to remember to tell him that. It'll make him feel better."

"What are you up to this weekend?" Digger's leaning across Harper again, interrupting my conversation with Moira.

Before I can tell him that my only plans involve writing, Harper interjects, "That's his way of checking to see if you can help him paint Moira's kitchen cabinets."

Digger nudges her in the side playfully. "I don't remember asking for an interpreter."

"Don't worry. She's always been a bit of a busybody," I declare. "I'm used to it." Before Harper can cry foul, I add, "I'd love to help paint cabinets. What time should I be there?"

Digger offers me a grateful smile. "Tomorrow at nine."

"I'll be there." Painting cabinets is not something I'd ever have agreed to help with back home—not that anyone would ask— but still, the answer would've been a hard no. And yet, here I am, happy to do it.

In the third inning, the kids get restless and beg their moms for cash so they can go down to the concession stand

and buy some popcorn and soda. I offer to treat since I haven't seen Lily and Liam in so long. I pull out a twenty and hand it to Liam, who leads the others off like a miniature army captain.

Instead of coming back right away, the four of them goof around behind the stands, and eventually start up their own mini-game of baseball with some of the other siblings in the empty diamond next to the one we're at. I can't help but think of how much freedom a small town like this affords children. It's the way all kids should grow up.

The game flies by and I realize I can't remember the last time I had so much fun. Easy conversation flows among us, and we share lots of laughs over the course of the evening.

When the game ends, Jack announces that he's got a date and gets up and walks toward the dugout to congratulate Wyatt on his way out. The rest of the kids come running back up the steps, looking dirty and wild-eyed.

"Can we go for ice cream now, Mom?" Ash asks Moira.

She nods her head, which sets off loud cheers. Glancing at me, she explains, "It's our tradition. After wins, we eat ice cream to celebrate. After losses, it helps ease the pain."

"So either way, everyone gets some ice cream."

"When you're the mom, you get to make some rules that work in your favor," Moira says, standing up. "You coming?"

"I'd never turn down ice cream."

I wish I'd had a mom like Moira when I was a kid. Mine would only let me eat ice cream once a month and she carefully portioned it out to the half cup serving size suggested on the back of the carton. I used to dream about calling Child Protective Services on her.

After Moira collects Wyatt, we set off as a big group down the sidewalk toward the general store (which Liam, the resident ice cream connoisseur, assures me is THE BEST ICE CREAM EVER).

Somehow, Moira and I end up at the back of the pack, strolling leisurely next to one another. I have an inexplicable urge to slip my fingers through hers, but I don't.

"You're quiet all of a sudden," she says.

"I was just thinking about how much I'm enjoying myself," I tell her. "I've needed a break for a long time, and this is just what the doctor ordered."

"You're not bored? I'd think Friday nights in L.A. would be a lot more exciting."

I shake my head. "Most of my Friday nights are spent at home by myself watching sports or at the office trying to put out whatever fires my clients are starting. Sometimes literal fires."

Moira laughs. "Your job sounds so much more interesting than mine."

"If by interesting, you mean insane, you're right."

"But there must be some parts that are glamorous, right?" she asks. "Upscale restaurants, nightclubs with A-list celebrities…"

"It was fun for a while, but I'm totally over that part of my life. Wild nights out get old."

"I could see that," she says. "Although in my case, I can count all the wild nights out I've had on one hand, so they still hold a lot of appeal."

Passing by a small bookshop, Moira stops in front of a window display of James Patterson's latest. "That's going to be you soon."

My pulse races at the thought of being a bestseller,

then I remember that blinking cursor on my screen all week waiting for me to type the first sentence. "I have to write the book first."

"You're going to find your groove, and before you know it, your great life will only get better." She sounds far more confident in my abilities than I am.

Staring into her blue eyes, I suddenly long to tuck her hair behind her ear and lower my lips to hers. There's something in her expression that suggests she might not mind me doing that. Or is that wishful thinking?

Thankfully, before I can act on such an impulse, Digger calls out, "Come on, you two!"

Moira jolts and her feet immediately answer the call to action. I'm left wondering if we were really on the verge of a moment, or if I just made that up.

Chapter 9

Moira

The boys are sitting at the breakfast table, eating waffles faster than I can cook them. The kitchen is an absolute mess, what with the cupboard doors and drawer fronts gone. Digger disassembled everything yesterday and took them out to the garage to sand them and prep them for painting. Glancing at the clock, I realize he and Ethan will be here in about half an hour.

"I'm next!" Colton shouts out as Wyatt shoves his plate in my direction.

"No, I'm next!" Ash nudges past him.

"I'm next," I tell them in my best no-nonsense mom voice. "I made each of you two waffles already and if you want more, you can make them yourselves."

"What?" they gasp in unison. "You never let us cook," my oldest says.

"About that," I tell them. "Things are going to change. I can't keep up on everything that I need to do and I'm not about to raise three sons who expect the women in their lives to take care of them. As of today, you three are in training."

"Sweet!" Colton shouts while Ash and Wyatt exchange worried glances.

I open the lid to the waffle maker and put the offering on my plate. Then I push the recipe book in their direction. "Grandma Adele's specialty. Follow the directions and if you have any questions, just ask."

I watch them closely as they measure out ingredients and fight over the whisk. Having sons is hard, but it's a lot tougher when you're a control freak like I am. Once I'm done eating, and the boys are elbow deep in making the rest of their breakfast, I get up and walk into the entry hall and pick up all the mail that came in over the week.

Sitting back at the table, I sort bills, coupons, and other sundry missives. The last envelope I open is from Wyatt's coach, Dalton Phillips. I wonder what he wants. I pull out a single sheet of paper and read carefully as a pit the size of the Grand Canyon starts to form in my stomach.

"Wyatt, why didn't you tell me about this fundraiser your baseball team is part of?"

My son spins around on his heels, flinging waffle batter through the air. "I totally forgot! Isn't it cool? The team that raises the most money gets free tickets to a Dodgers game, and we even get a tour of the dugout!"

"I can see how that's exciting," I tell him haltingly. "But according to Coach's flyer, even if your team sells the most raffle tickets, you'll still have to pay for your own airfare and lodging once you get to Los Angeles."

He shrugs nonchalantly. "Yeah, but how much can that be? Fifty dollars? A hundred? I can make that by doing odd jobs around the neighborhood."

I look down at the sheet. "More like five hundred

dollars. Look, I'm not trying to burst your bubble, but I don't have that kind of money to pay for your ticket to California, and even if I did, that wouldn't be enough because I'm not about to let you go without me."

"Coach Dalton and his wife will be there. I'd be fine."

He turns around to take his waffle out, when Ash announces, "You'd need two thousand dollars, Mom, because Colton and I would be going, too."

"You'd stay with Grandpa Jack and Uncle Digger," Wyatt snarls.

"No way! If you're going to California, then so are we!" Colton joins the fray.

"No one's going to California," I tell them. "I'm sorry, Wyatt, but there's just no way. Not this summer anyway."

"That's not fair, Mom," he pouts, crossing his arms across his chest. He looks just like a tiny, furious version of Everett. Like a knife to my heart, he adds, "Just because you're poor doesn't mean we should have to be poor, too."

All kinds of feelings rush through my nervous system. Anger at Everett for leaving us with no life insurance; anger at myself for not making enough to give my boys the extras; and finally, anger at the kids for not appreciating how hard I work to give them the things I do. I mean, seriously, the baseball uniform and shoes strapped my June budget enough.

Inhaling deeply, I hold my breath for a count of five before exhaling. When I'm slightly calmer, I tell the kids, "We may not be rich, but we're not poor. We have clothes on our backs and shoes on our feet, and a roof over our heads." Such as it is. "Just because I can't afford to take off work and fly you all to California doesn't mean you don't have a good life." Take that, you little rug rats.

Ash shrugs. "It's cool with me. I'm not even sure where California is."

"I'm good, too." Colton nods while spooning batter onto the waffle iron.

"Well, I'm *not* good!" Wyatt shouts. "I'm going to raise as much money as I can and I'm going! I don't care if I have to ask Uncle Digger for the money."

I point my finger in his direction with sharp jabbing motions. "You will not ask Uncle Digger. He's already giving us a water heater and is painting our kitchen, which, believe me, we need a lot more than we need a vacation."

"Then I'll ask Aunt Harper," he threatens. "She's got loads of money."

I find myself longing to be a parent in the eighties who could spank freely. "You will do no such thing, young man, and if you go against my orders and ask anyway, I'll ground you until you're in high school." His glare is so menacing, I add, "Don't cross me, Wyatt. I told you how it's going to be and that's it. End of discussion."

Instead of responding, he storms out of the house, making sure to slam the front door on his way out. I turn to the twins and demand, "Do you two have anything you want to fight with me about? Because, let me warn you, if you do, things will not go your way."

I'm practically shaking with rage when Colton puts his spatula down and walks toward me. Throwing his arms around my waist, he says, "I love you, Mom. I know you're doing the best you can."

Ash joins in, holding on as tight as his brother. "I love you too, Mom."

And just like that, I burst into tears again—this is becoming an alarming habit. My seven-year-old sons are comforting me. I'm proud and ashamed all at once. If Everett were still alive, he could have taken Wyatt and I could have stayed home with the twins. We would have had two incomes, so even if we'd had to scrimp a little, we could have done it.

"What would you think about us selling this house?" I ask them, wiping my eyes.

"Just so Wyatt could go to Los Angeles?" Colton asks, pulling away from me.

"That seems a little extreme, Mom," Ash says.

"No, not so Wyatt can go to California." At this point, even if I had the money, I wouldn't let him go after that scene he just made. "I was thinking we could move into a smaller house that needs less work. It would free up time for us to do more fun things."

"I like it here," Ash says.

"Me, too," Colton hurries to add.

Slumping back into my chair, I say, "Okay." I'll leave it for now. After all, Digger and Ethan will be here in a few minutes to paint. Maybe I just need to start seeing some improvements to start liking this house again.

A knock at the front door interrupts my thoughts. I hurry over to answer it, only to see Ethan standing on the other side of the screen. He's wearing ripped jeans and a gray T-shirt, and he looks far too handsome for my own good. His boyish smile appears as I push the door open for him.

"Is this where the painting party is happening?"

All sorts of feelings bubble up inside me as I stare at his gorgeous face, not the least of which is a longing to kiss him. It's so strong, it nearly knocks me on my butt. Where the heck did that come from? I should only be thinking about how grateful I am that Ethan is helping me out. Not only is he here to paint, but he's renting a table at the diner.

As he steps inside, I get a hint of his aftershave, and

I'm back to longing again. Suddenly, I'm afraid my feelings for him are going to become another complication in my life.

And the last thing I need are more complications.

Chapter 10

Ethan

"Am I too early?" I ask, noticing how flustered Moira seems. She's dressed in an old T-shirt that nearly swallows her up and a pair of shorts that barely poke out from the hem of her shirt. Her hair is up in a ponytail, and she doesn't have any makeup on, but somehow, she's as appealing as a movie star on the red carpet.

"Not at all. It's just been a hectic morning. Come on in," she says, stepping aside to let me in.

Juno, their golden retriever, greets me like we're long-lost friends. I crouch down to pet her. "Hey, girl, how have you been?" When Prisha and I stayed here last summer, Juno decided to honor me by sleeping on my bed.

She rubs her head against my thigh to let me know all is well in her doggie world. After a minute, Moira leads the way into the kitchen where the twins are gobbling up some waffles.

"Did you eat?" she asks.

"Yup, I'm all fueled up and ready to paint."

"Digger and Harper stopped at the hardware store to get the paint mixed. They should be here in a few minutes," she says. "Can I get you a cup of coffee?"

"Only if it's already made."

"It is." She reaches into a cabinet for a mug. "Ash, Colt, you boys head outside and see if you can find your brother. I'll do the dishes."

The boys move so fast, I have to step aside to avoid being mowed down. Juno follows them. When the door slams behind them, Moira releases a ragged sigh while she pours my coffee. Handing it to me, she explains, "Wyatt is upset with me this morning."

I don't want to pry, so I say, "That'll happen with kids."

She opens the ancient burnished-yellow dishwasher and starts to load the dishes on the counter. Setting my coffee down, I get up and carry over the plates and cutlery that are littering the table.

"You don't have to help," she says.

"I thought that's why I was here."

She takes a glass from my hand. "Thank you." Her fingertip brushes against my skin, warming me from head to heel. She startles like she's just been on the receiving end of an electric shock. She hurriedly turns her attention back to the dishes.

I'm almost one hundred percent certain, Moira Bishop is not immune to my charms. She makes me feel like a middle schooler in the throes of my first crush. Maybe I should just pass her a note. *Do you like any boy in this room? Circle Yes or No.*

The front door opens, and Ash sticks his head in. "Wyatt's down at the creek. We're going to race sticks for a while."

"That's fine. Just stay out of the water. There's enough laundry to do this weekend as it is."

He gives her a thumbs up before racing across the front lawn. Moira looks over at me. "What do you suppose the chances are that any of them come home dry?"

"Based on my recollection of being that age, I'm going to say five percent."

"You must be an optimist," she says wryly.

Moira scrubs the waffle maker while I wipe the counters and table. After a few minutes, the work is done. She takes a deep breath. "Thank you. Cleanup is much easier with a little help. I've been training the boys, but they seem to leave more messes than they start with."

The door opens and Digger and Harper walk in. Harper announces, "Liam and Lily saw the boys and ran down to the creek to join them."

Digger adds, "I'm thinking it might be easier to just let them play. With the four of us working, we should be done in no time."

"That's a great idea," Moira replies. "This way the kids can get as wet as they want, and I don't have to worry about who's going to spill paint first."

It's quickly decided that Digger and I will paint the doors and drawer fronts in the garage while Moira and Harper paint the frames in the kitchen. I'm slightly disappointed I won't be working with Moira, but I suppose it's for the best. After all, I'm pretty sure that even if she did like me as more than a friend, she's probably got no time for a man in her life—definitely not one who isn't going to stick around.

The morning flies by. A couple of hours into painting, Wyatt wanders into the garage and plunks himself down on an overturned bucket. He sighs heavily.

"You sound like you have the weight of the world on your shoulders," Digger tells him.

"Nah, I'm fine."

"Something's bugging you. Otherwise, you'd be playing with the other kids right now."

"I'm not supposed to talk to you about it because Mom doesn't want you *fixing* it for me." Wyatt makes finger quotations around the word fixing.

Digger stops painting for a second. "Tell me. You know I'm always happy to help in any way that I can."

Shaking his head determinedly, Wyatt says, "No way. Mom's madder at me now than the time I gave Travis Sinclair the super nut cruncher."

Before I can insert myself into the conversation and ask if a nut cruncher is what I think it is, Colton walks in and declares, "He's mad because his team is going to try to win a trip to LA to see a Dodgers game, but it doesn't include the airfare and hotel so Mom said he can't go."

Ash walks in right after his twin. "Wyatt yelled at Mom and told her he was going to ask Auntie Harper on account of her being rich and all. Mom practically blew a gasket."

"I never said that!" Wyatt tells him with a scowl.

"Did, too!"

"Fine, but only because Mom wasn't even letting me *try* to come up with another plan!" Wyatt says. "She's so mean sometimes."

"None of that kind of talk," Digger tells him. "Your mom's got a lot on her plate. She's doing the best she can."

"I know, but she should at least let me try to raise the money, shouldn't she?" he asks.

"If she said no, I'm sure she has a good reason," Digger answers.

Ash nods his head. "She's upset because the house is

too old and too big and needs so much work. She actually had a huge cry about it after Wyatt ran out." He makes a little *tsk*ing sound, then adds, "Haven't seen her do that in a long time."

Wyatt's face turns bright red and he tries to blink back the tears that spring to his eyes. "Why'd my dad have to be a stupid crab fisherman? Why couldn't he have had a normal job like … like … being a dentist or something? Then he'd still be alive, and we could afford things like trips and stuff."

Digger puts down his brush and walks over to his nephew. He folds him into a big hug while he sobs.

I keep working, knowing it's none of my business, but I can't help feeling choked up at the scene that's playing out. I can't imagine how hard it is to grow up with only one parent. Both of mine worked a lot, but at least we always knew they were there if we needed them.

After a couple of minutes, Wyatt pulls back and wipes the tears off his cheeks.

"Feel better?" Digger asks.

Nodding, Wyatt says, "A little."

"Listen, I can't make any promises, but maybe if you write out a plan for how you'd raise the money, your mom might listen. Of course, you'll have to apologize first," he tells him. "And you have to treat your mom with respect which means no yelling, no matter how upset you are."

"Okay, Uncle Digger," he says. "You're right." After a second, he asks, "Do you really think she might let me go? I mean, if I had a really good plan and could raise the money myself?"

"It's worth a shot, but remember, the final decision is hers."

Wyatt beams like the spotlight on the Hollywood sign

at night. "Thanks. I'm going to see what I can come up with." He races out of the garage.

The twins follow him out, leaving Digger and me alone. Digger looks at me and shakes his head. "I wish they had it easier."

"I can't even begin to imagine how tough being a single parent would be. They're lucky to have you in their lives though. I wouldn't have had any idea what to say to Wyatt, but you handled him really well."

"Years of practice. Wyatt was only three when Everett died, and the twins never knew him, so I'm the only father-like figure they've ever had."

The rest of the day is spent brightening up Moira's kitchen. When we finally stop for some pizza, my back aches and my hands are cramped from painting for hours on end, but even so, I feel good. I've helped someone who really needed it, which is a real departure from cleaning up messes after spoiled rich people.

We eat out in the backyard at an old wooden picnic table while the last coat of paint dries. We'll hang the cupboard doors back on after supper.

The kids make short work of their dinner, then get back to zipping around the yard playing while the grown-ups sip beer from cans and gush about how great the kitchen is going to look.

Moira seems a lot happier than she was this morning. "I can't tell you how grateful I am that you would all spend your day helping me with this. It was such a big job, I wouldn't have even known where to start, and now it's done."

"We're happy to help," Harper says. "Really. It's been a fun day."

"Agreed," I tell her. "Really fun." Glancing over at the kids, I watch as Wyatt trots down the back steps of the house. I know exactly what he's up to and for his sake, I hope he's successful. He's holding some papers in his hand. Walking over to us, he says, "Mom, I know I sounded like a spoiled baby this morning and I'm really sorry."

Moira nods her head once. "Thank you. I appreciate your saying that.

He offers her a winning smile. "I've come up with a plan to raise the money myself."

She purses her lips tightly. "What kind of plan?"

"I'm going to start my own business. It's called Wasp Be Gone. All I need are some empty plastic bottles, some jam, and some water to make the traps. I can take them door-to-door around town and sell them to people."

Pointing to the page, he says, "My customers can choose to either buy the traps and take care of mainte-nance themselves, or they can pick the full-service package, and I'll go every week to get rid of the dead wasps and set the traps again."

I can't help but grin at how proud of his idea he is. I find myself cheering for him internally.

"For those who don't want my wasp removal service, I'm also going to offer dog walking, weeding, and mowing lawns, but for that one, I'd need you to let me use the mower. I'll pay for the gas of course." He stops and smiles, hope shining in his eyes while he waits for an answer.

Moira sighs, looking down at his proposal. "You think you can win the competition *and* make a thousand dollars in six weeks?"

He shrugs. "I can try. I really want to do this, Mom," he says. "I can't be the only guy who won't get to go if we win. It's the *Dodgers.* We'll get to run around on the field after the game and meet the players and everything."

"What about the hotel? That'll be extra."

"You could stay at my place," I say without thinking.

All eyes turn to me, which makes me wonder if I should have kept my mouth shut.

Moira seems angry, confirming that it isn't my place to interfere. I think fast. "Sorry, I know this isn't my business. I just mean that if Wyatt was able to come up with the flight money, I have enough room for everyone at my house and you're more than welcome to stay there. In fact, I have to zip home for a few days later this summer, so I could go with you, and even show you guys around a little." I hold up both hands. "But only if it's one hundred percent okay with you, Moira."

Wyatt grins at me, then at his mom. He's positively shaking with excitement.

Digger interjects, "We could use your services at the lodge, Wyatt. I'll take twenty of those traps as soon as you can get them to me."

Wyatt's eyes grow wide, and his grin expands to his ears. "See, Mom? This could work."

She gives each of us a dirty look, before telling her son, "I'll think about it."

He nods enthusiastically. "You're the best mom ever and if you say yes to this, I'll never complain about doing my chores again."

I lift my beer to my mouth to hide the smirk that's trying to overtake my face. I'm sure I used that line before on my own parents a time or two.

Wyatt closes out his presentation with a quick hug, before running off to where the other kids have started a paddle ball competition.

Moira gives Digger a look. "There's no way he can earn enough money for both of us."

"What if he can?" Digger asks.

She counters with, "What if he can't?"

"If he can't, Grandpa Jack, Harper and I can pitch in

for flights for all the boys' birthdays. That way you can have a family vacation."

She shakes her head adamantly. "No dice. If he can't do it, we don't go. That's final." Digger opens his mouth, but she cuts him off. "If he can't do it, it will be a tough lesson, but it's one he's going to have to learn. Better now while he's young, than later."

"The kids don't ask for a lot, Moira," Digger tells her. "Let us help give them this. Besides, I think a break from your regular life will be good for you, too."

"I'm not budging, Digger. And I don't want to hear anything more about it." She picks up her beer and takes a long pull, then gives me a look that lets me know I screwed up. Moira Bishop is one tough woman in an even tougher position in life.

Chapter 11

Moira

"Girl, if you slam that coffee pot down one more time, it's gonna shatter," Abigail says, calling me out on my intensity which, to be honest, is on the extreme side today.

"Have you ever had someone determined to interfere with your life who has no place doing so?" I spin around and demand.

We've just finished the morning rush and there are no customers in urgent need of anything, so she sits down at the counter. "Who's butting into your business now? If it's that Sissy Sinclair again, I'd be happy to arrange a tire slashing incident." Sissy's hatred of me is well known around town.

My eyebrows raise toward my hairline. "You'd commit a crime for me? I'm touched."

"Better yet"—she rests her elbows on the counter—"I'd commit a felony. Who needs whacking?"

A burst of laughter escapes me. "You know that guy Ethan, who's been in here a couple times?"

"The good-looking lawyer with a butt you could bounce a quarter off?"

"I don't know about the butt, but yeah, that's him." Pouring myself a cup of coffee, I explain, "He was over helping paint my kitchen on Saturday, and he offered to let the kids and me stay at his house in LA if Wyatt's baseball team can sell enough raffle tickets to win a trip there, and if Wyatt can make enough money for airfare."

"The fiend!" She slaps her hands on the countertop so loudly I jump. "He painted your kitchen and then dared make you a generous offer?" She pretends to scribble something on her notepad and jokes, "I'll have him removed from Alaska within the hour."

I roll my eyes. "I'm not explaining myself very well. First off, I do know it was very kind of him to help with the painting this weekend and I am grateful. But, while he, Harper, and Digger were there, this whole thing about the baseball trip came up. I'd already told Wyatt that even if his team won the competition, we didn't have money for him to go see the Dodgers. I hoped that would put the matter to bed, but it didn't."

After a big sigh, I conclude, "Instead, everyone seemed hell bent on making me eat my words. First, Ethan offered to put us up at his house, then Digger said that he and Harper would pay. When I said no, he offered to give my determined son enough work at the lodge to get him the money that way."

Abigail takes a sip of water before saying, "You do realize that by its very definition, family is there to help. I mean, where would Danny and I be if my parents hadn't given us the down payment for our house?" Before I can answer, she says, "We'd still be renting. Do you think we even once thought about saying no?" Shaking her head like she's successfully engaged her inner propeller, she adds, "We did not."

"Yeah, but that's your *parents*. That's different."

"Your parents are gone, so you don't get any help from them. Why shouldn't you take it where you can get it?"

"It's one thing to let Digger help, but I'm not looking for handouts from strangers." I'm sticking to my guns on this one.

Pushing off the stool, Abigail says, "The man rented a room from you last year for a week and he's your soon-to-be sister-in-law's best friend. He's not a stranger."

Wouldn't you know it, the door opens and Ethan strolls into the diner. I wondered when he'd planned to start his booth rental. I don't work Sundays, so I don't know if he came in yesterday, but he's here now.

"Morning!" Abigail calls out. "Sit wherever you'd like, and I'll be right over to get your order."

I try to look busy refilling sugars while whispering to Abigail, "He's going to rent a booth here to write a novel. I'm not sure he's going to be eating a lot."

She nods her head. "Either way, I bet he could use a cup of coffee." She picks up the pot and walks over to the table where Ethan has set up shop. He's sitting on the side that's facing me which is more than a little uncomfortable. How in the world am I going to go about my business day in and day out with him here?

After ten minutes or so, I realize that I need to go over and say hello. The man did work at my house all day on Saturday. The very least I owe him is a pleasant work environment. Putting a blueberry muffin onto a plate, I pick up the coffee pot and walk over to him. "Good morning, Ethan, how are you today?"

He looks up from his keyboard. "I was wondering if you were going to say hello."

He could have just as easily said hello to me, but I don't point that out. "Sorry, I was doing some side work to prepare for the lunch rush."

"Are you still mad at me?" he asks while adding a sugar packet to the coffee I just poured.

"I'm not mad at you," I lie. "I'm mad at my son who won't take no for an answer."

He nods his head. "Pushing boundaries is a kid's job. It's one of the basic tenets of childhood."

"I brought you a muffin," I say, putting it down in front of him. "It's on the house."

He opens a new tab on his computer. "Thanks. Do you have PayPal or Venmo? I can transfer my first month's rent to you now."

After giving him my PayPal address, I say, "I feel kind of bad about taking your money." Not so bad that I won't take it, but still.

"Just wait until you see how much coffee I drink. You'll be doubling my rent next month."

I stare at him, quietly taking inventory of his features. Ethan Caplan is one good-looking man. Light sandy brown hair, green eyes that crinkle in the corners like he spends a lot of time smiling, and a jaw so chiseled you could probably cut bread with it. "I'm not looking for a relationship," I blurt out. The heat of embarrassment immediately creeps from the base of my neck all the way up to my face.

He smiles kindly. "And you're telling me this, why?"

"I'm just … I mean … It's just that …" I want to crawl under the table and die. *Why in the world did I say that?*

He takes me off the hook by saying, "You're a beautiful woman, Moira, but I'm not looking for a relationship, either. What do you say we keep things at the friend level?"

"Sure, that's great." I practically run away from him before he can respond. I must be the biggest idiot in a five-hundred-mile radius.

The lunch rush comes and goes, as I work hard to ignore Ethan's occasional gaze. Suddenly, a thousand dollars a month doesn't feel like enough to put up with his presence. The truth is that if I could go back in time and live my life over, Ethan is exactly the kind of guy I could see myself going for.

The landline rings, breaking into my reverie, and I reach over to pull the receiver off the wall. "The Diner, what can I do for you?"

"Is this THE diner? In Gamble, Alaska?" a semi-nasally female voice asks.

"It is," I tell her. "We're the only diner in town."

"This is Rose Caplan," she whispers like she doesn't want to be overheard. "I think my son Ethan is working on his book there somewhere. He's not picking up his phone."

"Would you like me to get him?" I can't help but wonder why Rose Caplan is tracking her son down. I hope there isn't an emergency.

"Please just tell him that I expect him to answer the phone when I call. Oh, and you might want to mention that his father has finally lost his mind."

"Should I tell him how?" It's none of my business, but I kind of want to know.

"Harriet Eckle talked Isaac into taking swing dancing lessons with her and now he's prancing around the house like some lothario of yore. It's disgusting."

"Oh …" I seriously don't know what else to say.

"I've decided to take Ethan's advice and book a trip for us to keep my husband from making a fool of himself."

"I see …"

"Tell Ethan we're coming up there to see him in Alaska. Isaac and I will stay with him for a while, and he can take us sight-seeing. I'll let him know as soon as I book our tickets."

"Um, okay …"

"I mean, honestly, that boy isn't really writing a book, is he? He should be here at home working and finding a nice young thing to help him make me a grandmother. But is he? No."

I have no idea what to say, so I settle on, "I'll give him the message."

"You do that, dear, and make sure to tell him that I want to see a bear. Not up close and personal, but close enough to get a good picture. I'll show it to Harriet when I let her know she'd better keep her hands to herself."

Suddenly, I'm looking forward to talking to Ethan again. I want to get the skinny on his mom. She sounds like a real character.

Chapter 12

Ethan

The first line of my novel doesn't want to be written, so I decide to start with the second and see where that takes me. Twenty minutes in, I Google "how to write a thriller."

I'm too distracted by what just happened with Moira to concentrate on any of the advice I find. Watching the object of my preoccupation talk on the phone, I realize I must be sending her the wrong vibes. Why else would she blurt out that she's not looking for a relationship?

Even though I'm not looking for love, my ego is still bruised. I don't know who to feel worse for—me, for firmly getting put into the friend zone before I even had a chance to pull out my best moves, or her, for looking so humiliated after preemptively shooting me down.

Me. I feel worse for myself.

Glancing up, I notice Moira coming my way with a strange look on her face. She looks like she's trying not to laugh, which is odd considering how embarrassed she was earlier. Stopping at my booth, she says, "So, umm … your mom just called. Apparently, you're not picking up your phone."

"My mother called here?" Either my father is dead, or Bristol Farms ran out of the good cheese.

"She's mad at you for not answering your phone."

"She doesn't seem to understand the concept of work hours. Sorry about that. I'll make sure she doesn't bother you again."

"It was no problem, really." Moira barely suppresses a giggle. "She asked me to take a message."

I close my eyes for a second and silently pray for peace. "I see."

"Rose says you need to pick up your phone from now on, in case there's an emergency. Also, she says your dad has finally lost his mind and has started taking dance lessons with someone named Harriet."

Rubbing my temples on both sides of my forehead to suppress the headache that's creeping closer, I ask, "Anything else?"

She nods her head. "It sounds like she doesn't approve of your writing a book, and she'd rather you come home and go back to your *real* job." Moira taps her chin with a pen while looking up at the ceiling as if trying to recall what else my mother said to her. "Oh yeah, and she and your dad are coming for a visit."

"Excuse me?" Icy fingers of dread shoot up my spine.

"She's booking a trip up here so you can show them around. She wants to see a bear … which seemed to have something to do with that Harriet person. I couldn't quite follow the logic, but if I had to guess, I'd say she plans on threatening Harriet with a mauling."

"This can't be happening …" My entire face is hot with embarrassment and dread.

"And yet, it is ..." She's full-on beaming now.

"Mothers, am I right?" I ask, before remembering that Moira's mom is not only dead, but she abandoned her family first. Also, Moira's a mother who's currently engaged in a battle of wills with one of her kids ...

Her expression falls. "Yeah, I hear they can be pretty tough."

"I'm sorry, Moira. That was insensitive of me."

"No worries." She sounds sincere. "I've had a long time to get over it." Grinning again, she adds, "But you should probably call your mom now."

Sighing dramatically, I push out of the booth. "I'll go outside and call her." I have no idea where this conversation is going to go, and I don't really love the idea of the other customers listening in. Moira steps aside so I can move around her, and seconds later, I'm standing out in the warmth of the sun waiting for my mom to pick up the phone.

In lieu of a greeting, she says, "I suppose you're going to lecture me."

"Would it help?" I ask.

"No."

"Then I won't bother, except to say that the woman who answered the phone at the diner doesn't have time to take messages for me. She especially doesn't have time to hear about Dad taking dance lessons with Harriet Eckle."

"Well, I had to do something. You weren't picking up."

My mother is so sure I'm in the wrong here, there's no point engaging in an argument. "I always call you back, Mom. But you know I can't always be at your beck and call. I do work."

"Psh, work. You're not working now." Not that she's psychic, but even if she were, that comment has less to do with my writer's block and more to do with the fact that I'm not currently "lawyering," as she calls it.

Do not take the bait, Ethan. Do not take the bait. "What's this about you coming to visit?"

"You're the one who said your dad and I should take a trip. I'm just following your advice."

"I was thinking about Greece or Spain. You know, places you've always wanted to see but have never made time for."

"Greece and Spain will always be there, but you won't always be in Alaska." Then she drops the mother of all bombs. "Plus, you have that nice big house for us to stay in."

No way are they staying with me. "You have no interest in seeing Alaska. You wouldn't even accept Harper's wedding invitation because you were worried you'd die of boredom."

"We love Harper, but not enough to fly across Canada like some kind of migrating birds. But you, you're enough reason, Ethan."

"I live on the other side of Beverly Hills from you, and it's been months since you've last come to my house."

"That's because there are so many great restaurants to eat at. Why would I subject myself to your cooking if I didn't have to?"

"There's only one diner, and one grocery store in Gamble. And no one serves anything remotely kosher here either."

"Kosher shmosher. It's not like your father and I are religious. We're booked on the six a.m. non-stop flight to Anchorage a week from Thursday. The plane lands at nine twenty-five your time." Without so much as taking a breath, she adds, "I'm assuming you can pick us up at the airport."

"It's a two-hour drive on a dirt road from here." The road is actually paved, but this is my last chance to get her to back out.

She pauses slightly before saying, "It'll be an adventure."

"Mom, please cancel the flight. You'll hate it here, and I won't have time to be your tour guide." I'm desperate for her to acquiesce.

"We're coming, and that's final. I'll text the flight details to you. Now, I have to run. I'm on my way out the door for Pilates. See you in a week."

"Mom, Mom …" Too late, she's already gone.

Isaac and Rose Caplan of Beverly Hills are about to descend upon the nice people of Gamble, Alaska, like a sizable earthquake. While I should be thinking of how to best shield the local citizenry from the onslaught heading their way, I'm more concerned about getting a good start on my book. I'm never going to hear the end of it otherwise.

Chapter 13

Moira

At twelve noon on the nose, I look out the window to see my three boys jumping off their bikes. They fly into the diner in a cloud of chaos and dust. A chorus of "Hi, Mom" greets me before they spot Ethan. Once that happens, their trajectory shifts, and they hurry to sit down with him.

I walk over and announce, "I don't think Ethan needs you kids distracting him from his work."

Ethan has already closed his laptop. He distributes menus to my sons and says, "Nonsense. A man needs to eat." Then he smiles brightly. "Plus, I told Wyatt I'd help him think of things his team can raffle off."

"I was thinking we could sell handshakes with Aunt Harper." Wyatt's eyes are veritably sparkling with dollar signs.

"I told you that you need to find a way to make money that doesn't infringe on anyone else." Plus, everyone in town has already met Harper. They've either stalked her at the market or gone to the lodge for a meal. A few have been so bold as to knock on her door. Meeting Harper Kennedy is the only claim to fame most of us will ever have.

"Mr. Sinclair is going to donate a free tune-up to the raffle." He's clearly trying to get me to sign up to volunteer for his raffle.

Dammit. It worked because I hear myself say, "I'll give you a free lunch for two."

My son scrunches up his face in disappointment. "I thought maybe you'd do free lunches for a month."

"How about if I raffle off my smart-mouth ten-year-old son?" *Put that in your pipe, kid.* I don't wait for him to answer before saying, "Today's lunch is club sandwiches with fruit."

Before Wyatt and I can start a full-out battle again, Colton asks, "Can I have french fries with my sandwich? I know you think they'll ruin my appetite for supper, but I'm starving. Mrs. Turner made us do all kinds of weeding this morning and my breakfast didn't last as long as it should have."

"Edna had you weed? Where?" Panic rips through me as I imagine every last flower ripped out of the flower bed.

Ash elbows his brother in the ribs. "It was supposed to be a surprise, you dunderhead."

"What kind of surprise?" Everyone knows I hate surprises, so I can't imagine why my neighbor thinks this time will be any different.

"A good one," Wyatt says. "But we promised we wouldn't say anything." He glares at Colton. "You're such a blabbermouth."

Before they can come to blows, I tell them, "You can all

have french fries." Turning to Ethan, I ask, "What would you like?"

"Same as the boys," he says with a wink. "But I might need extra fries for fuel."

By the time I turn around to put their order in, five more tables have sat themselves. Abigail has already been to most of them.

Luckily, the rest of the day flies by and it's four o'clock before I know it. Taking off my apron, I call out to Ethan, "See you tomorrow."

"You're heading out?" He scoots out of his booth. "I should probably be going, too."

"You got big plans or something?"

He laughs. "Big plans for Lily," he tells me. "I promised I'd take her out to get her toenails painted. She claims she doesn't get enough one-on-one time with me." Putting his laptop into a tote, he asks, "You wouldn't happen to know a good place to get your nails done in town?"

"The Rinse 'n Repeat is the only place that does manicures and pedicures. I've never had one there though, so I don't know if they're any good."

"Lily's not picky," he says.

My whole nervous system fills with warm fuzzies. "You're pretty close to Harper's kids, aren't you?"

"I'm their godfather." Then, in a Marlon Brando-esque tone, he says, "Nothing is more important than family."

The more I talk to Ethan, the more attractive he gets. Which is bad, *so* bad, as we clearly aren't meant for each other. "You two have fun," I say. "And tell Lily I'm jealous."

"Why don't you join us?" he asks, his eyes flicking down to my lips for the briefest of moments.

Blushing, I say, "I wouldn't want to horn in on Lily's time with you." Looking down at my nails, I realize how in need I am of a little TLC. "Besides, I need to relieve Edna. She likes to get home soon, so she has enough time to put dinner on the table for Ed."

"In that case, I should let you get going."

Not wanting the conversation to end just yet, I ask, "What color are you getting?"

"Excuse me?" he asks, looking confused.

"Nail polish. I'm wondering what color of nail polish you're getting."

"I think I'll just get them trimmed. As much as I love Lily, I'm not about to walk around Gamble with pink sparkly nails."

"That would be a good way to get the small-town tongues wagging," I tell him.

"I bet, and as I'd like to avoid that, I think I'll stay with my original plan."

Leading the way out the front door, I tell Ethan, "Good luck with that. When these people want to gossip, nothing stops them." Realizing I sound like a negative Nelly, I change the subject. "Have a great night."

"You, too."

Neither one of us seems to want to walk away. We just stand in front of the diner staring at each other. I finally say, "Thanks for being nice to my boys. But please feel free to tell them if you're too busy to eat lunch with them. You'll have to be firm though, because they don't pick up on subtlety very well."

"I enjoy hanging out with them," he says. "I bet they're a great influence on Liam."

"Ah, yes, the little man in socks and sandals," I tease. "I think my boys are making an impact on him. Just last week Liam burped at the table so loudly, I thought Harper would faint."

"I would have paid money to see that," Ethan laughs.

When we finally part ways, Ethan goes to his car, and I head to mine. I think about how lucky Harper's kids are to have a man like Ethan in their lives. He would make a great father. A pang of something that feels like longing rips through me and I start to wonder if I might enjoy having a husband again. I miss adult conversation in the evenings. Not like Everett and I talked about much more than his job and random gossip that was spreading around town, but it was nice to have another adult around.

On my way home, I decide tonight is going to be what Grandma Adele used to call Emergency Supper—which is essentially any box of cereal you have accompanied by a piece of fruit. I just don't have the energy to take care of another person today. In fact, I might just crawl into bed and give that romance novel another crack. Becoming someone else for the night sounds like just the ticket. Heck, I'd even take an hour.

Pulling into my driveway, my mouth practically hits my knees. What in the world have my kids been up to?

Chapter 14

Ethan

"You're sure you want to get a pedicure here?" I murmur to Lily, who's holding my hand as we stand in the doorway of the Rinse 'n Repeat. This place isn't exactly giving off spa vibes. There's a country song blasting out of the speakers about a man lamenting his fate of "looking at the world through a windshield." The walls are prison gray and instead of massage chairs, they appear to be using folding chairs.

Lily tilts her head to the side and looks at me from under her blonde eyelashes. With a smile, she says, "We can't neglect our feet during flip-flop season."

I stare at the three metal chairs and nod. "Pedis it is." The woman behind the counter grins at me like Lily and I are the cutest thing she's ever seen. She leads us over to the chairs before pouring water into the basins. "I'm Rhonda. It'll take me a minute to get your foot baths filled. Why don't you pick out your colors?"

Lily tugs at my arm and leads me to a wall of nail polish bottles in every color under the sun. "I think I'll get blue."

"Blue is my favorite," I tell her.

Her eyes light up. "You should do the same one."

"I was thinking I'd skip the polish."

Her eyes roll up. "Men."

"Exactly," I tell her. "Can't live with 'em, can't live without 'em."

We're soon sipping bottled water and letting our feet soak in massage baths. Not what I'd call luxurious, but not a total miss. After all, I'm with one of my favorite people in the world.

Said companion sighs as soon as Rhonda plugs her foot bath in, and it starts to vibrate. "Mom thinks you have a crush on Moira. True or false?"

My cheeks heat up. "False."

Leveling me with a surprisingly condescending glare for a five-year-old, Lily continues, "Really? Because it seems like you really like her."

"Moira is a beautiful woman and I really like spending time with her. But I am not looking for a girlfriend right now, and she's not looking for anyone either. So, we're going to be friends."

"You're not getting any younger, you know," Lily says, taking a sip of her water.

Ouch. "That's not very nice," I tell her.

Cocking one eyebrow, she says, "Someone's got to tell you the truth, Uncle Ethan. And I'm not going to lie to you. Mommy says lying is for dogs."

"Right, well, thanks, but I've almost been married once, and I don't think it's for me."

"You can't let Paige ruin the rest of your life. There are plenty of nice women in the world who would love to marry you." I'm pretty sure she's overheard Harper say these exact words. Prisha too.

"Thanks, but no thanks. I've been there, almost done that, didn't like how it turned out."

"That's just silly, Uncle Ethan. If I had given up on swimming the first time I got scared, I'd be missing out on a lot of fun."

Fidgeting in my chair, I suddenly realize how powerful little kids can be at making you take a good hard look at your choices. Unfortunately, Paige wasn't just a simple fear of the deep end that I could get over as soon as I jumped in.

I was so damn sure she was *the one*, that I went out and bought the biggest ring I could find. I booked the Hollywood Bowl and had The Ivy pack us the fanciest picnic you've ever seen. While we sat on the stage to eat, a string quartet serenaded us. Afterwards, I dropped to one knee to declare my love only to get kicked in the gut in return. It seems that while Paige was making a good show of loving me as much as I loved her, she was only biding her time until someone better came along. Someone better turned out to be a music producer that she was engaged to only a month later.

Needing to distract myself from the memory, I decide to change the subject. "While you're giving out free advice, you wouldn't happen to know anything about writing a book, would you?"

"What's the book about?" she asks.

"It's a thriller. Do you know what that means?" I ask, forgetting that her father has starred in a dozen of them.

"Ah, yeah," she says, pulling out the sarcastic tone more often heard from fourteen-year-olds. "It means it's scary, but not all bloody and stuff."

"Exactly," I tell her. "To be honest, I'm having trouble getting the whole story going."

"Start with the bad guy."

"What?"

"Figure out who the bad guy is, what he's going to do that's bad. At least that's what Uncle Dan told Dad when he was visiting us in the Hamptons."

The Uncle Dan in question is *that* Dan—author of *The Da Vinci Code*. "That's actually some pretty solid advice."

"He knows what he's talking about," she says, patting my knee.

After taking Lily back to the lodge and having supper with Harper's family, I zip back to my cabin. My mind is swirling with ideas. I hurry inside, just as a crack of thunder rips through the air causing the small hairs on the back up my neck to stand at attention. "The mood is set," I mumble ominously.

Grabbing my notebook, I jot down everything I can think of about my villain—Stacey Simpson, a small-town woman whose husband is a chronic cheater. She decides to go all Snow White's stepmom on every young, good-looking woman in a hundred-mile radius. But she doesn't expect the feisty bakery owner to put up such a struggle …

It's well after midnight when I stop, and the rain is still coming down. I not only have my villain sorted out, but I've also got my heroine, too. Single mom Melinda Brown, whose husband died in a tragic logging accident. Melinda makes the best muffins in town, and when the incompetent sheriff, who's addicted to her baking, keeps coming in and spilling the beans about the investigation, Melinda learns more about the murders than anyone else in town. As all the victims are single women under forty, she starts to worry her safety might be in jeopardy. She decides that if she's going to survive, she's going to have to solve the case herself.

After what feels like hours, I stand up to stretch out the stiffness in my back. Charged by the progress I'm making, I walk over to the window and watch as the lightning shifts across the surface of the water. Maybe I'll have Stacey confront Melinda in a lake setting on a night just like this.

I finally pull myself away from the window and head into the bedroom. Closing the blackout blinds, I say a silent plea that my dreams will be filled with plot twists for my book. My subconscious has other ideas.

Instead of drama and intrigue, my night's full of thoughts of Moira. I dream about taking a boat ride together before hiking up to a romantic mountain retreat. We laugh and hold hands while talking about everything under the sun. It's by far the best dream I've ever had. When I wake up, I'm overcome with longing to see her again.

After throwing on a hoodie to soak up the rain—it's still going strong—I quickly tie my sneakers and run out the door to the diner. Moira smiles at me when I walk in. She arrives at my booth with a mug and the coffee pot just as I sit down.

"How was the pedicure?"

"Pretty good," I tell her. "Although, I was expecting a massage chair."

She looks at me with a blank expression. So, I explain, "Big cushy chair that massages your head, neck, back and butt while you get your feet done."

She raises an eyebrow. "I had no idea you were kinky." She pours my coffee. "Did Lily manage to talk you into getting polish?"

"Thankfully, no."

"Lily is lucky to have you."

Shrugging, I tell her, "Actually, it's a good thing I took her. She single-handedly cured my writer's block. I'm considering making her my co-author."

"Seriously?" Moira asks with a grin.

"Turns out she knows a lot more than the average five-year-old about thrillers. I was up half the night getting my ideas down."

Moira chuckles. "Good for you. Now, what can I get you for breakfast so you can be all fueled to keep going?"

"Oatmeal, please, with a side of whatever fruit you've got." I explain, "If my stomach is too full, I'm going to get drowsy, and I need to make some major progress before my parents get here." I immediately feel silly for admitting that, so I add, "Because I'll be busy showing them around. Not because I need their approval or anything."

"You're your own man and all." Moira tries and fails to suppress a giggle.

"I'm a successful lawyer, for God's sake. I don't have to justify my time to my mother." We both laugh this time.

"Still, it's probably a huge relief to have a break-through before they get here, right?"

"Yes," I murmur, feeling completely sheepish.

The moment we just shared makes me almost forget that I've been friend-zoned. I sternly remind myself that friends don't kiss the way I want to kiss Moira.

Clearing her throat, she says, "Okay, one oatmeal coming up."

"You're the best," I tell her before opening my laptop. I get straight to work, intent on channeling all the feelings I have for one sassy diner owner into my writing.

Fingers crossed.

Chapter 15

Moira

The next several days start to form a delightful pattern. Ethan arrives at the diner for breakfast every morning, my boys join him for lunch, and then the two of us walk out together at the end of my shift. I've really started looking forward to work.

Digger picks Wyatt up after lunch to take him back to the lodge to make money for the trip—that is, if his age bracket wins the most raffle sales. Although, the way he's going, you'd think it was in the bag.

Meanwhile, the twins go home, where under Edna's supervision, they keep digging up my front yard like they're looking for buried treasure. They won't tell me why they're doing it and it's making me crazy.

The boys and I are supposed to have Sunday dinner at the lodge today, but other than that, I'm planning to relax. And by that, I mean get caught up on laundry, tidy the house, dust, and vacuum. But when I'm done with all of that, I'm going to sit out on the back deck and read.

I'm just turning on the washing machine when my phone pings.

Digger: *There's a problem with the house so I can't make the monthly grocery run to Anchorage today. Can you wait a few days for supplies?*

As regular restaurant supply deliveries don't happen in our corner of Alaska, Digger usually makes the run for both my diner and the lodge.

Sighing, I realize my entire day is about to take a sharp turn. I'm in for four hours of driving plus lifting, lugging, and loading several carts full of groceries, only to come back and unload at both the lodge and the diner.

Me: *I'm almost out of everything at the diner, so I'll make the trip.*

Digger: *Thanks. Drop the boys off here so you can take the truck. Grandpa'll watch them.*

Me: *Okay, I'll be there in about an hour.*

Digger: *Ethan is here and he's wondering if he can go with you. He wants to do some research for his book.*

Me: *Yes, please. I could use help loading everything in the truck.*

Not only have I come to love seeing Ethan, but it will also make the trip a lot less boring having someone to talk to. I spend the next forty-five minutes getting ready, and by the time I'm done, I look pretty darn great. I try to convince myself I'm doing it for me—after all, a gal likes to feel girly occasionally.

Outside, the boys are making all kinds of racket, and I

rush to the window to let them know we're leaving for the lodge in a few minutes. Then I run downstairs to change the laundry and load the dishwasher so I can have it run while I'm gone. As much as I bemoan the fact that my life is busy, I know the day will come when the boys leave and I'm left totally alone. The quiet will be deafening.

Thoughts like this make me wonder if I should listen to Digger and Grandpa Jack and start opening myself up to a man in my life. Yet, the only man that comes to mind is Ethan and we're practically from different galaxies.

I climb into the driver's seat with my blown-out hair, my face full of makeup, and wearing the new sundress I bought online. The kids pile in after me.

"I thought you were going to Costco," Wyatt says, buckling himself in.

"I am."

"Then how come you look like you're going to a wedding?"

"I don't look that dressed up, do I?" Panic sets in that Ethan is going to think I did this for him. I mean, I did, sort of, but I don't want him to know that.

"You look totally fancy," Ash says.

"I just … felt like getting a little done up today is all."

"Why?" Colton asks.

"Sometimes a woman wants to make herself look nice. Can we drop it already?"

By the time we pull up in front of the lodge, I'm worn out by the boys and their relentless questioning of why I'm wearing makeup and a dress. As soon as I park, they take off to find Lily and Liam, and I give myself a quick once-over in the rearview mirror. I suddenly feel silly. Maybe I am too dressed up. There's no way Ethan won't see through me. On the other hand, what's to see if he could see through me? It's not like I know what I want from him.

Forcing myself out of the car, I spot him standing next to Digger's big truck, tossing the keys in the air.

When he sees me, his reaction tells me I have nothing to feel self-conscious about. He tosses the keys up and lets them fall to the ground right next to him. His mouth drops open and even though he's got sunglasses on, I'm guessing his eyes are popping out of his head. Letting out a long whistle, he says, "You look like a Vogue cover."

I offer a small curtsy. "You don't look half bad yourself."

In fact, he looks good. So good in a pair of jeans with a light blue linen button-down rolled up at the sleeves, and loafers. He's effortlessly elegant, which is a characteristic you don't find in many of the men in Gamble. In fact, I don't think I've seen anyone around here pull off such a look.

Ethan opens the passenger door of Digger's truck for me. "Have you eaten lunch?"

"I had a late breakfast with the boys," I tell him.

After closing the door behind me, he hurries around to his side and gets in. Leaning over the backseat, he pulls out an adorable wicker picnic hamper. "Harper packed us some cheese and crackers, grapes, and shortbread in case we get peckish."

"Shortbread? I'm guessing it's Grandpa Jack's," I tell him. "In which case it'll be the best shortbread you've ever tasted."

"Really? Harper said yours is better."

"I said the best *you've* ever had. Not the best there is. Mine *is* the best."

He puts the truck into reverse and angles around until he's turned the opposite direction. "I don't suppose you'd make me yours sometime."

"I could be persuaded," I tell him flirtatiously. "All it will cost you is some help at Costco today."

"What kind of help are you looking for?" he asks, grinning at me.

"I'm doing the big shop today and I could use your muscles."

"Conveniently, I happen to have some available." He winks before turning on the sound system. The strains of a swing band fill the cab.

"I loved Squirrel Nut Zippers when I was a kid!" I tell him over the old-school music blasting through the speakers. "It always makes me want to dance."

His foot hits the brake before shifting into park.

"What are you doing?"

"I thought you said you wanted to dance." His hand is on the door handle. "Just as friends, of course."

"Not here! Not now!" I sound as alarmed as I feel.

"Why not? We have time."

"Don't be silly, Ethan. What would people think if they saw us swing dancing in the parking lot?"

"If they had a brain in their head, they'd come out and join in." He leaves his door open so the song "Suits" blasts from the speakers. Then he comes over to let me out. With a short bow, he takes my hand and spins me around in a circle that flings me to arm's length.

I barely keep my balance while releasing a squeal of surprise. Ethan really knows what he's doing. Way more than I do. Pulling me back into his arms, we whirl around in a circle before he says, "It's time to dip!"

Before I can tense up, he pulls me close, placing one hand on the small of my back and dropping me so low I'm worried my head might hit the ground. Laughter explodes out of my mouth as I hang there in the air.

Ethan pulls me up as fast as he dropped me and spins me out again. "How is it that you know how to do this?"

"My parents had a rule when I was a kid. I had to play at least one instrument, one sport, and take one kind of dancing lesson."

"You're kidding? That's so cool!" I'm huffing and puffing as we continue to shake our moneymakers. The song stops just as Ethan pulls me into his chest. He holds onto me like we're locked in a lovers' embrace, and it's positively delicious. The feeling of his body against mine, the scent of his aftershave, the boyish grin on his face.

Staring down at me, he croons, "If this were a date, I'd be kissing you right now."

"Really?" My voice is all breathy like I'm not getting enough oxygen.

He holds tighter before releasing me, and I almost hit the ground. "Alas, buddies don't do that kind of thing. Now hurry up and get into the car. We've got some shopping to do."

My stomach lurches painfully. I do *not* want to be Ethan Caplan's buddy. Not in the slightest. But what's the alternative? I tell you what, there isn't one.

Once I'm back in the passenger seat, Ethan turns down the stereo. "You're a pretty good dancer yourself."

"That's only because I was letting you lead," I tell him. Before I explain my penchant for taking over the man's role, I hurry to ask, "What instrument do you play?"

"Piano. I have a thing for ragtime."

"Seriously? That's so cool! I play a mean kazoo," I brag before asking, "What sport did you play?"

"Baseball." He smiles devilishly.

"Were you any good?"

"I went to UCLA on a partial ride." He shrugs his eyebrows cockily.

"Wow. So yes, you *were* good."

"How about you? Did you play any sports?"

"I used to run track," I tell him.

"And were *you* any good?"

"Not at all. I quickly concluded that the only way I'd willingly run fast is if my life depended upon it. Since no one was chasing me with a butcher's knife, I didn't last longer than one season."

Ethan shoots me the side-eye. "I have a feeling you're not giving yourself enough credit."

The heat of a blush covers my cheeks. "Why?"

"I've noticed you have a tendency to sell yourself short."

"There's not much to sell," I answer in a light tone.

"I disagree. You're a successful businesswoman, a great mom, and you reportedly make the best shortbread in town. Although the jury is out on the last one until I have a chance to judge it myself."

I grin at him, then lean my head against the seat and stare out the window, watching the trees zip by as we head up the road. There's something so domestic about what we're doing right now. Him driving, and me in the passenger seat for a change. We're going to the city to get groceries. It's just a simple thing, but somehow doing it with him makes my heart ache. As much as I tell myself I don't want a man in my life, I know there are so many ways my life would be better if I had a man exactly like Ethan.

Chapter 16

Ethan

"You weren't kidding about how many groceries we were getting," I tell Moira as I shut the tailgate. We've been through the line-up twice already, both times with large flatbed carts.

"One trip was for the diner and the other for the lodge. Both should last a month. Although, we only got enough perishables for a week," she says. "Digger picks those up with his float plane when he makes trips to Anchorage to drop off guests."

I stare at her a moment longer than I should, imagining myself pulling her into my arms. I try to force myself back to reality. "I can't seem to take my eyes off of you." I rub the back of my neck nervously. "Sorry."

"I don't mind as much as you might think," she whispers, her cheeks flooding with color. "It's kind of nice to be appreciated."

"Even if it's just by a *friend*?"

Nodding, she glances down at my mouth, then back up at my eyes. "Yes."

We gaze into each other's eyes a little longer, then she asks, "So, what do you need to see?"

I'm tempted to answer, "More of you, perhaps in significantly less clothing," but I don't think that's what she meant. But for the life of me, I don't know what she's asking.

As though reading my thoughts, she clarifies, "For your book. Digger said you wanted to come along so you could do some research."

"Oh, right, that." I feel slightly guilty on account of it being a total lie. I just wanted to spend some one-on-one time with Moira. "I want to write a chapter set in a nice restaurant here in town. It's sort of a romantic scene so …"

After a moment, she says, "There's a place on the shore called the Parched Moose. They have a great menu and when the weather's nice, you can sit out on the deck and watch the tide come and go while you eat."

"The Parched Moose, eh?"

"Don't let the name fool you. It's been written up in *Gourmet* magazine."

"Do we have time to stop for supper?" I ask, hoping she doesn't see through my excuse.

"Let me call Digger and Harper to check on the boys. If they haven't gotten into too much trouble, I'm game."

After we get into the truck, I start to follow the directions on my map app while Moira calls the lodge. "Hey, Harper, I just wanted to see how things are going there."

After a pause, she adds, "Ethan and I were thinking of stopping for a bite before we come back."

She laughs a little, then says, "Get your mind out of the gutter, lady." Another pause, then, "You sure? That wasn't the plan." Pause. "Okay, well, I appreciate it. That'll give us more time so I can show Ethan around town for his research." Her last comment before hanging up is, "Not going to happen, bye!" It doesn't take a brain surgeon to figure out what Harper was suggesting.

Moira tosses her phone into her handbag. "Looks like I'm off mom duty until the morning."

"Really?" I'm sure my tone sounds far too hopeful. "What was that about Harper's mind being in the gutter? You've piqued my curiosity."

Bursting out laughing, Moira says, "I'm not telling you what she said."

"I'll have to ask her myself then."

"You'll regret it, trust me."

I grin at Moira and shrug. "We'll see."

Not ten minutes later, Moira and I walk into the Parched Moose. It's got an old lodge feel with stone and wood accents, a trophy black bear in the lobby and an enormous moose head hanging on the wall above the fireplace. It's a beautiful, warm evening, so we elect to eat outside on the patio.

As we follow the hostess through the dining room, I'm pretty sure people assume Moira and I are a couple. Even though that's not the case, I still feel a sense of pride just being with her.

As expected, our table overlooks the ocean. The sound of the waves rolling in creates a calming atmosphere. Taking a deep breath of fresh air, I suddenly feel alive in a way I haven't in years. I take Moira's advice and order the crab-stuffed halibut, and we decide to split a bottle of Marsanne.

Once our first glass is poured, I tell her, "You're going to have to drink the lion's share of it if I'm driving back to Gamble."

"I think I can handle it," she says with a smirk.

My heart pounds in my chest just looking at her. Moira in a diner uniform, or shorts and an oversized T-shirt is enough to make me stare, but all dolled up? I have to force myself not to blurt out exactly what I'm thinking. It's like the purest form of torture to be so near her without any hope that things will progress between us.

"Can I ask you a personal question?" she says. "It's one I hate answering, so if you don't want to, just don't."

"Okay, deal."

She holds her glass to her lips but stalls before she takes a sip. "Why are you single?"

"Life's easier this way," I tell her.

She nods, but I can see in her eyes that she's not buying it. "Did you ever want to get married?"

"Yes. Actually, I always assumed I'd get married and have a family someday, but it didn't work out that way." I glance out at the water. "I got as far as proposing a few years ago, but it turns out the woman I thought I loved didn't feel the same way about our future as I did. She was trying to think of a way to break it off with me while I was busy making plans for us."

"That must have been hard. I'm sorry."

"The real gut punch was that she wound up engaged to another guy a month later."

"That's brutal."

"C'est la vie." I try to sound nonchalant. "That was four years ago. I'm over it, but I also decided that staying single is in my best interest. How about you? Do you ever miss having a man into your life?"

"I have three men in my life. Five, if you count Digger and Grandpa Jack." After a thoughtful pause, she says, "But yeah, I guess I miss some things."

"Like what?" Our server returns to refill our wine, so she pauses her thought until he leaves.

Then Moira picks up her glass and takes a sip. "It's the little things, like sitting in the passenger seat instead of driving all the time or … having someone to talk to about grown-up things like paying bills. Or having someone to talk to about the boys. When things are going bad and I'm worried, I could use the moral support, and when things are going well and I'm proud of them, I want someone to feel my joy. I've got my grandpa and Digger, but that's different, you know?"

My heart aches for her. "I'm sure it is."

She shakes her head sadly. "But I've been there, done that, and I'm still picking up the pieces."

"I don't want to pry," I say, realizing I'm about to do just that. "But were you and Everett happy?"

She tips her head back and forth in a non-committal fashion. "We did the best we could. We were young and strapped for cash, so that didn't exactly make life easier. But it's not like I had great role models in the marriage department."

"Not exactly a ringing endorsement for the institution of matrimony," I say in a gentle tone.

She takes a deep breath. "It wasn't what I thought marriage would be like. Everett seemed to think I was an accessory he could put on and take off at will. I assumed it would be more like the lovey-dovey couples in the movies. I suppose I didn't try to change things because, unlike my mother, he wasn't abandoning me."

"Do you ever want to go down that road again?"

"It's not like there's a line of men in Gamble waiting to date a single mom with three rowdy boys."

I'm sure what she says is the truth. Most men in my experience would rather have their own kids than marry into a ready-made family. But I don't confirm that. "That's a shame because any man would be lucky to end up with you and your boys."

Moira scoffs. "I doubt many guys would see it that way."

"I do."

A moment of intensity passes between us that's so raw and honest it steals my breath away. I can tell that Moira wants the same thing I do, but as quickly as hope fills her eyes, it disappears. She turns away, and gazes out over the ocean.

Our meals arrive in time to save me from doing something stupid like pulling her into my arms and kissing her with the heat of a thousand suns. "This looks great," I tell her. Taking a bite, I discover it tastes as good as it looks. The fish is cooked to perfection and the dill cream sauce is light and flavorful. Mashed potatoes and roasted veggies round out the meal, each bite better than the last.

We eat in silence if you don't include all the groans of appreciation. Taking a break to let my food digest, I tell Moira, "My parents will make you think they can barely stand each other, but they're the strongest couple I know."

"Pardon me?" she asks, looking confused.

"I was thinking about what you said earlier about your parents … and you and Everett."

"And you wanted me to know you had good role models." Her eyes narrow in confusion.

"I don't know why I need you to know that, but I do." I feel a bit foolish.

Giving me a doubtful look, she says, "Even though your dad is taking dancing lessons with some woman named Harriet?"

"He's only doing that to get my mom's attention. And

it looks like it worked. She's going on vacation with him ... to visit me." *I've sunk my own ship.*

Moira laughs. "Well then, I can't wait to meet them. They sound very interesting."

"They really are. They drive me nuts a lot of the time, but their hearts are in the right place. They're going to love you," I tell her. "In fact, I wouldn't be surprised if my mom tries to play matchmaker."

Moira's smile fades. "I'm pretty sure they aren't going to want you to get involved with a woman with as much baggage as I have."

"You haven't seen my mother's luggage collection," I tease. Moira smiles, seemingly against her will.

We finish our meal, but neither of us has room for dessert. "So, what do we do from here?" I ask.

"Go home and unload the truck. Even with all hands on deck, it will take at least an hour."

"In that case, I guess we should get back on the road." I slip cash into the payment folder before standing up to pull Moira's chair out for her. I gently put my hand on the small of her back and lead her out of the restaurant. There's a shift in the air between us, as she leans into my fingertips. For the first time in years, I realize that I want more. I want her. And not just for one night.

Chapter 17

Moira

As soon as Ethan and I hit the main road, I close my eyes and pretend to sleep. I'm one hundred percent on emotional overload, and I'm about to lose consciousness for real, when the angel on my shoulder whispers, "Let him in, he's the one."

I silently remind her that Ethan only wants to be friends. "He's just as afraid as you are," she replies. "Set your worries aside and I promise everything will work out."

Not to be ignored, the devil on my other shoulder practically yells, "It'll never work! He'll never leave Los Angeles for you. He's rich and you're poor ..."

I'm sure he'd go on and on, but the angel retaliates with, "Love is not determined by finances."

"He could have anyone. Why would he pick her?" That damn devil hits the nail on the head, and it hurts.

"Why wouldn't he pick her? She's smart and beautiful and plucky ..."

"Poor, overburdened, has a derelict house, three kids … and let's not get started on those stretch marks."

I inwardly tell them both to shut up, but peace does not find me. My brain starts to play a kind of travelogue of my life.

When I was a child, my only dream was to get married and have kids someday—kids that I would never leave. I thought I could heal my own wounds by being the mother I wished I'd had. It wasn't until I'd become such a mother that I realized that would only get me so far.

I don't recall if my parents had a happy marriage before Mom left. All I remember is her leaving, and the mess she left in her wake. Dad started drinking *a lot*. He wasn't a mean drunk, just a melancholy one. After a couple of years, we moved in with Grandpa Jack and Grandma Adele and we started treating them like our parents. I don't think our dad even noticed.

I didn't cry when my dad died. I'd mourned him long before his spirit left this world. I did, however, hope that he and my mother would meet on the other side and finally find peace together.

Conversely, when Grandma Adele died a few years later, I cried so much you could have filled a lake with my tears. I was only in my mid-twenties and suddenly I was the old lady of my family. I was going to have to traverse the rocky road of womanhood without the gentle and guiding hand of any maternal figure.

I cried when Everett died, but along with the grief, I was rocked to the core that I was solely responsible for the lives of three children. I spent way more time stuck in the phase of anger than sadness. I'm not mad anymore though, just kind of numb. My four-year marriage has become nothing more than a vague memory, like I'd watched it in a movie instead of living it myself.

When I graduated from high school, Grandpa Jack had asked me what I wanted to be when I grew up. I answered, "Happy." Remembering that sets off a PowerPoint presentation in my head. Happy times pop up as still photos. Yet for every one of them, there was an underlying feeling of unsettledness.

Maybe that's what life is. Maybe no one is happy all the time and you just have to string enough moments together to have something beautiful to show when it's all done. I feel the truck start to slow down until it stops altogether.

Opening my eyes, I look over at Ethan. "Why are we stopped? Are we out of gas or something?"

He reaches over and touches my face. "You're crying."

I scrub my hands over my eyes and discover that I am. "I must have been having a bad dream," I tell him while blinking back the rest of the tears that are trying to escape.

"I don't think that's it." His concern practically undoes me. He places his palm over my hand; his skin is warm and comforting. "You can talk to me, Moira."

Blinking quickly, I answer, "It's just that our conversation earlier kind of got to me. For the most part, I manage to get through my days without thinking about what I'm missing, but lately, I can't seem to stop. I don't know what's different, but I've been walking around in a funk for weeks."

Instead of saying anything, he rubs his thumb over the back of my hand, encouraging me to go on.

"I'm lonely," I practically choke. I'm simultaneously embarrassed and relieved to admit that out loud to someone who cares. "I *want* to share my life with someone —the right someone this time around. But so far, he hasn't shown up, and even if he did, I wouldn't have the first clue anymore how to be with a man. I just feel so … stuck, you know? I've been trapped in this place in my life for so long,

I don't know how to move forward. Does that make sense?"

He nods slowly. "I know it's not the same, but for the last couple of years, I've felt a lot like that. I woke up every day and did what was expected of me, but it all felt wrong. After a while it just started eating away at me until I felt that if I didn't make a drastic change, I was going to explode."

"What finally made you decide to take a break?"

"One of my clients said something to me that really hit home. I thought I'd been hiding my dissatisfaction well, but she noticed. She told me that being chronically miserable is life's way of telling you that you need to make a change. She said the only way to do that is to figure out what's missing." He pauses momentarily before adding, "To put it simply, any happiness in my career was missing. It took me nearly a year to get my sabbatical sorted out, but here I am."

"I can't take a sabbatical from raising my kids. But I suppose there might be something I can do about being lonely." I stare at him intently.

"Of course, you can," he says, making me want to lean in and kiss him. Instead, I look down at our hands, letting myself enjoy the feeling of such a simple touch.

"Which client gave you such great advice? If you can tell me, that is." God knows he's probably signed so many nondisclosure agreements he can't say much.

"Ellie Fansworthy," he says.

"No way!" Ellie is like the Oprah of the millennial generation. She doesn't have a television show. Instead, she came to fame on YouTube before practically taking over the world on TikTok. She's created such hashtags as #wantitgetit, #youdoyou, #makeupyourmind, and #boardyourvision

"Are you a fan of hers?" he asks.

"I like watching her videos. They make me feel hopeful. But I've never made a bucket list or done a vision board or anything like that."

"Honestly, I used to think what she does is a bunch of woo-woo nonsense, but now I'm not so sure," he tells me. "It's hard to believe that just gluing some pictures on a piece of cardboard will change your life, but I think it has something to do with prioritizing what you want. The first step to any success is realizing that you want it."

"If *you* don't change, nothing will change," I say, repeating Ellie's famous tagline.

"Exactly. Can I tell you a secret?"

"Yes."

When he speaks again, he lets the words rush out. "I don't ever want to go back to practicing law. This writing thing may not work out—I'm mean, let's face it, it's a total long shot. But deep down, I know my days at the firm are over."

A tiny glimmer of hope sparks at his words. It's not like he's started house hunting in Alaska, or even hinted that he wants to move out of LA. And yet, a flicker of warmth builds inside of me. "That's huge, Ethan."

He swallows hard. "I know. I spent my entire adult life getting where I am today so the thought of giving it up is more than a little scary. But after taking this break, I know it's what I have to do."

"Good for you for figuring that out," I say, meaning it.

"I'm still working on the rest, but my point in telling you this wasn't to talk about me. I just wanted to help you get unstuck." He twists his body toward me. "You want someone to share your life with, but you're understandably worried you've forgotten how to be in a relationship."

"Among other things." My whole body heats up as I confess to that.

"What if you used me as a practice boyfriend while I'm here? Just to get your feet wet in the whole dating scene. We'd both go in knowing that whatever happens between us has an expiration date. But even so, I think we'd both benefit."

"So, we'd just try to enjoy being together for a short time?" If we were really deciding to be a couple, I'd be jumping in his lap right now.

"No pressure, no expectations. Just me treating you like a queen so that when you get out into the dating world, you'll know how you should be treated."

Every cell in my body is singing *yes, yes, yes*. "That's quite an offer. But as tempting as it is, I'm afraid it would be too confusing for the boys." What I really mean is, it would be too confusing to me, and I'm terrified of crossing the line and getting my heart broken.

"We'll tell them we're just friends," he says, his eyes flicking down to my mouth. "You're an amazing and beautiful woman, Moira. Let me help you feel special, even if it's just for a while."

My heart pounds in my chest like a bongo drum solo. The attraction between us is undeniable and a voice inside my head is begging me to give myself this one gift this one time. "It sounds reckless ..."

"Maybe a little recklessness is what you need for once in your life," he murmurs, leaning in. "Maybe it's what I need, too."

I react on instinct before I can let my brain take over. Leaning as close to him as I can get with the armrest between us, I close my eyes, and press my mouth against his in an achingly tender kiss.

He kisses me back, gently, carefully, tilting my head so

he can deepen our connection. A surge of passion hits me, the likes of which I'm not sure I've ever felt. All reason leaves my head and the only thought left is that I don't want this feeling to ever end.

We stay like this, our mouths moving together in perfect unison for a long time, before Ethan finally pulls back and rests his forehead against mine. "Is that a yes?"

Chapter 18

Ethan

My heart bangs in my chest while I wait for Moira's answer. I shouldn't be pursuing her. I promised myself I wouldn't. And yet, I've never wanted anything more in my life than to just kiss her and be near her. I'm aching to show her how perfect she is and to give her a taste of what a good relationship should be like. Truth be told, I'd like to experience that for myself, too.

"Let's enjoy whatever time we've got together," she whispers.

Closing the distance between us, I kiss her again. Even though I want Moira with every fiber of my being, I'm not going to try to get her into bed. The whole point of this experiment is to treat her like a queen, not to leave her worse off than before she met me.

Moira puts her hands against my chest and pushes slightly. "We should go."

I lift her hand and brush my lips across her knuckles.

"You can change your mind if you want. Just tell me. I promise I'll understand." I hope to God she doesn't, as we've just opened the floodgates, and I'd have a hell of a time closing them again.

"You, too," she says, turning to face the windshield. "We're both mature adults who know what we're doing. I don't think either of us is in any danger here." She sounds like she's trying to convince herself.

Holding hands all the way back to Gamble, I wish I could stop time right now, before things get complicated. Before we eventually have to say goodbye.

When we pull up in front of the lodge, Digger walks out with his bouncy Great Dane, Otis, and Moira's boys in tow. Moira slips her hand from mine and points at her brother. "If we're really going to do this, we need to keep it a secret from that guy right there."

"Agreed." My mind races through a dozen scenarios of him finding out that I'm going to be his sister's practice boyfriend, and they all end at my funeral.

As soon as we get out of the truck, the boys greet Moira with big hugs. Digger says, "I'll unload the supplies, both here and at the diner, so you can go home and enjoy some kid-free time."

"Need any help?" I hope he says no.

He shakes his head. "You've done enough already." I know he means my accompanying Moira to Anchorage, but if he knew what we just agreed to, his response could definitely be construed as threatening.

As Moira and I walk to our cars, I lean in and whisper, "Want some company? I could drive over to your place instead of going home?"

Her eyes open so wide they look like they're in jeopardy of popping out of her head. "I … um … that is to say … I think I need some time alone."

"You've got it, lady. This whole experiment is so that you can finally take care of *you*."

Once she gets behind the wheel, she looks up at me and says, "Thank you for today. I enjoyed every second of it."

"Same here," I tell her, wondering if I've ever had a better time. "See you tomorrow morning?"

"You know where to find me." I watch her drive off, feeling like a teenager in the first throes of love as I drive back to my cabin. Except all images of Beth Steinberg—my first love—are replaced with Moira's visage. I warn myself not to get too carried away, but I'm still going to enjoy this pretend relationship. I'm going to cherish every moment she and I spend together, and I'm going to prove to her that she deserves only the best.

I could never do that if I was really trying for a future with Moira. Images of Paige still burn too hotly. But maybe a pretend relationship will help me see that happily-ever-after is a possibility for me too.

Once I'm inside my cabin, I pull out my phone to see if I have any messages. There haven't been many since I left town. The office doesn't call and the few friends I have outside of work have lives as busy as mine used to be. It was an accomplishment for us to see each other every couple of months or so.

So, imagine my surprise when I find I have seven missed calls. All from my mother.

Message one: *Ethan, your father and I have decided to rent a car at the airport. As much as I'd love to have you pick us up, we should have our own vehicle in case of emergency. Love you, bye.*

Message two: *Ethan, it's your mother. What's the weather like in Alaska right now? I don't want to overpack but I'm not sure if I should bring more shorts or more pants. Let me know.*

Message three: *I haven't heard from you so I'm going to*

pack mostly capri pants. That way my butt won't stick to the leather of a hot car and if it's cool, most of my legs will be covered.

Message four: *Ethan Adam Caplan, where are you? You need to be better about calling me back. I called the diner, but no one is picking up. Have you been mauled by a bear? Call me the second you get this message!*

Message five: *If you got mauled by a bear, I'm never going to forgive you.*

Message six: *I've called every hospital in a two-hundred-mile radius from Gamble and they don't have any John Does that fit your description. I can only take that to mean you are good and truly dead, and all before making me a grandmother. This smarts, Ethan, it really does.*

The last message came in a couple of minutes before I got in. It's my dad this time. *Call back as soon as you can, Ethan. Your mom's blood pressure has shot up a hundred points in the last hour.*

I hit redial and wait for twelve rings until the phone is answered. "I could have been mauled by a bear waiting for you to answer the phone," I joke.

"Ethan, finally. I had to go lie down in a dark room," my mother says. "Where have you been?"

"I went to Anchorage to help a friend."

"What friend? Your only friend there is Harper and if you meant Harper, you would have just said Harper."

"Digger's sister, Moira."

"The one from the diner?"

"Yes, that Moira."

"Is she single?"

"Why? Are you thinking of switching teams?" I ask. I know I'm being a bit of an ass, but honestly, there's only so much prying a man can take.

With a big sigh, Mom says, "I can see you're in a

mood, which frankly, I don't appreciate. Not after what you put me through today."

"I'm fine, Mom. I haven't been mauled by a bear, I'm not dead in a ditch. I simply was out for most of the afternoon and evening. Okay?"

"Fine," she says quietly. "But is she?"

I know exactly what she means, but I intend to make her meddling as painful as possible. "Is who what?"

"Is this Moira person single? And if so, does she want to have children?" she asks, her voice rising.

"She is single, and she has three children. I have no idea if she wants any more of them," I tell her, walking upstairs to the bedroom. "Why don't I have her call you so you can ask her yourself?"

"Don't get snippy, mister," Mom says.

"I'm sorry, Mom, but I just get kind of sick of you assuming you know what I want better than I do."

Her voice softens. "Maybe I do. When it comes to love, anyway."

"Not everyone needs to fall in love to have a fulfilling life," I tell her.

"I'm not talking about anyone. I'm talking about my son, who I know better than anyone. I know you would be happier if you found your soulmate," she says. "You may balk at that idea, but it's true. You're not enjoying your career, you're alone too much, and you need more."

I think about her words. Being with Moira and the kids would definitely be more. But I'm not about to even think about that. And I'm certainly not going to leave any hint for her that anything could happen. "You're forgetting how intense my career is. It's twenty-four-seven, Mom. Nonstop. It's not exactly conducive to having a healthy work-life balance."

"And *you're* forgetting that I had a pretty intense career

myself," she answers. "And I still raised you and made a wonderful life with your father that was completely separate from my work. Someday, when you're retired, you'll need people in your life, Ethan. And your dad and I won't be here then."

"Sure you will," I say lightly.

"Joke all you want, but at the end of the day, life is about who we love and how we love them."

Damn. She's got me there, doesn't she? "Okay, Mom. I promise to think about what you've said. But I need you to promise to back off."

"That really doesn't come naturally for me." She lets out a loud yawn. "Okay, I've got to go to bed. It's late here."

"Good night, Mom. Love you."

"Good night, sweetie. I'm glad you're not dead in a ditch."

Chapter 19

Moira

Filling up the bathtub with bubbles, I try to make sense out of what happened between me and Ethan tonight. Did we really decide to secretly date? What good could come from such a thing? I can't seem to answer that question though, because my body is still humming from all the delicious kisses we shared. So, so yummy.

Slipping out of my robe, I step into the hot water while silently thanking Digger for the new heater. After slowly lowering myself until I'm fully submerged, I start a negotiation with both the angel and devil who have started once again barraging me with their opinions.

Angel: You can't do this! You should never engage in this kind of intimacy without thinking of the long term.

Devil: Ride him like a bull in the rodeo, girl. YEE-HA!!!

Angel: *Do not* listen to that rogue. You can be friends

with Ethan but nothing more. Do not make this harder on yourself.

Devil (smirking): Make it harder, so much harder!

I tell them both to shut up before explaining that I'm not going to jump into bed with anyone, but I am going to let Ethan keep kissing me like I'm the only thing in the world that matters. It's such a novel experience that I cannot let myself pass up what might be an opportunity of a lifetime.

Everett was my first everything. My first boyfriend, first kiss, the only guy I've ever slept with. And while things were physically okay between us, there were not the kind of fireworks involved that I experienced from Ethan's kisses.

Everett was more he-man than sensitive and caring. For instance, when Wyatt was born, I wanted him in the hospital room with me, but he told me that was woman's stuff and that he'd be down at the bar waiting to hear the news.

Down at the bar. It's like Everett lived in a 1950s male chauvinist world where there were such things as "man's work" and "woman's work." To be honest, there are still more than a few people in Gamble who think like that. While I was madder at my husband than I had ever been, I let him go and gave birth to our son with only medical staff to share the experience.

When I found out I was pregnant with the twins, I told Everett that come hell or high water I was not going to do it alone this time. He begrudgingly agreed, then went off and died on me.

Ethan would be the kind of guy who would sit right next to his wife, rubbing her back and offering her ice chips. I feel a momentary pang of jealousy for the woman who's going to be lucky enough to win him for the long haul. But for now, I'm going to enjoy and appreciate his company every chance I get.

When I finally get out of the tub and dry off, I crawl into bed and pick up the phone without thinking.

"Hello?" Ethan's groggy voice says.

"Did I wake you?"

"Not at all." He seems to force himself to sound more alert.

"I just wanted to thank you for today. I had a wonderful time."

"I did too, Moira. It was the best day I can remember having."

"I also want to remind you that we can't hold hands or kiss in public, or the whole town will know about us within seconds."

"But we can still do those things in private?" He sounds so hopeful.

"Yes." Although I'm not sure how often we'll be able to find time to spend alone. With a full-time job, three kids, and nosy family members, I'm usually surrounded.

"Are you going to bed now?" he asks.

"I just crawled in."

"Can you put me on speaker and put the phone on the pillow next to you?"

Oh, my God, he doesn't think we're going to have phone sex, does he? My body heats up at the thought, even though I have no intention of doing such a thing. "I'm getting pretty sleepy," I tell him, hoping he'll take the hint.

"Me, too," he says. "I just thought that we could talk until one of us conks out."

"That's nice." Of course, he wasn't thinking phone sex. What kind of perv am I? Ethan is way too gentlemanly for such a thing. I put the phone on speaker and then lay it on the pillow next to mine. "Tell me about what it was like growing up in LA."

"It wasn't normal, that's for sure," he says. "My dad was a talent agent and my mom a casting director, so I'm afraid Hollywood is the family business."

"That must have been so exciting."

"I guess it was. Sylvester Stallone used to come to supper sometimes and bring a variety of women until he met his wife. Steven Spielberg and his family often invited us to their Seder."

"What's that?" I ask.

"It's the Jewish Passover meal. My family isn't particularly religious, but we still observe the Jewish holidays. What about your family? Do you have any special traditions?"

"We celebrate the typical American holidays." I snuggle under my blanket.

"What's your favorite?" he asks.

"Thanksgiving."

"What do you love about it?"

"It's not about presents. It's about being with the people you love." I yawn, then say, "At the end of the day, isn't that what life is about?"

Ethan's voice is low and comforting. "My mom said something very similar to me this evening. She said life is about who we love and how we love them."

"She's right. I don't think anyone ever gets to the end of their lives wishing they'd worked more."

"We're getting pretty deep tonight," Ethan says, his tone light.

"Okay, change of topic," I tell him. "What's your favorite time of day and why?"

"Early morning." Before I can ask why, he says.

"Everything is quiet and the world is full of possibilities. You?"

"Same. I like to get up before the boys every day and have a few minutes to sip my coffee and stare out the kitchen window at the creek and the woods. It's so peaceful." I trace my fingertip around my phone, wishing he really was lying next to me.

"Favorite season," he says.

"Autumn."

"Because pumpkin spice everything?" he asks.

I laugh. "Obviously. But also because of the colors and the crisp air. Fall is short here but absolutely breathtaking."

"I can't wait to see it for myself. Fall in L.A. looks a lot like the other seasons, to be honest."

"What's your favorite then?"

"Winter somewhere other than SoCal. I love the snow. I try to head up to Aspen every year to ski."

"If you love snow and skiing, you're in the right place. There are some terrific hills near here," I tell him, imagining us out on the slopes together on a sunny afternoon.

"Do you ski?" he asks.

"I used to, but I haven't had much of a chance since I had the boys," I say. "I want them to learn though."

"Maybe I could teach them while I'm here."

"That sounds wonderful." My eyelids grow heavy, but I'm not ready to say goodnight yet. "Describe your perfect day."

"Workday or weekend?"

"Workday."

"Hmm…okay. I'd get up early and sit outside while I have a coffee. Then go for a run, have a quick shower, then sit down and work on my novel. After work, I'd want to eat supper with someone I care about."

"Restaurant or cooking it yourself?"

"Cooking together," he says.

Best. Answer. Ever. "That sounds nice. What happens next?"

"After supper, we go outside to watch the sunset and sip some wine, then curl up on the couch to watch a movie."

"That does sound like a perfect day," I say, realizing how much I want the life he's talking about. "I have to say I'm surprised someone like you would consider that a perfect day."

"Really, why?"

"I don't know. I guess because I thought yours would include something bigger, like surfing or yachting."

"Those are fun things for the weekend," he says. "But now it's your turn. What's your perfect day?"

"You already described it. I would add to it that the kids get along and do their homework without me having to nag them. And I'd swap out writing for a really great day at the diner," I tell him.

"You must like your work then," he says.

"I really do. I'm lucky to have terrific staff, and for the most part, the regulars are good to me, with some exceptions," I tell him, turning over and shutting off my bedside lamp. "The recipes we use were my Grandma Adele's, so sharing her creations with people makes me feel like she's still with us."

"You must miss her."

"Every day. Yet, she's still with us in a lot of ways. Ash has her smile. The way his mouth curves a little more on the left than the right when he finds something amusing is pure Grandma," I say. "She would have loved you. She was a real sucker for a handsome gentleman." *And so am I.*

"Is that how you'd describe me?" he asks, and I can hear the smile in his voice.

"It is."

We talk for another half hour or so, and Ethan tells me a little about his childhood and college life. The entire time I fight to stay awake just to hear more, but eventually I give in. The last thing I hear before I drift off is Ethan's voice.

"Close your eyes and rest. I'll be right here next to you."

I have never in my life felt so cherished and cared for. I can't comprehend that a man like Ethan has come into my life only to leave it. It makes my heart ache, while at the same time it makes me want to get to know every little thing about him before he does.

I hear his breath on the pillow next to mine, and it lulls me to sleep. Something happened today that has changed me. It's deep and profound, yet I can't quite seem to define it further. All I know is that Ethan Caplan is a treasure and I'm going to enjoy every moment that I get to spend with him.

Chapter 20

Ethan

"How'd you sleep?" I ask Moira as soon as she makes her way over to my table with the coffee pot and a mug.

"Really well." She smiles flirtatiously. "It usually takes me forever to fall asleep."

"I bored you to death with all that talk about my childhood, didn't I?"

She pours my coffee, then shakes her head. "No, what you did was help me think about something nice for a change. Usually, I'm awake going over my ever-growing to-do list."

"Good. You look beautiful, by the way," I tell her, while looking down at my menu so my infatuated expression doesn't give us away. I don't know how we're going to keep up the act of being just friends in public because it's all I can do to tear my eyes away from her.

"You don't look so bad yourself."

The door opens and four elderly folks walk in. "You

want oatmeal today?" Moira asks while eyeing the newcomers. By the looks of it, she has another few minutes before they get to their booth.

"Whenever you have a chance. I'm not in a rush."

Over the next hour, the diner gets busy while I fall into the zone. I write quickly, cruising through a particularly tense scene in which Stacey Simpson sits in her car outside the bakery watching the heroine mop the floors before locking up. Every few minutes I look up from the screen and spot Moira. Happiness fills my body.

When things finally slow down, Moira drops what I'm guessing is my bill on the table, but instead of my check it's a note. On it is written, *meet me in the supply closet in two minutes*. A grin spreads across my face. Hello! I pretend to keep working, but there's no way I can concentrate.

I hear Moira tell Abigail that she's going to the ladies' room. She glides by me, flashing a covert smile. After a moment, I stretch my legs and follow. As I near the closet, she reaches an arm out and yanks me inside with her, then she kicks the door shut with her foot.

Wrapping her arms around my neck, she tentatively touches her lips to mine. Placing my hands on her hips, I pull her close, and we spend the next several minutes like this. We kiss each other senseless and I'm seriously considering telling her that I'm no longer in this relationship as a temporary thing. But before I can say anything, she says, "That was fun, but I'd better get back to work."

"If you're not doing anything tonight, maybe I can pop over after the kids are in bed and we could watch a movie or something?"

She grins up at me. "Is watching a movie code for making out on my couch? 'Cause if it is, I'm in."

Yeah, I'm seriously thinking I should make a real play

for Moira. This pretend thing is already feeling like a sham and it hasn't even been twenty-four hours.

The morning passes quickly and I'm having a horrible time concentrating. Also, I'm pretty sure Abigail is on to us. She's been walking around glancing between Moira and me with a very curious expression on her face. I think that might have something to do with her witnessing our exit from the storage closet. Together.

At noon, the boys come piling into the diner and make a beeline for my table. I manage to put my laptop away before they take over. Wyatt sits next to me, as he tends to do, and Ash and Colton sit across from us. "What have you fellas been up to this morning?" I ask them.

"I caught a cricket and put him in a jar, but Colton felt sorry for him and let him out when I went in the house to use the bathroom," Ash says, glaring at his twin.

"You had him out in the sun. He was going to fry," Colton tells him.

"He was fine."

"Was not."

"Was, too."

Moira zips over, carrying empty plates from a table she just cleared. In a low (and surprisingly menacing) tone she says, "Knock it off, the pair of you, or you'll be on dish duty in the kitchen all afternoon."

They shut their mouths immediately.

"That's better. Tuna melts on whole wheat and a side of fruit for each of you. What about you, Ethan?"

"I'll have the same."

After she disappears into the kitchen, I glance over at Wyatt. He looks a little down in the mouth. "You okay, Wyatt?"

Shrugging, he says, "One of the kids on the five to eight-year-old team has a grandpa who owns a Denny's in

Anchorage. He's offering free coffee to anyone who buys a raffle ticket. He's sold hundreds of tickets just this week."

"Oh, man, so it's not looking good for your team to win."

He sighs and rests his chin on his fist. "Not unless we come up with something real amazing."

"Amazing, like, say, the actual jersey LeBron James wore in *Space Jam*?"

His eyes light up. "Do you know someone who has that?"

"*I* have it. It's signed, framed, and authenticated," I tell him. "I'd be happy to part with it, for a good cause." I like Wyatt a lot, but the thought of taking him and his mom to LA is where my real investment lies. I want to see Moira in my hometown and get a feel for how she likes it. If I want to make her my girlfriend for real, I've got to see what she thinks of where I've spent my life.

Wyatt beams at me. "So if people buy tickets from us, they get a ticket for the jersey, too?"

"Exactly," I answer. "All we have to do is get a flyer with the details and a roll of tickets to distribute to your teammates. I can have the flyers made up by tomorrow and have the jersey shipped here within a few days. Maybe your mom will let us put it on display in the diner to create some buzz."

"You're the best, Ethan!"

"I want you to win." I'd like to see a lot of good things happen for this family.

"You and Aunt Harper have the best lives," he says longingly.

"We've definitely been lucky, but life in Hollywood isn't all it's cracked up to be."

Narrowing his eyes, he says, "It's got to be better than here."

"Different, but not better. Gamble's got a lot going for it too."

"Yeah, right."

"No, seriously—there's no smog here, you don't have to sit in traffic for hours every time you want to go somewhere, and you don't have to worry about getting mugged if you find yourself in the wrong part of town late at night."

"But there aren't any famous people here," he answers. I have to suppress a smile because I'm willing to bet that he never even thought about famous people before Harper came to town.

"Famous people are just people, like everyone else, Wyatt. And a lot of them—Harper excluded—aren't all that nice. They've gotten so used to everyone giving them whatever they want, whenever they want it, that they can be difficult to be around."

"Is that why you came up here? To get away from them?" Ash asks.

"In a way, yes. I've been there my whole life and I needed a change of scenery," I tell him. "When you boys grow up, you'll probably want to go see the world, and while that's a good thing, what you've got here is pretty special, too, and I predict you'll only learn to appreciate it more."

He gives me a skeptical look. "If it's so special, why don't you move here?"

"I … well … because my job is there," I say, unable to come up with a better answer. The truth is that I may have to go back to practicing law, at least until I can come up with something else.

"I thought you wanted to be a writer," Wyatt says. "Can't you do that anywhere?"

"I do, but it's a bit of a long shot."

Moira appears with our lunches, saving me from further questions from the peanut gallery. As I eat, I find myself amused at the fact that a ten-year-old was able to back me into a corner so easily. It's a sure sign that my days as an entertainment lawyer are over. I may have to become a real estate lawyer or something.

Chapter 21

Moira

At five o'clock, I grab my purse from behind the counter and tell Abigail, "I'm heading out. I'll see you in the morning."

"You going out on a date with lover boy?" She puckers up her lips together in a kissy face.

Halting in my tracks, I stutter, "L—lover boy? Who's that?"

She shoots me a look of such incredulity, I almost confess on the spot. "Ethan? The writer who sits at table six day in and day out and stares at you like he wants to eat you for dinner?"

"What? No!" I wave my hand in front of my face as though batting at a swarm of mosquitos. "Don't be ridiculous. We're just friends." I compound my lie by adding, "Actually, we aren't even that. He's *Harper's* friend."

Abigail shakes her head, causing her thick, black ponytail to bounce around her shoulders. "You lie like a frozen dog turd."

I do, but I don't want her to know that. "I don't have time for a man, Abigail. You know that."

She rolls her eyes. "You don't have time for a tall, rich, and handsome lawyer? Shoot, Moira, *I* have time for him, and I'm happily married."

Nervous laughter erupts out of my mouth. "Then maybe *you* should date him."

"Maybe I will," she taunts.

"Have a good time!" I wave as I turn around and stride toward the front door. Almost immediately, I feel Ethan behind me. Before he can say anything, I practically hiss, "Turn in the other direction and walk away from me. Abigail is onto us."

"I was thinking the same thing. Your excuse for us both walking out of the storage closet at the same time didn't sound overly convincing."

"Why? I might have needed your help reaching the toilet paper."

He shakes his head. "The toilet paper was on the bottom shelf."

"Drive down the road and make the turn for your cabin. I'll meet you there," I tell him.

Ethan does as he's been bid, but I sit in my truck for a minute, wondering what the heck I've gotten myself involved in. I'm not sure I can casually date, let alone a guy like him. He's the kind of man my Grandma Adele used to call a game changer. Meaning he makes an impact. And boy howdy, what an impact he's making.

I pull out of the parking lot and drive the short distance to the road where Ethan lives. My senses are on hyper alert, and my skin feels like it's being invaded by an army of ants. I'm either prickling with fear or excitement.

Maybe a little bit of both. When I see Ethan's car parked by the side of the road, I veer off and park behind him.

Turning off the ignition, I take a deep breath and put my hand on the door handle to get out, but he's already there, opening it for me. Reaching into the car, he asks, "Why don't you just come up to my place?"

"Not possible."

His eyebrows arch in question, so I explain, "As the latest resident of Gamble, you're currently the most interesting person in town." I take his hand and let him help me out. "I'm willing to bet more than one pair of binoculars are aimed at your front door."

"Seriously?"

"Yup. People are going to be trying to figure you out, and until they do, they're going to have their eyes trained on you."

Once I'm on my feet, Ethan pulls me into his arms and holds me closely. "That's creepy."

"That's life in a small town."

Resting his chin on my head, he asks, "Have you ever thought about living somewhere else?"

"I've thought about it, but my whole support system is in Gamble, so I'd be a fool to leave that behind. A single mother needs all the help she can get."

"What if you had a support system somewhere else?"

"If you're asking what I'd do if Grandpa and Digger moved, I'd probably follow them. But there's no way that's ever going to happen. They're both set in their ways."

"I get that," he says, as my stomach suddenly drops.

He's telling me that he's set in his ways, too. Which, once again, makes this short-term dating thing a bad idea.

I don't have time to let doubt take center stage in my brain because Ethan lowers his lips to mine in the most soul-searing kiss I've ever experienced. The burn starts at my feet and slowly moves all the way up to my brain. That's when a serious malfunction of my thought process occurs, and I no longer wonder at the logistics of what we're doing. There are times in life where you have to live for the moment. And if this isn't one of those times, I don't know what is.

It feels so good to be in Ethan's arms, so right. It feels like it's where I was always meant to be. If not for old Mrs. Martin driving by and honking, I might have stayed there forever. *So much for finding a more secluded spot.*

Instinctually, I lower my head onto Ethan's chest, hoping to hide from her until she passes by.

"Who was that?" he asks.

"Sissy Sinclair's grandmother. Hopefully, she didn't see me." That's when it hits me that my truck is sitting out in plain sight, and there's no chance she didn't see that. Super. My already undeserved reputation in town is about to get even more interesting.

"Is there any place in Gamble where we can be alone?" He sounds as frustrated as I feel.

"We could go for a hike," I suggest.

"When?" I love that he's so eager.

"How about on Saturday after two? Things slow down at the diner at that time, so Abigail can handle things on her own until the dinner shift shows up. The kids are going to go fishing with Digger, so they won't be around."

That's when Ethan smacks himself in the head. "My parents will be here tomorrow. I don't know how I'm going to sneak away from them so soon."

"Tell them that you're going up the mountain to help gather notes for a grisly murder scene," I suggest.

"I'll do my best, but just so you know, my mother is not the easiest person in the world to shake. When she wants something, she gets it."

She sounds like someone I'd like to meet. "Bring her along, then. Maybe she can give me some lessons." I eye him with intent.

He steps back with a wicked grin on his face. Running his hands up and down in front of his body, he asks, "Is there something here that you want?"

Yes, yes, yes, yesyesyesyesyesyes … but of course, I don't say that. Instead, I offer a slight shrug. "Maybe." Then I look at my watch. "Edna needs to get home, so I'd better hustle. I'll text you once the boys go to bed."

He reaches out as if to grab me, but I speed up to stay out of his reach. If I let Ethan get his hands on me again, I'll be hard pressed to ever walk away. Driving home feels like I've tuned into the Ethan channel. He's all I can think about until I pull into my driveway.

That's where I'm greeted by total mayhem. The twins are running around screaming, Wyatt is lying on the ground like he's been hit by a brick, and Edna's heading in my direction as fast as her seventy-something legs will carry her.

I barely have the car in park before I get out. "What happened?"

"Well, there's good news and bad news. What do you want first?" She huffs as she stops to catch her breath.

"Always the bad," I tell her. I hate having good news ruined by bad.

"I think Wyatt might have a concussion."

"What? How?"

"He stepped on a rake and the handle hit him in the head so hard, he dropped."

Hurrying over to my son, I ask, "What in the heck was he doing with a rake?" My boys aren't known for their love of yard work. The only reason I can get them to mow is because that job pays five bucks.

Kneeling next to Wyatt, he beams up at me and asks, "Do you like it?"

"Do I like what, honey?"

"That's the good news," Edna says. And then, with a flourish, she gestures toward the front of the house. "The boys and I put in a proper flower garden for you!"

I turn and look, and sure enough, in the very place I've always wanted a garden, there is one. It's full of bright blooms and plants. There's even a garden gnome statue lying in his own little hammock. "But why? I mean, it's lovely, but what's the occasion?"

"My cousin from Anchorage came down and brought me all kinds of flowers. But I'm full up with them, so the boys and I decided to plant you a garden."

"Edna, I don't know what to say. Thank you." People don't normally do things for me for no reason. Outside of my family, that is.

"That's why we've been digging up the front yard," Wyatt says, still lying on his back. He suddenly rolls over and throws up all over the place.

As I rub his back, Edna says, "Yup, it's a concussion. You'd better take him to the hospital. I'll take the twins home with me."

Colton had a concussion when he got hit in the head with a baseball. I can only hope we're not in for a night of vomiting, but one thing's sure, we're going to be stuck at the hospital for several hours.

It looks like my plans with Ethan will have to be postponed.

Chapter 22

Ethan

My parents arrive today. I've decided that I'm sort of happy they're coming, even though it's going to make it considerably more difficult to sneak in some time with Moira. We missed out on our "movie date" because of Wyatt's concussion. Moira took some time off work to stay with him, and suddenly it's Thursday.

I'm currently sitting on the porch at the lodge, waiting for my parents to pull up. I told them to come here first, since it's a lot easier to find than my cabin, not to mention it means they get to see Harper, Lily, and Liam. My mom adores the three of them so much, she went into serious mourning when Harper and Digger ended up together. As soon as Mom heard Harper's marriage had ended, she started texting and calling me non-stop to "get in there before someone else does."

The front door opens, and Harper walks outside and

sits down on the Adirondack chair next to mine. "You going to tell me what's going on?"

"Umm … sure. But I thought you knew that my parents were arriving in a few minutes."

Looking annoyed, she says, "Don't play dumb with me, mister. I know you far too well. What's going on with you and Moira?"

"Nothing." My cheeks suddenly heat up like I'm standing too close to a bonfire. "Other than a very nice friendship, that is."

"Uh-huh." She doesn't sound convinced. "Those were her exact words when I asked her this morning."

"Could it be that she has the same answer because it's the truth?"

"Not when the two of you look as guilty as sin," Harper teases, lightly punching my arm. "Plus, Abigail told me she saw you two coming out of the storage closet together."

"It was …research for my book. I'm writing a scene where the villain hides in a closet, so Moira was kind enough to show me hers."

"I'll just bet she did," Harper laughs. Clearing her throat, she adds, "And what's your excuse for the fact that Mrs. Martin saw the two of you kissing on the side of the road?"

I freeze for a second, feeling like one of my clients caught in the headlights of a police car.

"You're so busted," she says. "Relax. I'm not about to lecture you on playing with fire. You're both adults. I'm sure you know what you're doing."

"I appreciate the vote of confidence."

"I do have one question though."

"Which is?" I ask.

"Are you considering staying in Gamble permanently?"

"Honestly, Harper, I haven't even had a chance to think that far ahead. Moira and I have decided to enjoy our friendship for what it is. We both know it has to end." *Unless she crawls under my Paige radar and decides to go all in.* "I just wanted to remind her what it feels like to be treated like a queen, so when she's ready to get back into the dating game, she won't settle for someone who doesn't deserve her."

"That's the most ridiculous thing I've ever heard," Harper says as a black sedan pulls into the parking lot. My parents have arrived.

"Maybe so, but please don't tell anyone about this. Not even Digger."

"Your secret is safe with me, but I don't know how much longer you'll be able to keep things on the down low. Mrs. Martin has already been up here to start gossiping about what she saw, and I'm willing to bet we were one of many stops on her list."

"Oh, no, who did she tell?"

"Digger and Jack." One of Harper's eyebrows is arched in the way it does when she's trying to get one of her kids to confess to some transgression. "But don't worry, they didn't believe her. In fact, Jack told her that she'd better get her eyes checked or the police would take away her driver's license again."

We hear the slam of car doors and Harper and I both jump to our feet. "Moira and I are just enjoying living a little," I say as we walk down the steps.

"Just make sure you don't *live* so much that one of you gets hurt," she says, waving to my mom.

"I thought you weren't going to lecture me," I mutter.

"I was lying," she says with a big grin.

Before I can respond, my mother comes at us like they just opened the doors for the annual Bloomingdale's blowout sale. She's practically sprinting.

She heads toward Harper first. In lieu of a standard greeting, she goes with, "Why in the hell would you want to live way up here?"

Before Harper can answer, my mom's gaze darts behind us. Her eyes nearly pop out of her head, and when I turn, I see Digger walking out of the lodge. "Forget I asked. I get it now."

"Hi, Mom," I interject before giving her a big hug.

"Hi, yourself," she says, holding onto me tightly. "Next time you go on sabbatical, can you make it in San Diego or something? The trip up here was ridiculous."

My dad makes his way over to us and gives Harper a kiss on her cheek, then gives me a hug. "It was fine, Rose. In fact, it was fun."

"It was fine until we got off the plane in Anchorage and had to spend two hours on that bumpy road. I'm pretty sure my teeth might fall out." She points her finger at Dad sharply. "If they do, I'm getting implants, and those run around two thousand, per tooth."

My dad looks down at her lovingly. "Honey, you can have whatever you want, whenever you want it."

"Oh, pish," Mom says to him. "Quit making light of my suffering."

Harper stifles a laugh, then says, "I've missed you two."

They both turn to her, and then in unison say, "You, too, sweetheart."

Digger walks over to Harper and wraps an arm around her waist. Harper says, "Rose, Isaac, this is my fiancé, Digger. Digger, these are my dear friends, Rose and Isaac."

"It's a pleasure to meet you both," Digger says.

"Harper has had nothing but wonderful things to say about you."

"She says a lot of nice things about you, too," Mom tells him. She's staring so intently, you'd think she was checking him for lice. "I was praying Ethan would wind up with Harper. If you hadn't swooped in so fast, he might have had a chance."

Digger smiles easily before saying, "Sorry, but this lady was meant for me." He's clearly so confident in his relationship that nothing my mom has to say will bother him.

I turn to Digger. "My mom can't understand the concept of men and women just being friends."

"I can, too!" Mom says. "It's just that I love Harper and the kids so much, I wanted them for myself." She looks at Digger and points to me with her thumb. "This one's never going to give me grandkids."

Harper gives her a thoughtful look. "So, you wouldn't mind if Ethan, say, fell for someone who already had children for you to spoil."

I glare at Harper, while my mother says, "Hell, at this point, I'd take a couple of grand-dogs, a parrot, or even a gerbil."

"I hear grand-gerbils are all the rage now," Harper teases.

Digger gestures toward the lodge. "You two must be hungry after your long trip. Would you like to come inside for lunch?"

Harper interrupts. "That won't work, honey. The restaurant is closed right now."

Digger looks at her oddly. "Yes, but I own the place, I can open it."

Harper waves her hand in front of her face. "Nonsense. Why don't we just take them over to Moira's place?" Digger shrugs in agreement.

Two things. One—I have a feeling my friend has every intention of involving herself in my love life. And two—get ready, Gamble, because Rose and Isaac have arrived.

Chapter 23

Moira

Even though it's only been three days, I miss Ethan way more than I should.

After the hospital confirmed Wyatt's concussion, I took a few days off work to spend with him, as I can't stand the thought of leaving my kids when they're hurt. Edna takes great care of them, but I'm their mother. That privilege should be mine.

Once I passed the twenty-four-hour concussion danger zone on Tuesday afternoon, I asked Edna to come by for an hour so I could hit the only crafting store in a thirty-mile radius. As per Ellie Fansworthy's advice, I bought supplies to make my own vision board. While it's not something I would normally see myself doing, I've reached the point in my life where something has to be done.

At the Hobby Hut, I bought a white foam board, some scissors with fancy edges, and packages of stickers. At the checkout counter, I added several magazines that I was confident would have the kinds of pictures that would adequately portray my greatest desires.

When I got home, the boys questioned what I was doing, so I lied and told them that I was working on a project for Digger. Luckily, their complete lack of interest in all things crafty took over and they didn't ask another thing about it.

I've spent hours cutting out pictures of happy families, full-on with a dad. I cut out pictures of houses that aren't in horrible need of repair. I cut out pictures of indulgences, like people eating in beautiful restaurants, getting massages, and simply smiling. I cut out pictures of airplanes, yachts, and white sand beaches dotted with little tiki huts. Even though this vision board thing might be a total washout, I've enjoyed every single moment of putting my wildest dreams on display.

I've learned a lot about myself, too. I've discovered that I have a wide array of dreams that I haven't let myself think about since I was a child. When my mom left, everything in my life got put on hold. I no longer talked about going to Paris someday or owning a fancy restaurant. It's as though when she left to pursue her dreams, she packed up all of mine and took them away with her.

Every time I look at my vision board, it rekindles my ability to feel excitement and possibility. I've left enough space on it that I'm going to continue adding to it, and when this one's full, I'll make another one. I'll fill my bedroom walls with them if I have to.

"Mooooooooooooom!" Colton runs into my room and jumps on my bed on top of me.

"Is the house on fire?" I demand.

"Nope." He crawls under the covers next to me and lays his head on my pillow.

"Then why are you so fired up?" I ask, pulling him close.

"I like having you home. I don't want you to go back to work today."

"Oh, honey, I like being home, too. But you know that I need to work to keep a roof over our heads."

"I suppose." He doesn't sound like he's buying it.

Before I can respond, Ash and Wyatt walk in. Once they see their brother in bed with me, they jump in as well. "This is nice," I tell them. "I miss snuggling with my boys."

"You're the best, Mom," Wyatt says. "Thanks for staying home with us."

"It's almost like we're a real family," Ash adds.

"We *are* a real family," I say a bit harshly.

Colton says, "Sure, we are. Ash just means that it's nice to have a mom around."

I feel like I've just been hacked in half with a cleaver. "A lot of moms work," I tell my boys.

"Sure, but you know, they have dads to help make up for it." Wyatt stares at me like he knows they've just hurt me, but he doesn't seem to know how to make it better.

"Do you have any memories of your dad, Wy?" I ask him.

He shakes his head. "Not really. I mean, I see pictures and feel like maybe there's something there, but it's probably just the picture making me think that."

"Ash and I have never had a dad," Colton announces. "It looks really cool, too."

"And stupid Travis Sinclair is always rubbing it in our faces," Ash adds.

"Excuse me?" I'm positively boiling in anger. "What does he say?"

After several moments of silence, Wyatt answers, "He tells us that if our dad wasn't so stupid, he would have never fallen off the boat and drowned and then we wouldn't have to be raised by the neighbor while our mom slings hash."

I sit bolt upright and scoot the boys aside.

Colton demands, "Where are you going?"

"Not only do I have to work today," I tell them. "But I'm going to pay Travis's mom a visit. It's high time that woman learns how to shut her vile mouth."

"But she didn't say it, Travis did," Colton says.

"You don't think Travis came upon those opinions on his own, do you?" Shaking my head, I say, "She's been badmouthing me my whole life."

"Are you going to punch her?" Wyatt wants to know. "Because if you are, we want to come."

"Girl fight!" Ash adds excitedly.

"I want to go with you and give that turd Travis a piece of my mind," Colton says.

I force myself to take three deep breaths. Ellie Fansworthy suggests five, but I'm not that patient. "I think I should talk to Sissy on my own first," I tell the boys. "I don't want to fight her. I just want her family to leave mine alone."

Lies. I want to fight her. I'd start by tying her to a tree and egging her, then I'd move into covering her with honey and leaving her for the wildlife to finish off. But I can't tell my kids that.

The boys release a series of grunts which I take to mean they understand. "Can we come in for lunch today?" Wyatt asks.

"You know you can," I tell him. "In fact, you can spend the afternoon at the diner if you want. You can play at the park across the street or bring a book to read."

My suggestion is met by a chorus of cheers that fills me with both love and sadness. We don't have a bad life, and the boys have Digger and Grandpa Jack as male role models, but clearly, they want more.

Once we're all out of bed, I say, "You can even have breakfast at the diner, if you want. I think we should celebrate Wyatt's return to health with Lloyd's famous pigs in a blanket. What do you say?"

More cheers.

The boys run off to get dressed while I do the same. I call Edna and tell her we won't need her today, then I pile the kids into the truck and take them into work. My confrontation with Sissy will have to wait.

As per my new pledge to focus more on the positive, I start a silent litany of my blessings. I'm thankful for my children, for our health, for our house (such as it is), for Digger and Grandpa Jack. I'm grateful for my business, for Edna and her husband, and for the beautiful state in which I live. I'm grateful to have friends like Harper and Ethan who took a day to help paint my kitchen.

I ask the boys what they're grateful for.

Colton says, "I'm grateful for you, Mom. I'm grateful for baseball and for frogs and that school is out for the summer!"

"Same," Ash says, clearly not wanting to be put on the spot of having to come up with his own list.

"What about you, Wyatt?" I ask my eldest, who is currently staring thoughtfully out the window.

He's quiet for a moment before saying, "I'm grateful for you and the twins, for Uncle Digger, and Grandpa Jack. I'm grateful for fishing and fireworks and for …"

He stops mid-sentence, so I encouraged him to continue, "And what?"

Shaking his head, he sighs loudly. "I'm grateful for Ethan. I know he's just a friend, but I like him a lot, Mom. He's doing so much to help my team win the contest to see the Dodgers, and you know, I just think he's super cool."

A voice in my head starts screaming, "Abort! Abort!" It's warning me to stop what's going on with me and Ethan before things go so far that he leaves us all with broken hearts.

The selfish side of me doesn't agree. *As long as the kids never guess what's really going on, what can it hurt to keep seeing Ethan?*

I don't let myself answer that question though, because the truth is, it can hurt everything.

Chapter 24

Ethan

It's early Friday morning, and it's already shaping up to be a hot day. My parents and I are sipping coffees on the deck overlooking the lake and listening to the occasional call of the local loon population.

Moira wasn't at work yesterday, so we turned around and had supper at the lodge instead of the diner. My parents didn't quite know what to make of that, but they went with it.

Happily, my mom hasn't started in on me about anything yet—like my book, when I'm going to go home and work again, or my complete failure at making her a grandmother. I suspect that's only because she's not fully caffeinated.

"How's the book coming?" my dad asks.

"Really well," I tell him. "I've been making some great progress."

"Good for you, son," he says. "Any chance you'll let me see what you've got so far?"

My stomach flips at the thought of letting anyone read what I've written. "It's just a first draft. I'd really like to wait until it's all done and polished before I let people read it."

"First drafts are supposed to be terrible." He knows what he's talking about. Dad was a talent agent for years and has read more than one manuscript written by a famous actor who felt they had a book in them. *Shocker, the number that actually did was surprisingly low.*

"You really should let your dad read it," mom interjects. "Most authors would kill to have someone with his experience give them notes."

She makes a good point. Even if he tells me I lack any discernible talent, it would be better to know now than to keep wasting my time. "You know what? That sounds good, Dad. Thank you."

He beams at me. "Just email it to me and I'll read it on my laptop. Now, don't let us interrupt you. You took the day off yesterday. Your mom and I can fend for ourselves today."

Mom nods her head firmly. "We promise to stay out of your way."

"Actually, I write at the diner," I tell them. "It's too quiet for me here."

"Get going," Mom says before adding, "We'll meet you there for lunch."

I try to look relaxed, but my stomach is doing flip-flops at the thought of my parents meeting Moira. I'll have to force myself to act nonchalant, so they don't get any ideas. "That sounds like a plan."

～

Two hours into my book and I'm still not able to focus. Apparently, I can't go three days away from Moira without totally losing my bearings. I keep looking up to make sure she's really here.

She's been busy so we haven't had a chance to talk much, but when she walks by, we manage to get in an entire conversation, one bit at a time. "I take it Wyatt's feeling better?" I ask, watching through the diner window as he and the twins race around playing tag in the park across the street.

She pours me a cup of coffee. "Kids bounce back so fast."

"I've missed you," I tell her quietly. "I thought you might be avoiding me."

She rests the coffee pot on the table. "I've missed you, too." I feel like she's on the verge of confessing something more when she suddenly changes topics. "Where are your parents? Don't tell me they hated it here so much, they took the first plane home."

Dare to dream. "They're doing some exploring this morning, but they'll be here for lunch," I tell her.

"Why do I suddenly feel nervous?" she asks.

"No need, they'll love you," I tell her. "In fact, my only worry is that my mom will see through us and start getting ideas."

Moira nods her head steadily while offering a small shrug. She's got something on her mind. Shooting me a nervous smile, she turns around to take care of her other tables.

Two hours later, my parents arrive, looking completely out of place. My mom's hair has been coiffed to perfection and her outfit screams "I just left Barney's and I'm on my way to lunch at Crustacean." My dad looks like he's about to play eighteen holes in his pink plaid pants and polo shirt. All eyes in the diner turn to them as they make their way over to my table, sliding into the booth across from me.

My dad glances around, before whispering, "What's everyone staring at?"

I lean toward them. "You're not the typical kind of people they're used to seeing around here."

Out of the corner of my eye, I notice Moira staring, too. She's busily running her fingers through her hair to tidy it up. The sight of her looking so nervous makes me realize she shouldn't have to meet my parents for the first time while she's serving them. Moira picks up two mugs and a pot of coffee and walks over to us with a bright smile plastered on her face.

Grinning up at her, I say, "Mom, Dad, this is Digger's sister, Moira Bishop. Moira, meet Isaac and Rose Caplan." Inside my head I hear a fictional television announcer say, *"Welcome to the Isaac and Rose Show!"*

Setting down the mugs, Moira shakes hands with both of my parents. "It's a pleasure to meet you. Your son has been a welcome addition to Gamble. He's been very generous with his time helping people out around here." She sounds like she's been rehearsing her lines.

My parents look confused by this description of me. They know me as a super busy entertainment lawyer who hires his whole life out because he doesn't even have time to pick up his own dry cleaning. Not as someone who goes out of his way to help others.

"Moira's being kind," I tell them. "I just lent a hand with some painting one day."

"He's also helping my son's baseball team raise money for a trip to see the Dodgers in LA," Moira nervously adds. "You've raised a fine person."

"Thank you." My mom continues to look totally confused, which isn't very flattering.

The front door bursts open and the boys come racing in. "Mom, I'm so thirsty, I could die," Ash announces, grabbing his throat with one hand for dramatic effect.

"I'm so hungry I could eat a bear," Colton adds. "I need food now or I'm going to faint."

The three of them rush over to my table, stopping short when they see my parents. "Where are we supposed to sit?" Wyatt asks, informing my parents they normally sit with me. That's going to be a discussion.

"How about at another table?" Moira rolls her eyes to the side to indicate the booth next to mine.

Before they leave, I perform quick introductions with my parents. I do my best not to laugh when Ash bows to them with a flourish like he's a courtier meeting a king and queen.

Moira tells the boys, "Don't you dare sit down before you wash your hands." As they thunder away, she turns to us. "Sorry about that. Now, can I get you some coffee?"

"No, thank you," my mom says. "We only drink it first thing in the morning, on account of Isaac's insomnia."

"What can I get for you, then?" Moira nervously shifts from foot to foot like she's getting ready to run.

"I'd like a cup of hot water with some lemon in it," Mom says. "It's a great digestive."

"I'd love an iced tea," my dad tells her.

"I'll be right back." Moira bolts toward the counter.

My mom stares at me for a second. "Those boys eat lunch with you every day?"

"They do," I tell her.

"Why?"

"It turns out I'm pretty cool."

"But they're so *wild*," she whispers.

"They're kids. That's how normal kids act." I feel a lot more defensive about Moira's boys than I should.

"I don't know about that," my mom says. "Running into a restaurant and yelling."

"Rose, their mom owns the diner, so for them, this place is as good as home," my dad tells her. "Besides, it's not like this is the Polo Lounge or something." His eyes shift around, taking in how very much this place isn't like any he's used to.

When the boys tumble down the hall from the bathroom, they make a beeline for the booth right behind me. My mother will now watch, and judge, every move they make.

"I started reading your book this morning," my dad announces, drawing all attention away from the boys.

My gut tightens in anticipation. "And …?"

"I think you've got something there, Ethan."

Relief washes over me, followed quickly by a flood of self-doubt. "You're not just saying that because I'm your son, are you?"

"You know me better than that," he says. "I didn't coddle you when you were a kid, I'm certainly not going to start now. Besides, the fact that you've got talent isn't exactly good news as far as your mother's concerned." They don't have to say that they've seen too many people try to make it and fail in Hollywood for me to know that's what they're worried about.

Behind us, the boys are involved in what sounds like a life-or-death tic-tac-toe game, based on their raised voices. "You cheated."

"Did not."

"Did, too."

"Did *not*."

"You went twice. That's cheating."

I glance up as Moira arrives at our table. She hurries to put our drinks down before performing the "swipe across the neck" gesture to tell her kids to cut it out, then rushes off.

I grin when I hear Wyatt say, "That's enough, you boneheads. Mom's getting mad."

My mom, who has indeed been watching them, asks, "Why are they here instead of at home?"

"Moira's husband passed away when she was pregnant with the twins. She's had a pretty hard time handling everything on her own."

My mom looks up at Moira as though examining a racehorse she's thinking of buying. "A pretty little thing like her widowed at such a young age…" she says, shaking her head. "She must be exhausted all the time."

"Pretty much."

My mom's face lights up. "Now I see why you were willing to drive all the way to Anchorage to help a 'friend,'" she says, pursing her lips. It takes me a minute to understand her meaning. I had completely forgotten about my mom's day of panic when I didn't answer the phone.

Chapter 25

Moira

Ethan's parents are formidable. They're not exactly scary, just highly unapproachable. I hurry to wrap up some fresh bread in a basket. Sliding it toward Abigail, I ask, "Would you mind taking this over to Ethan and his parents?"

She pulls the basket toward her. "His parents, huh?"

I nod while turning around to get the boys some milk. I should have Abigail take care of the kids' drinks, but I need a minute to pull my thoughts together. There is no reason under the sun that I should be nervous around the Caplans. They're just like any other customers. Okay, that's a lie, but they're still customers. I'm never nervous around customers.

Dropping the milk off with the boys, I tell them, "Today you're having BLTs on whole wheat toast with a side salad."

"We haven't had fries all week," Colton moans.

"And we're allowed to have them once a week," Ash reminds me.

"Fine, a side salad and fries," I tell them. Then I lean in and whisper, "Be good and don't embarrass Ethan in front of his parents."

This is the point where they should nod their heads like good little soldiers and carry on with their meal quietly. That's not what happens. Wyatt practically shouts, "Embarrass Ethan? He loves us! How could we embarrass him?"

Colton says, "She means no farting and burping."
Dear God.

"Or telling poop jokes!" Ash adds.

I stare at them like I'm trying to perform a Vulcan mind meld from *Star Trek*. "Stop. Shouting. Now."

Before they can reply, I feel someone standing over my shoulder. It's Isaac. He scoots into the booth next to Wyatt and declares, "I love a good poop joke. What have you got?"

Ash glances up at me like he's bursting at the seams. I shake my head, so Ash replies, "Mom won't let us tell any."

Isaac leans in like he's going to share his deepest, darkest secret. "Why does Piglet stink?"

The boys look up at me nervously before turning their attention back to him. He answers, "Because he plays with Pooh." Riotous laughter ensues.

I turn toward Ethan's table so they won't see me laugh. I will lose all credibility with my kids if I don't appear annoyed by such potty humor. Worse yet, I'll be opening myself up for a lot more of it and that *cannot* happen.

Smiling at Ethan and his mom, I tell them, "Our special today is curried chicken salad sandwiches with fried pickles with a frisée salad. Do you need a minute, or do you know what you'd like?"

Rose asks, "Are there raisins in the chicken salad?"

"No," I tell her, wondering who puts raisins in chicken salad.

"I'll have that," she says. "I'd like it on a croissant."

"Um …" We don't serve croissants, but in the back of my head I'm wondering if I have time to run to the market and get some.

"You should have it on the sourdough, Mom." Ethan to the rescue. "They make a fresh batch every day."

"Sure, fine." Rose stares at me with her penetrating gaze and asks, "How old are you?"

"Excuse me?"

"How old are you, dear. You look very young."

"Most days, I feel like I'm ninety," I tell her, only half-joking. "But I'm thirty-two."

She nudges Ethan, "What do you want to eat?"

"I'll have the same thing as the boys." His smile causes my stomach to flutter. I've missed him so much.

"Isaac!" Rose calls out. "What do you want to eat?"

"Same as you, hon!" he answers before starting another poop joke.

Abigail walks by, so I hand her their orders. "Can you give these to Lloyd? I need a minute." Without another word to Ethan and his mom, I head in the direction of the supply closet.

Once I'm inside, I pace around like a caged tiger. Ethan's parents are nice. Isaac is even telling my sons stupid kid jokes. That's good, right? No, it's not good! My kids shouldn't be getting to know Ethan's parents. We shouldn't be getting closer to people who aren't going to be in our lives. But they're friends of Harper's and *she's* going to be in our lives, so maybe…

Before I can come to a conclusion about what we should do, the door opens and Ethan sneaks in.

"What are you doing here? Did anyone see you?"

He steps closer and pulls me into his arms. "I've missed you."

He's so big and solid and warm. I let myself soak in the feel of him before answering, "I've missed you, too."

Tilting my head up to meet his, I'm thrilled when Ethan lowers his soft, full lips to mine. The touch is tentative at first, but soon deepens into something so raw and carnal, it robs the breath from my lungs. I want to kiss him forever.

After several moments, he lifts his head and asks, "What are you doing tonight?"

I should make up something so that I don't fall farther down the rabbit hole, but I can't seem to make my mouth say anything.

"I'm taking my parents over to Harper's for supper. We thought you and the boys might like to join us." I don't answer right away, so he adds, "Liam and Lily have really missed the kids these last few days."

"I suppose we could …" I know I don't sound too excited, but the truth is, I'm scared. I'm scared of how Ethan makes me feel, and I'm scared I'm incapable of any kind of casual relationship that includes the kind of kisses we share. Forget the kisses, I'm starting to have real feelings for Ethan and that terrifies the absolute crap out of me.

"Good," Ethan says. "Meet us up there right after work. I'm hoping you and I can sneak off to the woods for a bit and make up for lost time." He winks before releasing me from his hold. Then he walks out the door.

My feet feel like they've been superglued to the floor. I can't make them move. I hope Abigail is doing okay out there, because it looks like I might live in the supply closet now. Moments after Ethan leaves, there's a knock on the door before Isaac walks in.

"Oh, sorry. I thought this was the men's room. I could have sworn Ethan just came out of here."

"Next door down the hall," I tell him.

"That's the ladies' room."

"Across from that."

"If that's true, then my son either just walked out of here, or he was in the ladies' room."

Good lord, what do I tell him? My eyes shift around hoping to find some reason that it would make sense for Ethan to visit the supply closet. My gaze lands on a large package wrapped in brown paper that's propped against the wall. Abigail said something about a package arriving for Ethan. I point to it and say, "Ah, yes, well … this package arrived for your son, and he was just checking it out."

"It's still wrapped." Isaac looks confused. *Welcome to the club, buddy.*

"Oh, yeah, right … I guess he'll open it later." I stumble over my words like I've been drinking tequila for three days. FYI, I'm a "one tequila, two tequila, three tequila, floor" kind of gal. Although I skip stages two and three and fall over after one.

"What is it?" Isaac asks.

"Ethan said it was something for my son's baseball raffle." I'm breaking out into a cold sweat now.

Isaac smiles. "Okay, then. I guess I'll just head to the little boys' room." As he turns to leave, my knees give out from under me, and I crumple to the floor.

Abigail is the next person to join me. She stares at me curled up next to the toilet paper and asks, "Can you throw me a roll?"

I fire one off in her direction, hoping she'll leave without comment. No such luck. "You've been spending so much time in here lately, we should look into getting you a chair or something."

I grab ahold of the shelving unit next to me and stand up. "I'll try to remember to bring one in next time."

I reach behind her for the door handle. I stop short when she says, "You're allowed to fall in love again, you know?"

I simply nod my head and walk out the door. I know I'm allowed to fall in love again. I also know that I have to be a lot smarter about it the second time around, as it's not only my life my decision will affect.

I'm stressed to the point of breaking here and I don't know what to do. Actually, I know what I should do, but I don't think I have the strength to do it.

Chapter 26

Ethan

My dad, who's decided to eat lunch with the boys, has been giving me the "I know what's going on here" eyebrow raise ever since he came out of the supply closet. There's about a fifty-fifty chance he'll spill the beans to my mom, which means I have to talk to him before that can happen.

Moira is clearly freaking out, which is most likely why she secluded herself in the supply closet in the first place.

Based on how carefully my mom has been observing us, I'm one hundred percent certain she's also jumping to conclusions. She's like Miss Marple from those Agatha Christie novels. But not in a sweet, elderly kind of way. More like an edgy Miss Marple who would as soon tie you up and beat a confession out of you than do the leg work of solving the crime on her own.

Meanwhile, I feel like a criminal, but not the cool, mastermind-type. More like the kind who gets handcuffed and dragged off to jail to rot in a cell full of rats.

When lunch is over, the kids stand up and Wyatt tells my dad, "Thanks for eating with us, Isaac. You're totally cool, like Ethan."

"Thanks for letting me sit with you boys. That's the most fun I've had in years." He gets up to return to my booth, while saying, "Before you go, your mom said you're raising money for your baseball team. Tell me about that."

Wyatt turns around. "The entire league is selling raffle tickets, and the team that sells the most wins a trip to LA to see the Dodgers. Ethan's donating a signed LeBron James jersey to my team's raffle, so I think we may have a shot at it."

"Not the one from *Space Jam*?" My dad looks at me with a twinkle in his eye.

"That's the one," I tell him.

"No!" my dad nearly shouts. "I've always wanted that jersey, and you told me you'd never give it up." Before I can remind him that he's not a basketball fan, he turns to Wyatt and asks, "How much are tickets?"

"A dollar each."

Pulling out his wallet, my dad asks, "Do you have the tickets on you? I'd like to buy some."

Clearly excited at the opportunity to boost his team's chance of winning, Wyatt says, "They're at home, but I can go get them and come right back if you want."

"You know what, Wyatt?" I interject. "We're all going to be at the lodge tonight for supper. Why don't you bring them then?"

"Okay, I will," he says. "See you later." He takes off in an excited dash for the door with the twins following close behind.

My dad grins after them. "Oh, to have that kind of energy again."

I worry my dad is going to say something about me

and Moira in the closet, but instead, he smiles at my mom. "We should get going, Rose. Let our future bestseller get back to work."

Instead of returning to the closet together, Moira avoids me all afternoon. It isn't until she heads out for the evening that I manage to talk to her again. Following her out the front door, I ask, "Are you okay? You've been kind of quiet."

"Ethan." She stands still like she's been tagged in that childhood game, statue maker. "I don't think we should go off on our own tonight. I'm worried your parents are going to guess there's something going on between us."

"Who cares what they think?" I mean, obviously *I* care, because I don't need them pressuring me, but I don't want Moira to worry about them.

"I don't want them sharing their suspicions with Digger and Grandpa Jack."

"Sissy Sinclair's grandmother already planted that seed." I explain, "She went right up to the lodge after she saw us kissing by the side of the road."

"Really? They didn't say a word to me."

I nod my head. "Apparently, they didn't believe her and told her she needed to get her eyeglass prescription updated."

"So, you're saying your parents are the only ones we have to fool."

"Yup."

That seems to lighten her mood considerably. "Okay then, I'll just head home and change. I'll see you up there in a few." There's almost a spring in her step as she walks away, which causes a warm feeling to permeate through my body.

This is the Moira I love.

Wait. What? I don't love Moira. I can't. It took me five

months to tell Paige that I loved her, and clearly that didn't turn out. What I meant to say is, this is the Moira I ... like.

It's a beautiful, warm evening, so we decide to have dinner on the deck. There's a kids' table and a grown-ups table. Surprise, surprise, my dad winds up sitting with the kids again. Jack occupies the adults with his entertaining and hilarious stories of life in Alaska.

After we're all so stuffed we can barely move, the kids hit the open space for an impromptu baseball game. Digger and I decide to join them, and we quickly form into two small teams. The evening passes far too quickly, and when Harper announces it's time for showers and bed for her kids, groans are heard from all participants, me included.

"Bedtime?" my mom asks, glancing at her watch. "How on earth can it be so late?"

"Midnight sun," I tell her.

"That's just incredible," she says, truly sounding impressed by such a foreign concept.

Moira stands and brushes imaginary crumbs off her shorts. "Come on, boys. We should get going, too."

Once again, my dad pulls his wallet out. He tells Wyatt, "I almost forgot about the raffle tickets."

Wyatt runs back up to the deck and starts digging around in Moira's purse. He returns with a thick roll of red tickets, his eyes brimming with hope and dollar signs.

"I want whatever I can get for a thousand," my dad declares.

Wyatt's eyes grow wide. "A thousand dollars?"

"Is that not enough?" My dad has no concept that this

kind of money is more than most kids ever think of. At least for kids that don't grow up in Beverly Hills.

"Yeah, no, I mean, that's a ton!" Wyatt exclaims. "But I don't have a thousand tickets here. I'll need to get more, and the drawing is tomorrow night."

My dad hands over the cash. "Just get them to me before the drawing."

Wyatt glances up at me as though looking for permission to take that kind of money. I nod at him. "My dad's a huge LeBron fan."

Beaming, Wyatt takes the money and hands my dad the roll of tickets. "There were five hundred, but I already sold fifty-five, so I'm going to owe you …"—he taps his head while thinking—"four hundred and forty-five. I think."

My dad nods. "Give them to Ethan, and he'll bring them home to me."

Wyatt blinks rapidly like he can't believe this just happened. "Thanks, Mr. Caplan!" He turns to me and adds, "You've got the best dad ever!"

"Yes, I do," I tell him, ruffling his hair.

We watch as he runs off to catch up with his brothers and Moira who are halfway to the parking lot by now. My dad puts a hand on my shoulder. "What a nice family."

"They sure are," I tell him. And even though Moira and I didn't get a chance to go off on our own, I still feel a world closer to her through her kids.

My dad interrupts my thoughts. "Their life would be a lot better off with you in it."

My heart stops for a second, knowing he's seeing the truth of what's going on between me and Moira. "We've both had a lot of disappointment, Dad. Me with Paige and Moira with her husband." For some reason I don't mention her parents. I guess it's my way of offering her a bit of dignity.

"So, what? You don't try because you've been let down in the past. That's the definition of quitter, son."

"I just don't want to disappoint her anymore," I tell him.

"Then don't. You're a big boy, Ethan. Don't make the mistake of not going after something you want because you're afraid." He punches me playfully on the shoulder while reciting his life's motto. "Wusses don't win wars."

"Smart people don't engage in battles they can't win," I counter.

"Anybody can win a battle if they have the proper motivation and determination."

We could go on like this all night. I finally ask my dad, "What would Mom think?"

"Who cares what she thinks? She's made her choices in life, it's time you do the same." He starts to walk up the stairs to the deck before turning back around. "Your mom and I love you, Ethan, and we'll always support you. We might give you hell at times, but that's only so you'll think things through before making a decision."

"You mean like taking time off to write a book?"

He nods his head. "I think you made the right choice there and I know you'll make the right choice regarding Moira."

Chapter 27

Moira

"You sold him *how* many tickets?" I slam a plate of Grandma Adele's famous scrambled eggs down in front of Wyatt.

"A thousand dollars' worth!" Ash answers before his brother can. "Can you believe it?"

"You cannot take that kind of money from Ethan's dad." I shake my spatula at Wyatt for emphasis.

"What? Why?" my oldest full-on sputters. "Of course, I can. He's a huge LeBron fan and he wants to win that jersey."

Colton interjects, "Geez, Mom, selling tickets is the whole point of a raffle."

I inhale deeply before saying, "Isaac doesn't even live in Gamble."

"So?" Wyatt shakes his head. "You're not making any sense, Mom. He doesn't have to live here to win something here."

My head starts to throb. It doesn't take much to realize that Isaac thinks there's something going on between me and his son and he's trying to help my kid because of it. And that's just not good.

"Why would Isaac pay a thousand dollars to win something that already belongs to his son?"

"Ethan gave it to me, Mom. He doesn't own it anymore, that's why." Wyatt's eyes are on the verge of tearing up.

"Fine," I concede. "But under no circumstances are you allowed to take anything more from him, do you understand?"

All three boys nod their heads. "He's a nice guy, Mom," Ash says.

"I'm sure he is," I tell them.

"Then why do you sound so mad at him?" Colton asks.

"I'm not mad." *I'm confused and scared, but I'm not mad.*

Edna walks through the front door as the boys head out to play. She kicks off her loafers before sitting down at the table. "I feel like I haven't talked to you in a month of Sundays," she greets.

I eye her subdued outfit—jeans and a T-shirt, and ask, "Is there something on your mind?"

She grunts a bit before saying, "The doctor found a spot on Ed's lung. He's going in for a biopsy next week."

Dropping my dish cloth, I hurry to the table and sit down next to her. "Oh, Edna, I'm so sorry. You must be scared to death."

She tips her head back and forth. "We're nervous, for sure. But my momma always told me that if you live long enough, you'll get everything."

"My grandmother used to say that none of us get out of here alive, so make the most of what you have while you have it," I say.

"That Adele was always the smart one." She smiles at me and adds, "Anyway, in a bid to make the most of life, Ed and I have decided to go away this week so we're not just sitting around and waiting. We're going to go to Anchorage and stay in a hotel and eat out and pretend we don't have a care in this world."

"That sounds like a wonderful idea," I tell her. "And don't worry about the boys, I'll take them up to the lodge in the mornings."

"I'm here today. We're going to leave tomorrow."

"Please let me know if there's anything I can do," I tell her. "Anything at all."

She smiles gently. "Honey, if it's cancer, and the worst happens, it will be sad, but not a huge tragedy. When you've lived as long as Ed and me, you recognize that at some point you're living on borrowed time."

"Still …"

She stands up and walks out of the kitchen. When she comes back, she's holding my vision board. "Tell me about this."

My face flushes with heat. "It's just something I made to help me figure out what I want in my life."

She points to the picture of a bride and groom. "You want to get married again?"

I nod my head tentatively. "I want a partner. Everett and I were not the best in that department, and I'd really like to share my life with someone."

"Well then, honey. If that's what you want, you gotta put yourself out there. From my experience, men do not tend to knock on your front door and whisk you off to a life in paradise."

"I know, Edna, and I'm starting to make some changes. It's just really important that I don't mess up and pick the wrong guy."

"Because of the boys?" she guesses accurately.

"It's a big responsibility choosing the man who will be their father figure."

"He'll be more than that, honey. He'll *be* their father."

Panic floods through my nervous system like food poisoning, causing my stomach to turn over. "I guess that's true."

"I'm not trying to upset you. Lord knows you've had enough of that. I just want you to get out of this rut you've been in. It's time."

On my way to work, I mull over my conversation with Edna, and think about all that this summer has brought so far. Wyatt's baseball league announces which team wins the tickets to the Dodgers game tonight.

If Wyatt's team wins, I'm going to go to LA with my kids and Ethan with an open mind. Ever since Ethan and I decided to date, I've been reminding myself that it's just a temporary thing. But maybe, just maybe, it can be something more. I realize that's putting a lot of expectations toward a trip to California, but Edna is right. I do have to put myself out there. I have to be brave and take risks.

Feeling a bit lighter in my step, I walk into the diner, determined to let myself fall for Ethan. Even if he leaves and nothing more happens between us, isn't it like Tennyson said, "It's better to have loved and lost, than never to have loved at all?"

I hurry to make the coffee and fill the creamers and sugar containers. As soon as Ethan walks in, I ask, "Could you meet me in the supply closet for a minute?"

He looks nervous. "Sure."

As soon as we're both inside, I shut the door behind him and lean against it. "I don't think we're doing a very good job of enjoying our time together."

"Excuse me?"

"You heard me. Now get over here and kiss me like you mean it."

Ethan is more than happy to oblige, and we spend the next several minutes in a bid to make up for lost time. It isn't until Abigail bangs on the door that we come up for air. "I'm pretty sure that toilet paper can arrange itself. I could use a little help out here."

I smile up at Ethan. "She's onto us."

I put my hand on the doorknob while he says, "Meet me back in here after the breakfast rush?"

"Wild elephants couldn't keep me away."

Life is short. It's also complicated, confusing, and terrifying, but most importantly, it's short. Even if I only have Ethan for a few months, I'm going to make the most of that time. I'll need those memories to get me through the lonely times ahead until someone else comes into my life.

Chapter 28

Ethan

My dad is almost as excited about Wyatt's game as the kids are. "Hurry up," he calls out to my mom and me. "I don't want to be late!"

"They don't announce the winner until after the game," I remind him.

"Maybe so, but I don't want to miss the game." He jangles his keys in his pocket like he does when he gets impatient.

"Good God, Isaac." My mom comes out of their bedroom while putting the back on one of her earrings. "You don't even know this boy. Why are you so worked up?"

"It's been a long time since we had any kids sports to watch. I've missed it. Plus, I *have* gotten to know Moira's boys and I like them a lot."

Mom grabs her purse off the table and joins us at the

front door. "Fine, but if I get bitten by a mosquito, I'm taking the car and leaving."

My dad looks up at me. "Let's drive separately."

My mom hits him on the arm. "We'll drive together, but I'm sitting in the car if I get swarmed." Sometimes I think my mom makes a fuss to remind herself that she's alive. Like if she doesn't fight back, life will just run her over.

On the way to the park, my dad announces, "This is a nice town, son. I can see why you wanted to come up here to write."

"Don't encourage him, Isaac," my mom warns.

"Don't encourage me to write or to like the town I'm writing in?" I ask for clarification.

"I don't want you to stay here when your sabbatical is over."

Don't beat around the bush, Mom.

"I can hardly stay here. I still have to work to make a living."

"Unless your book is a huge success!" I don't recall my dad being this excited about me writing a book before. I mean, yes, he said I should give it a try if I wanted to, but I don't recall any outright enthusiasm.

"That would be great, Dad, but once I'm done writing it, I'll need to get an agent and then they'll need to find a publisher, and then come the rewrites ... even if everything goes well, it'll still be a long time before the book is on the shelves."

"Oy vey, Ethan, you sound like we don't have any connections," my mom says. "Between the three of us, we know everyone who is anyone in Hollywood. Getting you an agent will be the easiest thing in the world."

"If I tell them who I am," I answer. Her look of total

confusion has me explaining, "We all know what it looks like to have someone take you on because you know somebody. It's a surefire way to sit around waiting for the rest of your life. I want an agent who believes in my book as much as I do and will do whatever it takes to get it sold."

"He's right," my dad tells her. "Remember that little Stein girl we helped get signed over at Unified Artists?" Before my mom can answer, he says, "She had the best agent in town who was so busy repping his star roster, he never gave her the time of day."

Nodding her head, my mom says, "I suppose. I know when someone asked me to cast an actor as a favor, I made sure they got the smallest role possible." And there you have it. Favors are the backbone of the Hollywood machine, but most people resent being asked. It's amazing anything ever gets made.

"Which is why I'm going to go back home after my sabbatical." I don't mention that I plan on leaving entertainment law. No sense in upsetting that apple cart until I have to. Parking the car right next to Moira's truck, I tell them, "I'll go grab us some hot dogs and sodas and meet you in the stands."

My dad gets out right away, but my mom doesn't. "I don't mean to sound negative, honey. It's just that I want what's best for you, and I'm nervous watching you go all rogue like this."

"Go rogue?"

"You know, going against the plan that was in place. Your dad and I come from a long line of people who pick a career and stay in it for life. It's the best way to have financial security."

"I get that, Mom. But haven't you ever been tempted to try something different?"

She shrugs nonchalantly. "I'm more of a pragmatist than a dreamer. Plus, I enjoyed my career."

"I guess I'm a dreamer," I tell her.

"I know it." She pats my knee almost like she's resigned to having such an oddball son. "I'll meet you out there."

Sitting in the car for a minute longer, I think about what my mom said. She makes being a dreamer sound like a bad thing, which might be true if I hadn't already saved a lot of money. But as it stands, I've lived the life expected of me, I've socked away a fabulous nest egg, and now, all I want to do is to make my dreams come true. I just need to figure out where Moira fits into my vision.

As I get out of the car, I spot Grandpa Jack standing in the concession line. I wave while jogging in his direction. "Hey, Jack."

"Ethan, how are you, son? Did your parents come with you?"

"They've already gone to sit down."

"The boys are so excited they can hardly stand still," he says. "Moira just about blew a gasket when she found out your dad bought all those tickets though." He shakes his head and leans in like he's about to divulge national secrets. "I'm going to have to thank him. That grand-daughter of mine would have disowned me if I did that."

"Do you think Wyatt's team has a shot?" I ask while making a mental note to tiptoe around Moira on the subject of my dad.

"I'd say so." Jack takes his food and turns. "See you over there."

By the time I join him, the game is in full swing. The players seem particularly fired up, which I'm sure has a lot to do with possibly meeting the Dodgers.

Moira scoots over and pats the bench next to her. I

hand my parents their food before sitting down. "There's a palpable energy in the air tonight," I tell her.

"The whole town is on pins and needles, waiting to hear who won the raffle." She leans in and giggles, "The kids all want it to be their team and the parents all want it to be someone else's."

"What? Why?"

"People plan their summer vacations a long time in advance and switching things around at the last minute so their kid can go to a baseball game in LA messes up the schedule." She doesn't mention the money, but I'm guessing that's part of it, as well.

"How's Wyatt doing making money for your airfare?"

"He's got enough for one ticket."

"So if they win, you won't be going?"

Without looking at me, she says, "I've decided to use the money you're paying me to rent a table at the diner. This really is a once in a lifetime opportunity and I don't want the boys to miss out if they don't have to."

"Nice!" I take a sip of my soda. "And with you all staying at my place, there won't be any extra expenses."

She looks at me out of the corner of her eye as a small smile crosses her mouth, but she doesn't say anything else.

Even though the game isn't a close one, it's exciting anyway. Wyatt's team wins eleven to four. You'd think they'd just took the World Series with all the cheering going on.

"Come on out here, kids!" The coach gestures for all the other teams to join them on the field. When they're all in place, he turns on the microphone he's holding and booms, "These boys have been working hard to raise enough money to revamp our baseball field."

Claps and whistles fill the cool evening air.

"First off, I'd like to tell you how much they earned and

what we're going to do with the money, and then I'll tell you which team won. The grand total brought in by the league so far is nine thousand and fifty-nine dollars."

Cheers!

"Which is enough to build a bigger concession stand, add more bleacher seating, and update the field and equipment. So, in a sense, all the kids are winners! Before we announce the team who gets to go see the Dodgers, we're going to draw the winner of the signed LeBron James jersey." The coach reaches into a bucket and pulls out a ticket. "The winner is Isaac Caplan. Come on up, Isaac and get your prize."

My dad jumps up and rushes down the stands to get his prize, looking much younger to me than I've seen him in a long time.

The coach keeps the crowd in suspense for the next several minutes, while he reads out the winners of the other prizes, then he finally says, "Okay, the moment we've all been waiting for!"

Someone starts to stamp their feet on the bleachers starting a kind of drumroll. Several more chime in until the coach holds a hand up. "The winners of the Dodger tickets are …" If tension could fuel a rocket, we'd all be halfway to the moon by now. "Our major division team, The Sluggers!!!"

"That's Wyatt's team!" Jack shouts.

Colton and Ash are jumping around, trying to figure the best way to get to their brother's side. They ultimately decide to hop off the back of the bleachers and go that way.

Moira slips her hand into mine and leans into me. "I guess this means we're going to California."

I squeeze her fingers tightly. "I guess it does. I promise

to make this the best family vacation you and the boys have ever had." *I cannot wait to show them around.*

"As it's the only time they've left Alaska, I can assure you it's already the best."

I feel more alive than I ever have, sitting here holding Moira's hand while the town whirls around us in excitement. The fear I have over a repeat of what happened with Paige seemingly fades away.

Chapter 29

Moira

The next two weeks fly by. I'm so busy with work and trying to make sure the boys have everything they need for our trip, I barely have time to worry about the closeness developing between me and Ethan. Now that we're all going to California together, he's been coming by the house at night for supper. Tonight, we're eating out in the yard.

The boys want to know everything about what we're going to do once they get there. Most of Wyatt's teammates are going with the coach and his wife as chaperones. They're only staying for three days. But because we're all going and have a place to stay, we'll be there for ten. Neither the boys nor I have ever gone away for that long. The whole thought is seriously wreaking havoc with my equilibrium.

"I want to go to Disneyland!" Colton jumps up and knocks over the folding chair he's sitting on.

"Disneyland is a given," Ethan tells him. He seems to notice the startled look in my eyes, because he adds, "I work with a lot of people from Disney. I can get us free tickets."

"Really?" Ash looks as surprised as he would have if Ethan had just sprouted wings and started to fly around.

"I can get us free tickets to Universal, too," he tells them proudly.

"Mom, I'm never going to want to go home!" Wyatt interjects.

"Can we go to the beach?" Ash wants to know.

"Sure, the Santa Monica Pier is only twenty minutes from my house," Ethan tells him.

"What else are we going to do?" Colton demands.

"I think we've planned enough for the moment," I say. "Now go burn off some of your energy while Ethan and I finish eating." They're off and running.

Before I can say anything about Disneyland, Ethan says, "I'm sorry if I've overstepped my bounds. I guess I'm just feeding off the boys' excitement."

"I never could have given them a trip like this on my own," I tell him. "They'll be talking about it for the rest of their lives." I lean over and give him a quick kiss. "Thank you, Ethan."

He puffs up in his seat. "Thank you for letting me do this for them. For you."

"What are your parents going to think?" I ask. We've seen Isaac and Rose a few times since the baseball game and while they've been very pleasant, I can't help but think Rose would hate the idea of her only son living so far away from her permanently.

"My parents love you guys," he says. "Also, they're going to stay here while we're gone so they won't get in our way."

"I thought they were only staying for a couple of weeks."

He leans back in his chair and takes a pull from his beer. "Digger told them about the cabin up the mountain and they want to spend a few days there. They also want to go out on a fishing charter and spend some time in Anchorage."

"I don't know them well, but that doesn't seem like stuff your parents would be into."

"It's amazing how much people can change when they open themselves up to new experiences." He winks at me.

"Like going to California?" I tease.

"Exactly." He pushes his chair back from the table. "Being that we're leaving in the morning, I'd better get myself home so you can get a good night's sleep."

"Who's going to sleep? The boys are so wired, I'm pretty sure they'll be running around all night. Plus, I've got laundry to do. So. Much. Laundry."

Ethan pulls me onto my feet and leans down so his hot breath caresses my earlobe. "I promise to make this the best and most relaxing trip you've ever had. And you won't have to do any laundry."

"I will if the boys get as dirty in California as they do here," I tell him.

"My housekeeper will do it for them," he says.

"You have a housekeeper?" Shock does not begin to cover how that makes me feel. We really do live in two different worlds.

"I do, but only because I'm always so busy, I don't have the time to do the things that Sandra does."

"Like?" I prompt.

"She keeps the house clean, does the laundry, picks up the dry cleaning, shops for food, makes meals, and coordinates the gardeners and any other repairs that need doing."

"So, Sandra is essentially your wife …"

He laughs. "Yup. She's my sixty-year-old wife."

"How big is your house?" I can't for the life of me imagine that Ethan really needs all that help.

"It's a standard four bed, three-and-a-half bath."

"Why do you need such a big house for only one person?"

Shrugging, he tells me, "It's a good investment. Plus, I figure that someday I'll get married and have a family."

The thought of us being that family pops into my mind and hope swells in my chest before I can stop it. Needing to push that feeling aside, I say, "I really should get to work on the laundry." We walk side by side to his truck and, for the first time since Wyatt's team won, I start to worry about this trip. I decided to enjoy this time with Ethan, and I have been, but that was before getting a glimpse into his real life.

"I'll meet you at the lodge at seven," he says. "It's nice of Digger to fly us to the airport."

"He's one of the good ones," I tell him. *Kind of like you.*

After Ethan drives off, I throw myself into getting ready for our trip. I fly around like a whirling dervish, so I won't have time to think about how nervous I am. It works. By the time I'm done doing laundry, packing, and making sure the house is in order, I can barely keep my eyes open. If I fall asleep right away, I'll get seven hours, which is perfect for me.

The only trouble is that once I crawl into bed, my brain wakes up like I've just drunk a pot of coffee. I imagine all kinds of horrific scenarios that keep me from getting any decent rest. Before I know it, my alarm is ringing, and the big day is here.

Today I'll finally get to see what Ethan's real life is like. I'm terrified I'm going to discover what I already know—that there's no place I could possibly fit in it.

Chapter 30

Ethan

I'm bursting with excitement as I pack my overnight bag. I'm not going to bother taking my Alaska clothes back to LA with me, not when I have a closetful at home.

I can't wait to show Moira and the boys everything LA has to offer—Disneyland and the Dodgers are only a fraction of what I want them to see. I want Moira to discover there's a new future for them—a life where she doesn't have to work another day, unless she wants to. A life of opportunities and the best schools for the boys.

I know I'm talking big talk for someone who's only known her a short time, but I feel strongly that the older you get, the less time you need to know if someone is right for you. And just because I once thought Paige was right for me doesn't mean that there isn't another woman out there for me.

Even if my writing career doesn't work out and I have to go back to practicing law, I wouldn't mind so long as I have Moira and the boys to come home to every night. It would all be worth it because my career wouldn't be the only thing I had. It would just be the thing I did to make life easier for the people I love. I haven't told Moira that I love her yet, because I know how skittish she is, but I'm hoping to show her while we're in California.

Later, when I crawl into bed, I envision us married, raising the boys together. We'd be a real family and do all the things families do, from bowling on Friday nights to taking vacations all over the world. Moira and I would sit next to each other at all the kids' sporting and music events, we'd go to parent-teacher conferences, and help with homework at the kitchen table.

I imagine taking the four of them to movie premieres and teaching them how to surf.

With laser focus, I see Moira walking down the aisle to stand with me under the chuppah, where we'll pledge our lives to each other. She will be a spectacularly beautiful bride. Suddenly, I know beyond a shadow of a doubt that this is what I want. That's why this trip is so important. I need Moira to see how perfect we are together and what an amazing life we could build.

I'm going to show her the magical side of LA and when the time is right, I'll propose. Who knows, if things go as well as I hope, we might even be engaged by the time we come home.

I never do fall into a deep sleep, and finally decide to just get up. After taking a quick shower, I make some toast and drink the better part of a pot of coffee.

As soon as I get to the dock, I discover that Moira and the boys are already there. They all rush me and start talking at once.

Laughing, I say, "Okay, guys, one at a time so I can hear you."

"This is my first plane ride ever," Colton says.

"Is not," Ash tells him. "We go on Uncle Digger's plane all the time."

"I meant a *big* plane, you goof," Colton says. "Are they going to serve us food? Mom says they don't do big meals anymore, but I'm going to get hungry."

"They'll serve something small, but if you want, we can pick up some sandwiches before we get to the gate."

"Do you have a pool?" Ash asks. "Mom said she wasn't sure if you had one, but you probably do because most rich people in Hollywood have them."

"You're not supposed to say he's rich," Wyatt mutters, rolling his eyes.

"Why not? Doesn't he know?" Ash asks.

"It's considered rude," Moira interjects sternly. Looking at me, she says, "Sorry about that."

"No problem," I tell her with a wink. Then I answer Ash. "I do have a swimming pool and you boys are welcome to use it, but only when there's an adult there to watch you."

Ash and Colton high five each other and say, "YES!" in unison.

"Are any of your famous friends going to come over while we're there?" Ash wants to know. "Also, do you know The Rock? Because I really want to meet The Rock."

The boys continue to chatter away as we walk down to the dock to where Digger is waiting next to the float plane. "Okay, everybody, load up," Moira says, already looking exasperated.

The kids clamber into the cabin while I help Digger put the luggage in the cargo compartment. Moira sighs and shakes her head. "You sure you still want to do this?"

"I've never been so sure of anything in my entire life."

The flight to Anchorage is a breeze and the boys are a

whirlwind of excitement when they get to the airport. "Look at that plane!" Wyatt yells as soon as we get to our gate.

"You think we'll crash?" Colton asks.

"Hey, maybe they'll give us parachutes to wear," Ash suggests.

Moira leans into my arm. "Too bad I didn't bring any earplugs. I don't think they're going to stop talking until we get there."

"Are you excited about the flight?" I ask her. "You don't look the least bit nervous."

"It takes more than a jet to scare me." She eyes her sons to indicate that they've made her fearless.

After we board and the kids freak out over how cool the inside of a big plane is, they all start to look a little weary.

"Did they get any sleep last night?" I ask Moira. She and I are sitting in the two seats on the side of the plane and the boys are in the three middle seats.

"Not much," she says. "None of us did."

As a result, all five of us fall asleep soon after takeoff, making the flight feel like a fraction of how long it really is. None of us wake up until the captain announces our descent into LAX. The boys can barely contain their shouts of delight whenever the plane drops or turns. Wyatt loudly declares, "Landings are the most dangerous times on a plane. We could all die!" He sounds ecstatic.

A lady in front of him turns around and glares at him, so he adds, "But we're good. I mean, heck, I can't die before going to a Dodgers game, can I?" That doesn't seem to make her any happier.

When LA comes into view, I can tell everyone, including Moira, is shocked with the way the city seems to stretch out forever. As I take it in with fresh eyes, I realize how intimidating this would feel to someone who has never left the state of Alaska. A city this big might feel like it would swallow you up.

Moira seems awfully quiet. I'm hoping it's just because she's tired from all the work it took to get ready for today, but if I had to guess, I'd say there's something else on her mind. When the plane finally reaches the gate, she sternly announces, "Boys, you need to listen to me. This airport is bigger than the entire town of Gamble. That means no wandering off—not even for a second. You stay with Ethan and me the entire time. Is that clear?"

They don't appear to be listening too intently, so I offer, "Let's divide and conquer. I'll watch the twins and you watch Wyatt, but we'll all stick together."

"Sounds good." Yet, she still looks worried.

We manage to get our bags and exit the airport without losing anyone, although there were a few dicey moments when all three boys jumped up on the shoeshine chairs and again when they caught sight of Cinnabon.

When we reach the sidewalk where the taxis are waiting, the mid-afternoon California sun hits us. Palm trees sway in the light breeze, but they don't do much to suppress the heat. Even though I love Alaska, I'm happy to be home again. There's an energy about LA that makes me feel like I can take on the world.

"Look! A limousine!" Wyatt shouts, pointing to a sleek black limo sitting in the cab line-up.

"Cool! I've never seen a limo before outside of the movies!" Colton says.

"Do you guys want to take that back to my place?" I ask.

"Seriously?!" Wyatt's eyes are practically popping out of his head.

"Yeah, of course," I tell him, as I push the luggage cart toward it.

"You can just get in a limo? Just like that?" Ash asks.

I point to the driver who's standing next to the car. "You see his sign?"

Colton shouts, "It says Ethan Caplan! That's you! Is that *your* limo?"

"It's the limo my assistant called and arranged to meet us," I tell him. "I figured we needed some extra room."

"Ethan …" Moira says, looking worried.

I shoot her a wink and a smile. "I promised this was going to be the best vacation you've ever had."

Once we pile in, the boys busy themselves checking out the mini-bar, the TV (which Moira tells them not to touch), and the sound system. Wyatt searches around on the satellite radio until he finds a song by Drake, then the three of them groove along as we cruise down the 405 to my house.

"You okay? You seem a little tense." Total understatement. Moira seems so brittle, I'm afraid she might shatter right in front of me.

She nods her head once. "I just don't want them to break anything."

"Trust me. We are not the rowdiest people to get in the back of this car."

"You sure?"

"Two words: bachelor party."

Wrinkling up her nose, Moira says, "Now I'm going to have to bleach them when we get to your place."

I chuckle. "How about we let them jump in the pool? Let the chlorine disinfect them, then they can shower before supper."

"They can burn off some energy, too." She turns her gaze out the window and starts chewing on her bottom lip.

"A penny for your thoughts," I tell her.

She turns to me. "I was just thinking how LA couldn't be more different than Gamble. It's like we're not even on the same planet."

Nodding, I say, "It's a lot to take in, isn't it?"

"Yeah." Moira shifts her gaze back to the window.

Then an idea hits me. They're not used to having a housekeeper, so I think it'll be better if I ease them into the SoCal lifestyle. I pull out my phone and text Sandra.

Me: *I'll be arriving in about twenty minutes with my guests. Why don't you take the rest of the day off?*

Sandra: *You don't have to ask me twice. Supper is in the fridge. I'll put heating instructions on it and then see you in the morning.*

When the driver pulls off the freeway and makes his way along street after street of mansions, the energy inside the car crackles. "Holy cow!" Wyatt whistles. "How rich *are* you?"

By the time the car pulls through the gates, the boys are clamoring to get out and start exploring. I take Moira's hand and give it a gentle squeeze. "Come on. Let's get your vacation started."

Chapter 31

Moira

Holy hell, Ethan's house looks like something straight out of a nighttime soap opera. Its modern design hosts a ton of windows that start at the ground floor and go straight up to the second-floor roof line. There are palm trees, fruit trees, and tropical-looking plants all over the place. It feels more like we've been dropped off at a luxury hotel than someone's private residence. Embarrassment over my own living situation hits me. Ethan must think I live in squalor.

"Come on, crew," Ethan shouts. "Grab your bags and I'll show you where your bedrooms are."

My boys turn into a pack of wild wolves running, jumping, and shouting in excitement. Meanwhile, I feel totally paralyzed. Ethan gets out of the limo before me and reaches in to take my hand. "Let's go, milady. I want to show you my home."

My sixty-year-old, run-down farmhouse is a home. This is a spectacular display of wealth, the disparity of which I'm not sure we can overcome. Ethan practically pulls me out of the car.

After he unlocks the front door, we wait while he walks in and goes straight to a keypad on the wall. There he punches in a series of numbers before we hear a loud beep. Of course, he has a security system with a place like this.

The living room is enormous with a vaulted ceiling as high as the two-story roof line. It's decorated with modern black and gray furniture, sleek chrome tables full of actual sculptures and giant coffee table books that probably take two people to lift. Believe me when I say that his supremely tasteful belongings make my collection of ceramic cows look ridiculous. The only pops of color come from the artwork hanging on the walls, which is probably worth more than my house and diner combined.

Ethan leads the way to an architectural steel staircase and starts to climb. "Come on, boys, your rooms are up here with mine. Your mom gets the guest suite downstairs that overlooks the rose garden."

"Do we each have our own rooms?" Wyatt wants to know.

"I was thinking the twins could share and you could have your own room. How does that sound?"

"I'd sleep outside in a doghouse if I had to. I mean, I bet your dog lives better than most people," Ash says.

"I don't have a dog," Ethan tells them. "I'd really like to get one someday, but I'm not home enough to really enjoy one."

"You have all of this and you're not home very much?" Colton shakes his head. "If I lived here, I'd never leave!"

"Boys," I warn them. "Use your manners."

I follow Ethan and the kids up the stairs, all the while reminding myself to keep breathing. The first door we come upon is where Wyatt will be staying. It's decorated in all navy and beige, with dark wood furniture. There's a giant king-size bed in the center of it. "This is *my* room?" Wyatt stands still for a full minute like he's lost his ability to speak.

Ethan says, "Ash, Colton, you're across the hallway." He leads them out the door to a room even bigger than Wyatt's. It's decorated in greens and grays and has two queen-size beds instead of one larger bed.

The twins immediately throw themselves on top of the duvets and start squirming like they have ants in their pants. Ethan leads me back out into the hall and calls to the kids, "Get your swimming suits on while I show your mom her room."

He takes my hand, and I follow him silently back down the stairs. I should compliment him on his beautiful home, but my tongue feels like it's tripled in size and won't let me make a sound.

Ethan leads me through an enormous kitchen, so bright and sparkling white, I'm tempted to put my sunglasses on. The marble island is bigger than my whole bedroom in Gamble. We walk down a small hallway that ends at a closed door. "This is your room." He opens the door on the most stunning image I have ever seen.

The floor is covered in a Tiffany blue carpet with an intricate white border, the bed has a sheer canopy the likes of which I dreamed about when I was a little girl, and the bedding is a pristine white covered with an array of light blue and white throw pillows. I walk across the room to the window like I'm being pulled by an invisible wire. Tears come to my eyes. "This is perfect, Ethan. Just perfect."

With a smile on his face, he says, "Put your swimming suit on and I'll meet you out back by the pool."

I have no idea how I'm going to find the pool, but I'm sure it's here somewhere. I put my suitcase on the bed and tentatively begin to unpack. There's no way I brought the right clothes with me. I mean, I'll probably look okay for the baseball game and Disneyland, but the rest of it? I'll look like Elly May Clampett (from the old *Beverly Hillbillies* show) in a room full of fashion models.

I hurry to put on the red one-piece I've worn for five years. It's faded and snagged and honestly looks so drab I'm tempted to say I forgot it. But the idea of playing with my kids forces me to get over myself and put it on. Throwing on an old T-shirt of Everett's, I open the bedroom door and pad through the house on bare feet. The tiles are deliciously cool, and the carpet is so soft it feels like I'm walking on clouds.

I hear everyone before I see them as I make my way through the house. Wyatt calls out, "Cannonball!" His war cry is followed by the inevitable splash. Two more follow which means all of my boys are living their best life.

There's a big, comfy family room on the other side of the kitchen. The whole back wall appears to be missing, and it leads out to the patio with an outdoor kitchen and seating area full-on with two couches and a giant square coffee table. *Who lives like this?*

I hear more splashing, which causes me to look up and beyond the immediate grandeur. A few short steps away is the most stunning swimming pool I've ever seen. The blue is dark, but not so dark as to obscure the terracotta brown and white tiles that adorn the edges. There are mini potted palms every eight feet or so surrounding it, which makes it feel like a secret garden. Sleek brown loungers surround the perimeter of the water, and beyond those are several modern statues framed by more tropical plants.

"Mom, look at me!" Ash calls from the diving board at the opposite side. He jumps up high and my mind's eye slows him down like a slow-motion scene in a movie. My son looks transcendently happy. I turn to look at Wyatt and Colton. They're all clearly ecstatic to be here.

Finally, I spot Ethan, who's taking off his robe. He calls out, "Let's go, Moira, last one in is a rotten papaya." Of course, he wouldn't say anything as common as a rotten egg. I pull my T-shirt off over my head and edge closer to the water.

I feel like I've taken too much nighttime cold medicine, but instead of falling into a fever dream, I've slipped into a fantasy, the likes of which I'm not sure I can absorb. I decide to let myself enjoy our time here. Ethan wants to give us the best vacation of our lives, and I need to let that happen. For my own sake, as much as for my children. I need to take their example and give into the pleasure of the moment, instead of constantly worrying about the future. We're in this incredible place with an incredible man. Even if it's not forever, we're here now, and maybe that's enough.

Chapter 32

Ethan

The muscles in my face are sore from smiling so much. Moira, the kids, and I spend what's left of the afternoon poolside. Moira seems to have shed the worries she had when we first arrived. We lay side-by-side on loungers while the boys play with a beach ball in the water when she lets out a happy sigh. "Remember when we talked about what a perfect day would be like?"

I grin over at her. "Is this it?"

She nods and smiles back.

"I'm so glad you're here."

"Me too. I can't remember ever being this relaxed."

At that exact moment, Colton climbs out of the pool and pads over to Moira. "I'm starving."

"And that concludes relaxing time for today," she says lightly, starting to get up.

"You stay right there. I'll run in and go see what's for supper," I tell her.

She lays back down with a grin. "You don't have to tell me twice."

I pop the lasagna that Sandra made in the oven, then have a quick shower and get changed. By the time I'm back in the kitchen, Moira and the boys are making their way inside to do the same. While they're gone, I take the big salad bowl out of the fridge and set out an assortment of salad dressings.

By the time my guests appear—the boys are in their pajamas—I have our dinner waiting on the patio table outside. Moira looks lovely in a black tank top and a long, patterned skirt. Her presence feels right here; it's almost like she came with the house and has always been here.

I uncork a bottle of Pinot Grigio and pour two glasses. Then I gesture to the outdoor fridge. "Boys, help your-selves to juice or soda."

Once we're all seated and the food has been dished up, the only sound is from forks and knives scraping against plates. Once we're finished, Ash, who always wants to know what's coming next, asks, "What's next?"

"I was thinking you could watch a movie in the screening room," I tell him.

"The *what*?" Colton demands.

"I can't wait to go home and tell Travis all about this trip. I want to rub his ugly face in it." Wyatt is wringing his hands together fiendishly like a villain from an old-time movie.

"Wyatt," Moira warns. All a mother has to do is say her kid's name in a certain tone to shut them right up. Moms are all-powerful that way. She turns to me and says, "That sounds perfect. It's been a long day and the boys need to settle down."

"What movie?" Colton asks.

"How about *Black Panther Two*?"

Wyatt narrows his eyes. "That one's not out yet."

"I know, but I have an advanced copy," I say with a shrug.

This news sets off cheers like I've just announced Ironman was coming back from the grave. I glance at Moira, who's shaking her head and laughing. "*Black Panther Two* it is."

The boys go nuts when they see the screening room. They hop over the lounging chairs and try out several before choosing their seats. I hurry to put the movie on for them so Moira and I can have some time alone.

Back in the kitchen, I load the dishwasher while she puts the leftovers in some glass containers. "What do you think of California so far?"

"It's amazing. Your home is …" She pauses as though looking for the right words in the middle of a word search puzzle. She finally settles on, "It's like something out of a magazine. To be honest, I'm a little nervous we're going to break some priceless artifact and I'll wind up having to turn the deed of the restaurant over to you to pay for it." She grimaces like she's only joking, but I can tell she's serious.

I dry my hands off on the nearest towel before pulling her into my arms. "There is nothing in this house I can't happily live without." Except for her and the boys. I can no longer imagine a future without them.

"Maybe so, but you bought all of this because you like it."

I give her a lingering kiss before murmuring, "Please stop worrying. You work so hard; you deserve a wonderful vacation. Let me give you that."

She lets her shoulders drop a little, then wraps her arms around my neck. "You're going to spoil me rotten, which is a problem, because I'm never going to want to go back to Gamble."

Catching her mouth in another kiss, I make this one count. I settle my hands on her hips and pull her closer to show her how very much she means to me. After several minutes, I force myself to stop. Leaning my forehead against hers, I say, "Want to go out back and gaze at the stars?"

"I would love nothing more."

Taking her hand, I lead her back out to the pool. Flipping on the switch starts the fountain that runs the entire length of the water. Turning on another starts the light show—blues and greens that slowly move into every other color of the rainbow.

"Holy cow!" Moira declares. "It looks like the water is on fire." I love the look of awe etched across her face.

"It's hooked up to the sound system and moves in tempo with the music," I tell her.

"The boys are going to flip over that."

Settling down on a chaise built for two, I pull her close. "I could sit out here every night with you."

She leans her head onto my shoulder and snuggles into me. I feel a sense of completion I never knew existed.

After the movie, the boys come out to find us. As expected, they spend several minutes running around the pool, investigating the fountain. I overhear Wyatt ask Colton, "What *doesn't* he have?"

Ash runs over to me and asks, "Do you want to read to us? We get a chapter every night before bed."

My heart feels full as I stand up so I can ruffle his hair. "Absolutely, buddy. What book are you reading?"

"*Captain Underpants and the Perilous Plot of Professor Poopypants,*" he announces.

Moira stretches like a cat before standing up. "Not

exactly the height of sophisticated literature, but the boys love it."

"It's exactly the kind of book I would have read at their age." After a beat, I add, "Actually, I have a feeling I'm going to enjoy it even now."

The five of us head into the house and go upstairs. We snuggle up on Wyatt's bed with Moira and me acting as the bookends to the three kids piled in the middle. As I start to read, I do funny voices for the characters, making sure the gross parts sound extra disgusting.

When we finish the chapter, Colton begs for one more. I'm having so much fun, I'm tempted to give in, but I don't. The last thing Moira needs is to feel like I've aligned myself against her.

"That's it, Mr. Nutter Butter," she says, scooting off the bed. "It's been a long day, and we need a gigantic sleep for Disneyland tomorrow."

"That's right," I add. "We want to be the first in every line." I won't tell them about the front-of-the-line passes until we get there.

Ash and Colton sprint across the hall. Moira follows them, while I get up and offer Wyatt a nighttime fist bump. He snuggles under his covers. "I wouldn't hate it if you gave me a hug."

Emotion fills my eyes, and I'm glad the room is dark. Clearing my throat, I tell him, "Sure thing." Then I lean down and wrap my arms around his skinny body. He hugs me back tightly like he really needs it.

When I turn to leave the room, I see Moira standing in the doorway. She looks every bit as emotional as I feel. She calls out, "Good night, Wyatt. I love you."

"Love you, too, Mom."

She takes my hand in hers and squeezes. "Thank you.

This has been the best day of the boys' life and it's all because of you."

I smile through the darkness. "I could say the same thing, except it's because of the four of you."

I lead her back down the stairs, and we settle ourselves on a sofa in the living room. "Would you like some more wine?"

Shaking her head, she says, "I'm good. I'm going to have to hit the hay soon. The boys will be up at the crack of dawn."

"Good point." I reach out and tuck a stray hair behind her ear.

"You're an amazing man, do you know that?"

"Aww, shucks," I answer with a wink.

"No, seriously. For Wyatt to ask for a hug is … huge." She sighs, then adds, "Terrifyingly huge."

"Why terrifying?" I ask, gazing into her eyes.

"Because you live here, and we live in a tiny town in Alaska."

"That's just geography."

She scoffs. "You sound like a lawyer."

"All I'm saying is that nothing is impossible." Leaning down, I narrow the distance between our mouths until our lips are almost brushing against each other. "You just have to believe."

She stares into my eyes as though searching for answers. She keeps staring as she stands up, only to sit back down. This time straddling my lap. Passion, longing, and need build between us as we explore each other's bodies over our clothes. I want this woman more than I've wanted anything in my life. The attraction isn't just physical either. It's everything, the whole package.

We could easily get carried away, but I don't want my first time with Moira to be when she's emotionally spent.

When she comes to my bed, it will be because she wants to be there and not because I've taken advantage of her exhaustion. I drop my head to break contact. "We should get some rest."

Her face falls. "Oh…yeah … I mean, yes. We definitely should."

She seems embarrassed as she jumps off my lap like she wishes she'd never been there.

"Moira, wait," I say, getting up and catching her hand before she can leave. She turns to me, and I see hurt in her eyes.

Cupping her cheek with one hand, I say, "I want our first time to be something worthy of you."

Nodding slightly, she says, "Okay."

"I mean it. If and when we do this, I'm going to take my time so I can show you what you mean to me. But tonight isn't that night. Not when you're so tired."

"You're right," she says, but she's not selling it. "We should get some sleep."

Lifting onto her tiptoes, she gives me a chaste kiss on the lips. "Good night, Ethan."

"Sweet dreams," I call after her, hoping that she knows I meant what I said.

I climb the stairs, content at having the people I've recently come to love under my roof. I stop by the boys' rooms and glance in to make sure they're resting well. When I crawl into my own bed, I let my mind reflect on the day. I have to force myself not to get too excited about this trip, but the truth is, it's too late for that. I'm already over the moon.

This is my big chance to show Moira how perfectly she and the boys fit here. Once they settle in, I'm sure she'll see it, too, and then it's just a matter of time before we're all together, permanently.

Chapter 33

Moira

I don't fit in here in the slightest. I always knew Ethan's life had to be spectacular, but I've never let myself really think about him *here*. I think about him in Gamble, wearing shorts and sandals and typing away at table six day after day. I think of him kissing me senseless in my living room after the boys go to sleep. But I've never really tried to picture him in his home, in his town.

It's way different than I could have ever imagined—probably because I couldn't imagine anything this … this … rich. I was on the verge of letting Ethan take me to bed tonight, but when he stopped things, I realized maybe he knows I don't belong here either. I know he said he wants our first time to be special, but he's such a gentleman, maybe he doesn't intend for there to be a first time. Not if he doesn't see a future for us.

Walking across the room, I open the window and stand there while the cool breeze blows past me. It's novel to see the sky so dark this time of year. As I stare out at the stars, the truth of my feelings slams into me like a Mack truck. I'm in love. And being in love for a single mom is beyond complicated.

I have so much more than just myself to think of. I have the boys. And while they seem to care about Ethan a great deal, they also care about Digger and Grandpa Jack. We all have a full life in Alaska that I can't imagine walking away from.

Feeling the weight of the day, I finally crawl into bed. For a brief second, I worry I'm going to toss and turn all night, but the minute I close my eyes, I go unconscious. I wake up after what feels like seconds, but I know it has been hours as it's light outside.

Stretching, my body snaps and pops into place. *Why is the house so quiet?* I look at the clock and see that it's nearly eight. Surely the boys are up and getting ready for Disneyland.

Throwing my legs over the side of the bed, I stand up and reach for the robe laying on the chair. I put it on and tie the sash while walking out the door. The smell of coffee is in the air, so Ethan must be up. I look out back, but he's not there, so I go upstairs and check on the kids. Wyatt isn't in his room, and the twins aren't in theirs. *Where is everyone?*

I look down the hall to the double doors that I'm guessing lead to the master bedroom. Should I look in there? I don't want to snoop, but I do want to know where everyone is.

The door is ajar, so I peek in. I feel like I just won the Showcase Showdown on the *Price is Right*. There, in the middle of the room, is the most enormous bed I've ever seen. It's bigger than a king and I never knew such a thing existed. Ethan and all three of my boys are sprawled out, sound asleep. I must be ovulating because I swear, I feel an egg drop.

Clearing my throat, I loudly announce, "Good morning, sleepy heads!"

There are moans and groans and shifting. Eventually Ethan replies, "Good morning. How did you sleep?"

"Like the dead. The night felt like it passed in the blink of an eye."

Wyatt moans loudly. "So tired …"

"I guess we can skip Disneyland …" I tell him, knowing exactly how he'll react.

He propels out of bed like he was lying on the business end of a catapult. Scratching his belly like a little man, he stretches. "Nope, I'm up. Let's go." He starts to pull his brothers out of bed by their feet.

"How did you guys all wind up here?" I ask.

"Possum fight," Ethan says.

"Excuse me?"

"There were a couple of possums fighting in the tree outside of the twins' room."

Colton adds, "It sounded like demons going at it."

"Or Thanos in a deathmatch with the Incredible Hulk!" Ash adds.

"It was seriously scary, Mom," Wyatt says.

"Why didn't you come get me?" I ask, feeling both grateful and hurt that I wasn't needed.

"None of us wanted to go down the stairs in the dark," Colton confesses.

Sliding to the edge of the bed, Ethan adds, "I was able to assure them that no one had crawled out of the bowels of hell."

I stare at him in his T-shirt and shorts, with his rumpled hair, and want nothing more than to crawl into bed with him, but then I force myself back to reality. "Who made the coffee?"

"Sandra sets it up before she leaves and puts it on a timer for me, so I wake up to fresh coffee."

"Who's Sandra again?" Wyatt asks grumpily.

"My housekeeper."

"You have a maid?" Ash demands. "Like a real, live servant?"

Ethan shakes his head and laughs. "You aren't long for this world if you call Sandra a servant to her face." He explains, "Sandra is the woman who makes my life run as smoothly as it does. I'd never be able to keep this place up without her."

"Does she come every day?" Colton wants to know.

"Monday through Friday," Ethan says. "She has the weekends off."

Wyatt looks at me with wonder. "Could you imagine having someone like that at home? That would be awesome!"

"We do have someone like that at home," I tell him. "Her name is Edna." Speaking of Edna, I make a mental note to text her and find out if they know the results of Ed's biopsy.

"Mrs. Turner makes *us* do the cleaning up," Ash says. "She doesn't do it for us."

"That's because she doesn't want you to grow up to be useless men who can't do the littlest things for themselves." Four sets of eyes turn to me in looks of pure shock. "That didn't come out right," I start to say, but Wyatt interrupts.

"God, Mom, that's mean. It sounds like you're calling Ethan useless."

"That's *not* what I'm saying …"

Colton interrupts this time. "I bet Ethan pays her way more than you pay Mrs. Turner." He's right about that.

The only thing Edna ever gets is free meals at the diner, and even then, she barely comes in to collect.

I turn to Ethan, who's still staring at me with a questioning look. "I just don't want the boys to expect other people to do things for them that they're perfectly capable of doing themselves."

His silence has me digging myself into a deeper pit. "I want them to be productive members of society ..." *How do I get this foot out of my mouth?*

Ethan comes to my rescue and tells the boys, "I think what your mother is saying is that you have to know how to take care of yourselves."

"Yes! That's exactly what I'm saying."

Ethan stands up. "Come on, kids. You can be my sous chefs and we'll show your mom how capable we really are. Let's go make her a breakfast she won't soon forget."

I'm so relieved this conversation is over that I step aside and let them walk by me.

After they're gone, I continue to stare at Ethan's giant bed. What would it have been like had he carried me up here last night? I guess I should be glad he didn't, because the boys wound up here, but even so, the thought of the two of us in bed has my heart racing overtime.

I'm going to have to work harder than ever to separate my emotions. While I want the kids to have a great time, I cannot risk a spectacular heartbreak for myself.

The problem is, it's already too late for that.

Chapter 34

Ethan

The next two days are every bit as magical as you'd expect them to be. We spent a full twelve hours at Disneyland the first day, not leaving until after the fireworks, then got up the next morning and did the same thing at California Adventure Park, where the boys couldn't get enough of the *Cars* ride (and I'm including myself as one of the boys). Moira surprised me by wanting to do all the rides—including the biggest drops and roller coasters. Seeing her laugh so much and just let loose has been incredible. I feel like she's letting go of her worries and allowing herself to just have fun. I can only hope she'll decide she wants a life more like this—with fewer worries and more joy.

In the evenings, we all swam in the pool, and Moira and I sat in the hot tub, letting the jets work on our sore legs while reliving the best parts of the day. I can honestly say I've never been this happy in my life. From the time I wake up until I go to sleep, I feel like I'm in exactly the right place, doing exactly the right thing, with exactly the right people.

The only downside of staying so busy is that Moira and I don't linger after the kids go to bed. There's no kissing and hugging—no canoodling at all. We're both so tired, sleep is the only thing that calls to us. I'm hoping to change that today.

Today's plan is to lounge around the house for the better part of the morning, then hit the beach in the afternoon. Crashing surf is the perfect antidote for the overstimulation of theme parks. But first, Prisha is coming over for brunch so she can see everyone again. She and I stayed at Moira's house last year, so she knows the family.

I'm a little nervous because I'm sure Prish and Harper have been talking nonstop about what's going on between me and Moira. While we've done our best to keep our feelings for each other private, Harper has made it clear she's not buying the "casual" that I'm selling. Therefore, I'm sure Prisha is going to have a lot of questions. And since she lacks a filter, some of those questions could be awkward.

Moira and the boys are playing cards outside on the patio table, and I'm in my office catching up on my writing, when the doorbell rings. I call out to Sandra that I'll get it, and when I pull the door open, Prisha is standing on the front step with a big grin.

"Hello, you," I say as we give each other a quick hug.

"So? What's this I hear about you turning into a family man overnight?" she asks before even stepping inside.

Unable to stop myself, I smile down at her. "I don't know what you're talking about."

She gives me a quizzical look. "Is this why you decided to take your sabbatical in Gamble? Because you were hoping something would happen with Moira?"

"I went to Gamble to write a book," I tell her. "A book which, you may be interested in knowing, is so good it's practically writing itself."

She rolls her eyes. "Yeah, yeah, you're Stephen King himself."

"I think you mean John Grisham."

Tipping her head to the side in a very "I'm over this conversation" kind of way, she says, "I don't care if you're the Easter Bunny. All I'm saying is that I think you had bigger plans than just writing when you flew off to Alaska." Her whole body seems to shiver at the very thought of the Last Frontier. "Now, where is everyone?" she demands.

"Follow me," I tell her, leading the way to the backyard. She stops at the kitchen island, where Sandra has set out an amazing spread of fruits and pastries, along with a chafing dish over a burner. Prisha plucks a strawberry off the platter and pops it in her mouth. Pointing to the covered dish, she says, "Sandra's famous waffles?"

"Of course."

"I'm going to woo that woman away from you if it's the last thing I do," she threatens. She's been saying that for years, but the truth is that Prisha's wife would never let that happen. Sheila fancies herself the only domestic diva needed in their household.

When we get outside, Moira and the boys are all laughing as they watch Ash do a little happy dance in his chair. He looks up at me. "I won the whole pot, Ethan!"

"I didn't realize you were playing for money," I tell him.

"Pennies, so I probably only made enough to buy a pack of gum, but I still won!"

Moira stands up and walks in our direction. "Prisha, it's wonderful to see you again." She opens her arms.

Taking the offered hug, my friend says, "You, too,

Moira. You look great. California is clearly agreeing with you." Then she turns her attention to the boys. After some fist bumps and hair ruffling, Prisha asks, "Have you guys had a chance to try Sandra's waffles yet?"

When they shake their heads, she tells them, "Well, they're ready and they're ah-maz-ing."

"Can we eat now?" Colton asks while he starts trotting toward the house.

"Of course. Let's go into the kitchen and plate up, then come back outside to eat."

Wyatt walks next to Prisha. "Ethan's place is the best. He's got a pool, a screening room, and we always get to eat outside. I'm *never* going to want to go home."

I catch the expression on Moira's face, which seems to be a cross between happiness and despair. When she notices me staring, she offers me a small smile and a wink. If I had to guess, I'd say she's worried about how the boys will feel when they go back to their regular lives. Which honestly is something I hope will only be until my sabbatical ends. Then we'll all come back to my house together.

Sandra is putting out a plate of bacon as we walk into the kitchen. I smile and say, "Thank you. It must be more fun to feed a group than just me."

"The only reason I came to work for you is that you promised I'd eventually have a family to take care of." She eyes the kids meaningfully. "Nice work."

"Do you come to work even when Ethan is in Alaska?" Colton wants to know.

Sandra nods her head. "To tell you the truth, it's not much different than when he's here."

"But what do you *do*?" Ash asks.

"Ash," Moira says in an embarrassed tone.

Sandra waves her hand as though not at all offended. "I clean, I let the gardeners and pool boy in, I change lightbulbs, I open and close windows, I make lists, I watch a lot of movies ..." She shrugs her eyebrows at me when she says that.

I smile at her. "She does crazy things like dusting the inside of cabinets and cleaning light fixtures. I came home early one day to find Sandra lying on the kitchen floor with a can of white paint. She was touching up the baseboards."

The boys stare at my housekeeper like they're looking at a real-life dragon. "We could use you in Alaska," Wyatt tells her.

"No kidding," Moira agrees.

The kids make short work of brunch, finishing every-thing on their plates while the adults go a little slower. After they run off to play, Prisha says, "So, Moira? You and Ethan?"

Moira blushes, then glances down at the table. "He's a great friend."

"That he is." Yeah, Prisha's not buying the whole friendship thing. "You must be pretty amazing yourself, because I never, in a thousand years, would have thought this guy would turn into a family man."

"He's going to be a great father someday."

Reaching out, I put my hand on Moira's. "Your kids are certainly selling me on the experience."

Prisha releases a bark of laughter. "I can hardly believe what I'm seeing."

"What?" Moira and I ask at the same time.

"Far be it from me to point out the obvious, but ..."

Oh God, I can't let Prisha point out the obvious. Historically, that has never gone well. Moira's eyes grow wide in anticipation of my friend's next words, so I hurry to interrupt. "It's obvious that I love having you here." I can't have Prisha declaring my feelings before I do. I still need some time to convince Moira that she belongs with me.

"Um, yeah," Prisha says. "He *loves* having you here."

Moira smiles politely. "We love being here."

The boys burst through the sliding doors at that exact moment in the direction of the pool. At the same time, Moira and I call out, "Walk!"

They slow down to the world's fastest speed walk, then torpedo themselves into the pool. Prisha bursts out laughing. "*Walk!*" she says, imitating me. "Oh my God, are you going to start with the dad jokes now?"

"Very funny," I tell her. "I just didn't want anyone to get hurt."

I glance over at Moira, but my face falls when I see her. She doesn't even look remotely amused. Pushing her chair back from the table, she says, "Excuse me." As she hurries toward the house, Prisha and I are left wondering what's going on in that beautiful head of hers.

Chapter 35

Moira

Somehow in a very short time, Ethan has started acting like a dad to the boys. As much as it fills my heart, it also terrifies me. I came to California hoping we might discover we had a future together, but now that I see his life here, I can't see myself in it. It's just too much, and my brain has become a war zone of conflicting emotions.

I have never wanted someone as badly as I want Ethan, and it's scaring the hell out of me. The pain of being left by the people I've counted on most keeps cropping up to remind me what's at stake. It's not just my heart, it's my boys too, and it's my job to protect them.

Everything here is a dream—the lavish lifestyle, the swaying palm trees, the never having to lift a finger. As much as I've been letting myself enjoy my time here, I know deep down that it can't be forever. And I'm scared to death by how much it's going to hurt when it's over.

Realizing I can't hide in my bedroom for the rest of the

day, I return to the patio. Ethan and Prisha are still at the table. "Hey," I call out. "Sorry about that, I had to use the restroom."

"You okay?" Prisha asks, not believing my excuse for a second.

"Of course! How could I not be good?" I sound positively maniacal.

"So, Moira, tell me, what's your favorite thing about California so far?" *Thank you, Prisha, for helping me push past the awkwardness.*

"It's so hard to know where to begin. It's all pretty spectacular," I tell her.

Ethan grins. "If I had to guess, I'd say it was the Dole Whip at Disney."

Prisha groans, "I know, right? Sheila and I bought season tickets one year just so we could stop in and get one whenever we wanted."

"And being that Anaheim is so conveniently located, that turned out to be, what, twice?" Ethan teases his friend.

"Three times, smarty pants." Prisha glares at him.

"Which works out to only what, a hundred bucks a whip?"

Ethan and Prisha have a wonderful friendship that I honestly envy. But, who in the world buys season passes to Disneyland so they can stop in for their favorite treat?

"What are you kids up to this afternoon?" Prisha asks.

"We're heading out to the beach. The boys are excited about miles of sand and warm water temperatures. I thought I'd give them their first surfing lesson."

"Nice." Prisha nods her head. "You going to your parents' place?"

"We are."

"I thought they lived in Beverly Hills." I stare at Ethan.

"They do, but when my sister and I were little, they

bought a beach house as an investment. It was nice to have a place to spend the weekends."

Prisha interjects with, "Wait until you see it. It's the house from *Summer Sands*."

"Their house is the one in *Summer Sands*?" I sound like I'm choking on a mouth full of marbles.

"My folks have been updating the place over the years," he says almost sheepishly.

"Ethan, that house is extraordinary! How can you sound so casual about it?"

He looks at me like I'm speaking Swahili. "It's just an investment."

Oh, yeah, well that makes total sense. *Not.* My idea of an investment is a new hot water heater or a new mattress. Both of which I got secondhand because I couldn't afford to *invest* in something new. "Maybe we should just stay here."

"Why?" Ethan asks.

"Because my boys aren't exactly careful, and I can't even begin to imagine what it would cost to replace something at that house. Besides, I don't want them thinking this is how real people live. How will they ever go home and settle back into normal life?"

Ethan's head snaps back. "Moira, you've met my parents, you know me, we're obviously real people."

"That's not what I meant …"

He nods his head, "I get that, but it sounds like you're calling us spoiled or entitled or something. I can assure you that we have all worked very hard for everything that we have." Oh yeah, I've pissed him off.

"*I* work hard," I tell him. "I'm at the diner fifty hours a week, and when I'm not there, I'm raising three kids and trying to make enough repairs to my house so that the roof doesn't fall down around us."

Ethan doesn't answer right away, and for once Prisha doesn't seem to have anything to say. A wave of guilt for being so harsh comes over me but before I can find a way to apologize, Ethan says, "I know you work hard, Moira. That's why I really wanted to make this a nice trip for you. If you'd rather go to a public beach, I'd be happy to oblige."

I've made a mess of things and I'm not quite sure how to back out of it. "I'm sorry," I finally say. "I'm just over-whelmed. All of this …"—I spokesmodel with my hands like I'm Vanna White about to turn over a new letter—"… is a lot to take in."

"Just treat it like any other vacation, hon," Prisha says. "Kick back and let Ethan be your own personal concierge."

Not only do I not go on vacations, but if I did, I certainly wouldn't be staying in a place with a concierge. "This is my first vacation since I was ten," I tell her. I don't mention that trip was to Anchorage where we stayed in a motel by the airport.

"Girl, then you need this. Just let go and enjoy." She picks up her phone and punches in a number. "Holland, babe, can you get to Malibu this afternoon? I need to treat a friend of mine to a massage and hot stone treatment."

Wait? What? My complaining about too much is getting me more? It's like I've stepped into an alternate dimension where up is down and less is more.

Before I can say anything, Prisha hangs up her phone. "You're all set. Holland will be there at three."

The only words that come out of my mouth are, "I've never had a massage." That is if you don't count the three-minute half-assed foot rubs Everett gave me when he wanted to have sex.

"I figured, babe. Which means you *really* need this."

"I'm not sure how comfortable I am having a man do it though." More accurately, I'm kind of freaking out at the thought.

Prisha waves her hand in front of her face. "Holland is a six-foot strapping Adonis …"

Now I feel nauseated.

She continues, "Who's been happily married to Charles for the last ten years."

"Oh, well, if that's the case, who am I to say no? Also, thank you very much."

Ethan stays remarkably silent on the subject until Prisha leaves. That's when he looks at me with hurt in his eyes and asks, "It's okay for Prisha to do something nice for you, but not me?"

"You've already done so much, Ethan. I just feel like the scoreboard is so weighted in your favor that I'll never be able to repay you."

"We're not playing a game, Moira. At least I'm not."

Before I can ask him what he means, Ash comes running over. "Can we go to the beach now?"

"Sure, buddy," Ethan says at the same time that I say, "In a bit."

Ash looks back and forth between us, clearly trying to decide who's in charge. To be honest, I'm not even sure anymore. Letting out a sigh, I concede, "Sure, let's get going."

Chapter 36

Ethan

I cannot remember a less enjoyable time at the beach house, which is saying something because I once had food poisoning and poison ivy at the same time when we were staying there. The tension between Moira and me is as thick as pancake batter.

We barely speak the entire day. Instead, we focus all of our attention on the children as a way to avoid each other. Turns out kids are quite handy in that regard.

Our surf lessons were cut short when Colton slipped on his surfboard and smashed his nose. There was blood everywhere. Unfortunately, Moira was only a few minutes into her massage at the time. As soon as she heard the commotion, she came rushing out in a robe and she took over for me.

After that, she quickly sent Holland home, then sat with Colton on a couch overlooking the veranda for a long time while I took Wyatt and Ash back out to play in the waves. Neither of them was keen to keep surfing.

We stopped for fish tacos on the way home from Malibu, along with shakes and churros. You need to be well-fueled to battle summer traffic on Pacific Coast Highway. By the time we got to my house, Colton was fast asleep, so I carried him up to his bed. I left while Moira tucked the other kids in.

I'm currently sitting outside under the stars by the pool while I sip a cold beer and wonder what the hell happened today. To say I'm hurt and angry would be an understatement. And while I'm not sure this is the best time to have it out with Moira, I can't imagine things getting better if we don't talk.

When I hear the patio door slide open behind me, I don't turn around. It isn't until Moira is standing next to me, dressed in jeans and a t-shirt, her hair wet from a shower, that I shift to look at her. "Hey," she says quietly.

"Hey." I take another sip of my beer, then set it on the side table next to the lounger. It's not one of the ones built for two, either. I'm in a single person lounge chair tonight. Moira's earlier behavior has dictated that choice.

"Can we talk?" Moira asks, sitting on the chair next to mine, facing me.

"I hope so. I'd really like to know what's wrong," I say.

"You're angry."

"A little bit, yeah," I tell her. "That stuff you said about how my parents and I live seemed a little uncalled for." I don't let her defend her actions; instead, I add, "All I've tried to do since I met you is to make your life better, and somehow you're pissed off about it."

She lets out a heavy sigh. "I'm not pissed off. I'm just … confused. I don't belong here, and neither do my kids."

"Why not? Why shouldn't you be able to have this kind of life?"

"Because none of this is real."

"There's that word again. What are you talking about?" I ask, narrowing my eyes at her. "I'm real, so clearly real people live like this. There isn't just one way of living in this world, Moira."

"I know," she practically whispers. "But this is never going to be *my* real life."

"Because you don't want it or because you've got some stupid voice in your brain telling you that you don't deserve it?" I ask, sitting up and turning my body so I'm facing her. My feet are planted firmly on the stone tile. "If it's the second one, you need to tell that voice to shut up already."

Tears spring to her eyes and she blinks quickly, setting her gaze on the night sky. "You don't understand. You could never understand. You grew up with two parents who love you and love each other. You had stability. Hell, you had two luxury houses. I grew up with an alcoholic father and a mother who abandoned us before overdosing and dying in an alley. Then, when I finally started to feel secure again, my grandma died. Then I got married and my husband died. Are you getting the theme of my life yet?"

"Just because you've been through hell doesn't mean your future has to be," I answer.

Moira groans. "I can't trust anything good that comes into my life because everyone *leaves*. Nobody sticks around, and you're not going to be any different."

"Well, thanks for deciding for me. It's sure nice to have someone else tell me what I'm going to do."

"You expect me to believe that you want the life I have? Are you going to come live in Gamble and we'll get married and live happily ever after?" she asks, raising her voice.

"Maybe," I answer, matching her angry tone. "Or maybe you and the boys could come live here."

"I'm not about to pack up the boys and take them away from our family and everything we know," she says, screwing up her face in disgust. "Is that what you thought? We'd spend a week here and see how much better it is than our real lives, and we'd just come running?"

"*Isn't* it better?" I ask. "You'd never have to work again if you didn't want to. You wouldn't be run off your feet anymore. Instead, you could enjoy life for once. Buy anything you want. Go anywhere. Would that be so terrible?"

"I never said I wanted any of this." Moira's voice shakes as she talks. "I'm sorry if you're disappointed, but you can't just swoop into my life and decide what's best for me and my kids. I'm an adult. I'm a mother. And *I* make the decisions for us. *I'm* the woman who stays up all night with them, holding a bucket when they're sick. *I* bandage up every scrape and kiss every boo-boo. *I'm* the one who's folded every pair of socks since they were born. Not *you*, some guy who we barely know who thinks he can just ride in on a white horse and save us from our crappy lives."

My head snaps back, as anger and rejection course through my veins. Clearly, Moira is not in love with me. In fact, she sounds like she can barely stand me. And if I know anything about her, it's that I'm not going to be able to change her mind.

No successful relationship starts with one person talking the other person into it. Ask me how I know? When I finally manage to speak, my voice is low and calm. "I had hoped for a different outcome, but believe me, my intentions were good. I promise I won't insult you with an offer of a future together again." Standing up, I tell her, "Thank you for finally being straight with me."

I walk back into the house before she can say anything. The truth is, I don't think my heart can take hearing anything else from her tonight.

Chapter 37

Moira

There's something to be said for not starting a fight you're not prepared to win. I didn't want to say the things I said to Ethan the way I said them. What I wanted to do was find out why he was being so nice to me and the boys when there was nothing in it for him. I mean, I practically threw myself at him the first night we were here, and he turned me down. To make matters worse, he hasn't made a move in that direction since. Now he's trying to make me believe that he wants a future with me? *Sorry, buddy, you can't play it both ways.*

I lay in bed for hours rehashing every horrible thing I said to him. I replay everything he said to me, focusing on the fact that he claims he wants the kids and me to live here with him. Truthfully, a life with Ethan would be nothing short of wonderful. But even if he means it right now, believing him would be the emotional equivalent of cliff diving with a blindfold on.

How can I know beyond a shadow of a doubt that he'll stick around? The answer is, I can't. All I know is we're totally different people, and while opposites may attract, there's no guarantee they'll stick.

I know Ethan works hard for what he has but I'm pretty sure he hasn't once fallen into bed so sore from his daily efforts that he can hardly move. The man doesn't even shop for his own groceries or mow his own grass.

I eventually fall into a fitful and disjointed sleep and feel like I've been hit by a truck when I finally wake up. Groaning, I roll over and look at the bedside clock. It's already after nine. I hurry to put on my robe and pad downstairs to check on the boys. They're all sitting at the kitchen table while Sandra fries up bacon and eggs for them.

"Good morning!" I call out, doing my best to keep my tone light.

The kids all turn to me and wave before going back to their conversation—could the Hulk take Thanos in an all-out battle?

Sandra smiles at me. "Good morning. Can I interest you in some breakfast?"

"I'd love some toast and juice," I tell her. "But I can get it myself."

"Nonsense. You're on vacation. You go sit with the boys and I'll bring it right over. Oh, and Ethan said to tell you he went for a run."

"Thanks." Instead of sitting down at the table, I pull out a stool at the island. "You and I have very similar jobs," I tell her. "I own a diner in Alaska, but I spend most of my time waiting on tables."

"So, you know how nice it feels to care for others." Her smile is bright as she hands me a mug of coffee.

"It's exhausting," I tell her while adding a spoonful of sugar to my cup.

"I imagine it is." Sandra cracks several eggs into a hot skillet before turning around so she's facing me. "But you work a lot harder than I do."

"From the way Ethan was talking, you single-handedly run his life." I say it as if it's a compliment, but inside I'm feeling pretty snarky.

Sandra pours four glasses of juice from a pitcher. "Taking care of Ethan is a piece of cake. I had four kids, a husband who worked sixty hours a week on the docks, and I worked part time as a telemarketer. *That* was a lot of work."

"How did you wind up here?"

"My sister Gloria used to clean for Ethan's mom. Rose hired me for two weeks to whip her son's household into shape. After that, he hired me on himself. I've been with him for six years."

"What does your husband think about it?"

"My job?" She shrugs her shoulders. "What's to think about? I make four times more working for Ethan than I've ever made before, and the work is a breeze. Honestly, I think Julio is jealous he didn't get the job." She lets out a melodious laugh.

"I don't mean to pry," I start to say, but then I think better of continuing.

"But …" Sandra encourages.

I sigh like I'm the Big Bad Wolf trying to blow one of the piglets' houses down. "Do you ever wonder why Ethan even needs a housekeeper? I mean, I guess I could understand a cleaning lady, but all this…" I wave my arms around the giant kitchen. "Doesn't it seem to be a lot for one person?"

"In your world and my world, maybe. But Ethan wants

a family, and this would be the perfect family home. It's only a matter of time before he gets married." She eyes me intently.

"I could never live like this," I say bluntly.

Sandra flips the eggs in the pan and counts to ten before turning them out onto the boys' plates. Then she adds the crisp bacon and toast that's sitting on the counter. She takes all three plates over to the table before coming back for the juice. Once that task is accomplished, she hands me the toast that just popped up, slides my juice across the counter, and sits down on a barstool next to me.

"Moira, I don't want to say anything I shouldn't but …" When I don't stop her, she adds, "I don't think you should pass up an easier life on principle. If Cinderella had done that, it would have been the worst fairy tale ever."

"But Ethan can't really want me. There's no way I'm his type, especially when he's dated movie stars."

"I think that if Ethan is telling you that you're his type, you should believe him."

"I don't think you quite understand how different our lives are."

Cocking her head to the side, she says, "Let me ask you something. Would you turn down the right man if he didn't have any money?"

"No, of course not."

"Then don't turn down the right man because he's wealthy. That would be plain crazy," she says, patting my arm.

"It's a little more complicated than that."

"Is it?" Sandra asks.

No. I'm just terrified. I pull off a piece of my toast and pop it in my mouth while I consider her advice. Maybe it really is a lot simpler than I'm making it.

Maybe this could be my life.

Chapter 38

Ethan

I run farther and faster than I have in years, needing to expel all the hurt Moira inflicted on me last night. When I get back home, I try to act like everything is fine, so I won't ruin Wyatt's big day out with the Dodgers. I've never been as mixed up as I am right now. The love I feel for Moira is real and it runs deep, but it can't work if she doesn't want it to.

Wiping the sweat off my brow, I turn the corner and my house comes into view. My very real house where I'll return to my very real life after Harper's wedding. I was up half the night thinking about things, trying to figure out if it's possible to still have a future with Moira, but I always wind up at the same conclusion—she doesn't want a life with me. Period.

I need to accept that. I'll go back to Gamble with her and the boys, then slowly extricate myself from their lives so that when I leave for good, it won't be so confusing for the kids. Just the thought of it breaks my heart. I was so sure we were on our way to becoming a family. Now I'm stuck cleaning up a mess that never felt like a mess —until now.

Stopping at my front gates, my heart pounds as I enter the code and I tell myself to check my feelings at the door because the only thing that matters is making the rest of the boys' trip a wonderful one. Who knows when they'll ever be able to take another one?

The sun is out in full force for the big game. Somehow, Moira and I pretend everything's fine while we go through the routine of getting everyone ready and out the door. During the drive over to Elysian Park, where Dodger Stadium is located, the atmosphere in my SUV is filled with boy excitement—mine included. Moira and I avoid all eye contact during the thirty-minute trip.

The Dodgers set aside a section of premium seats behind home plate for Wyatt's team and chaperones. Before the game starts, they even make a big announcement about the Sluggers being their special guests today.

Wyatt is in the front row with the rest of his team, while Moira and I are sitting a couple of rows back with the twins, who we've strategically placed between us. The first three innings pass quickly, with me trying to explain little things about the game, but Moira's boys know as much as I do, so that ends pretty quickly.

I should be enjoying this afternoon instead of counting the innings until it's over. I console myself that every minute that passes means I'm one step closer to putting an end to the torture of being with Moira and the boys.

By the time the fifth inning ends, the twins are a little

restless, so I offer to take them up to the concession stands for a treat. Moira hurries to stand up. "I'll come, too."

If I had to guess, I'd say it's because she's coming to the same realization as me—that either she's going to have to stop relying on me to help, or she doesn't want the kids to get any closer to me. Both are likely.

The four of us venture up the stairs, then make our way along the various stands while the boys try to decide between ice cream cones and popcorn. Ash picks ice cream and Colton, popcorn. "Should we divide and conquer?" I ask Moira, wanting to get back to the game.

"Sure," she says, digging around in her purse. "But I'm buying. You've treated enough."

She hands me a ten, and I take it, not wanting to argue.

Colton and I get through our line much faster than Ash and Moira, so we wait for them while I watch the game on one of the televisions.

"Ethan? Is that you?" a woman asks.

I turn to see Bridgette Hill in a fitted tank top that's practically bursting at the seams. Short shorts and over-sized sunglasses finish the look. Bridgette got her start modeling by landing herself on the cover of *Sports Illustrated Swimsuit Edition*. After several years gracing more covers than a person could count, she now has her own clothing line. She grins at me. "I thought it was you! I'm sitting a few rows back, and the entire game, I've been hoping you'd turn around so I could be sure."

Out of the corner of my eye, I see Moira staring at Bridgette. She looks none-too-pleased. The sight of her annoyance brings out something nasty in me, and I find myself giving Bridgette a kiss on the cheek—which is not what I'd normally do in this situation. "Bridgette, you look wonderful. It's been way too long."

She places her hand on my forearm and rubs it like a cat. "Yes, it has been. You look pretty terrific yourself, more relaxed or something."

"I've been taking some time off to enjoy the good life up in Alaska. I've been there for a couple of months."

"Good for you. You work way too hard." Bridgette glances down at Colton, who is shoveling popcorn in his mouth while he stares back and forth between us. "Who's this?"

Placing a hand on Colton's shoulder, I answer, "This is Colton Bishop, soon-to-be nephew of Harper's."

Her hand snaps back. "So the rumors are true then? Harper's getting remarried."

"Yup, to a hell of a good guy this time around," I tell her.

"I'm so glad. She's such a sweetheart. She deserves happiness." Then to Colton, she says, "You're going to love having Harper as an auntie. She's the best."

"Yup, she really is," Colton mumbles, allowing some bits of popcorn to fly out of his mouth.

"Is Harper here, too?" Bridgette asks.

"No, I'm here with Colton's family for a few days. His big brother's baseball team won a trip to see the game today. They've been staying at my place." I notice Moira and Ash are on their way to join our small circle, so I add, "Here's more of the gang now." When they arrive, I say, "Moira, Ash, this is my old friend, Bridgette Hill."

Bridgette playfully smacks me on the arm. "Be careful who you're calling old." Then she extends her hand to Moira. "Nice to meet you, Moira. I hear Harper's joining your family."

Moira offers her a polite smile. "She's marrying my big brother. We couldn't be happier." *Yeah, she doesn't seem very happy right now.*

"I *love* Harper," Bridgette gushes before turning her gaze back to me. "I've actually been hoping I'd run into you around town."

"You have some big contract you need me to look at?" I ask. I've done some legal work for Bridgette in the past.

"I thought maybe we could grab a drink or something." She noticeably leans into me, sending very non-business vibes.

Moira stiffens and I realize this is the perfect opportunity to show Moira that there are real women out there who don't eschew my attentions.

I grin down at Bridgette and croon, "I'd love that. I'm heading back to Alaska in a couple of days though, so how about I call you when I get back to town?"

Bridgette places her hand on my chest, then kisses my cheek with great care. "I can't wait," she says in a breathy tone.

"It's a date," I tell her while staring at Moira.

I know I'm being a jackass, but I don't care. I'm hurt and angry. Besides, maybe this will make Moira think that I can be happy without her. Even though I don't know if that will ever be possible.

The rest of the game is as tense as a rubber band right before its breaking point. Moira is frigidly cold every time we interact with each other, while I'm busy pretending everything is fine.

During the seventh-inning stretch, the Sluggers are taken out on the field to lead the crowd through "Take Me Out to the Ball Game." Then, after the game ends, they get to go to the dugout to meet the players, who take them onto the field with them to run around.

Now that the crowd is gone, Moira, the twins, and I walk down the steps and stand in the front row. Ash and Colton watch longingly as their brother has the time of his life.

"You okay, buddy?" I ask Colton.

He shrugs. "I kind of wish I was out there, too."

"Me, too," I tell him with a sad smile.

Wyatt must have some type of amazing big brother radar because when I look back at him, he's talking to one of the coaches for the Dodgers while pointing in our direction. The man nods, then Wyatt rushes over to us, shouting, "Ash! Colt! Come on!"

They immediately leap over the short wall that separates us from the field and take off like a couple of greyhounds, leaving Moira and me alone in an awkward silence.

After a couple of minutes, I can't take it anymore, so I say, "This will be a memory they'll never forget."

"They won't be the only ones," Moira says snippily, digging around in her purse. She pulls out her phone and starts videoing, effectively putting an end to our conversation.

I wish I knew how to fix whatever has happened between us. But Moira has made up her mind and I've learned that when a woman makes up her mind, there's no point in trying to change it. Paige taught me that.

The only move I have left is to accept reality.

Chapter 39

Moira

I'm so mad I could spit nails, and I'd direct every one of them at Ethan. He clearly has something going on with that supermodel or he wouldn't have been so touchy feely with her. Thank goodness I found out about his true character before making the giant-ass mistake of thinking I might really become his wife someday.

By the time Wyatt's team is saying goodbye to the Dodgers, there are very few cars left in the parking lot. What could have been an excruciating hour of getting out of Dodge, literally, is now pretty effortless.

The boys are talking a mile a minute with such intensity that Ethan has to yell to be heard over the fracas. "Where should we go for dinner? We can get great Chinese in Pasadena or head back to Beverly Hills and find something there."

"Is Pasadena closer to Beverly Hills or farther away?" I want to know.

"Farther away."

"Then my vote is Beverly Hills." I don't even turn my gaze in his direction. I don't want to be stuck in this car for one more minute than I have to.

He looks in the rear-view mirror at my boys and asks, "What are you kids in the mood for? Burgers? Pizza? Sushi?"

Great call, Einstein, kids are always in the mood for sushi. But I don't say anything. Let Ethan figure it out for himself.

Wyatt asks, "Can we go for steak? A steak would be the perfect end to this day!"

"Since when do we eat steak?" I sound harsher than I intend to.

"Don't you remember? Last summer Uncle Digger made buffalo steak. They were amazing!"

"I'm not sure the place I normally go to has buffalo steak, but I promise it has the best beef steak you've ever eaten," Ethan tells us. Before any further comment can be made, he pushes his phone button on the dash and says, "Call Maestro's."

The phone rings three times before a hostess answers. Ethan says, "Trina, this is Ethan Caplan. I'd like to speak to Tony."

Seconds later a deep voice greets, "Mr. Caplan, sir, how may I help you?"

"I have a carload of hungry boys looking for steak. Any chance you can fit us in tonight?"

We overhear shuffling papers as though he's searching through a reservation book. After several moments, he says, "I can fit you in at five thirty, but we're booked to closing after that."

Ethan replies, "We'll need a table for five, and thanks, Tony. You're the best."

"Anything for you, Mr. Caplan," the man says. Apparently, Ethan is used to this kind of bowing and scraping because he takes it very much as his due.

Once he hangs up, Ethan addresses the boys. "I don't suppose any of you brought suit coats?" A chorus of noes fills the air.

"Why do they need suit coats?" I demand.

"Maestro's has a dress code." His reply is curt.

"Then let's just go to a Sizzler or something." There's no way I can afford a place that requires a dress code.

Ethan looks at me. "I don't think there is a Sizzler in Beverly Hills."

"Of course." My tone is harsh. "Let's just go through a fast-food drive-through and be done with it."

"Moooooom, no!" Wyatt shouts from the back. "We want to try something new. Isn't that what this trip is all about?"

"I can't afford a place that requires you to wear a suit coat. Because that would mean buying dinner *and* the appropriate wardrobe."

"Aw, shucks," Wyatt says. "I guess you're right. Can we go to McDonald's then?"

"*I'm* buying dinner," Ethan declares. "I'm also buying the attire needed for it."

He's so authoritarian and bossy I want to yell at him, but I don't. Instead, I decide that he owes me a fancy dinner for the crap he pulled at Dodger Stadium. *Who agrees to go out with a supermodel in front of the woman who only hours before you were claiming to want to spend your life with?*

When I don't say anything, Ethan asks, "What sizes do the boys wear?"

"What, are you going to wave a magic wand and make them appear?" I demand.

"Yes." In the direction of the dashboard, he says, "Call Claire at Saks Fifth Avenue."

This time the phone is answered by a woman with a French accent. "Mr. Caplan," she gushes. "How can I help you?"

"Hi, Claire, I need three boys' suits and shoes to be picked up in thirty minutes. I'm going to need one, too. You know my size."

"May I ask the occasion?" she wants to know.

"Dinner at Maestro's. Oh, and I'm going to need a woman's dress and shoes, as well. I'm going to turn you over to Moira. She has all the sizes."

I spend the next five minutes telling this woman what sizes we all wear before she hangs up and gets busy shopping for us. This whole personal shopper, fancy dinner thing is just another reason why we aren't the right family for Ethan. Not that he wants us anymore.

We ride the rest of the way in complete silence. Well, Ethan and I do anyway. The boys are riding so high on the day they may never stop talking.

Ethan turns off Wilshire Boulevard before the imposing Saks Fifth Avenue building. He pulls into the valet parking and hands the valet his keys. "We'll only be about fifteen minutes." Then he leads the way as we trail behind him like a row of ugly ducklings. Seriously, I've never been into a department store fancier than Macy's and this place makes Macy's look like Walmart.

Ethan walks straight to the elevators and presses the button. Once we arrive at the menswear floor, he flags down a passing salesman. "We're here to see Claire."

Those appear to be the magic words that release the genie from the bottle, because an elegant woman around my age appears out of nowhere. She claps her hands, and her minions take the boys and Ethan off to get ready. Once they're gone, she turns to me. "Please follow me. I've pulled a couple dresses for you to choose from."

She takes me to a private dressing room with a rack holding five different dresses. "I understand you're in a bit of a hurry, so I asked someone from the cosmetic counter to come up and freshen your makeup for you." I barely refrain from asking her to turn a pumpkin and some rats into a horse-drawn carriage. I'm pretty sure she could do it.

The first thing I do when Claire leaves is to look at the price tags on the dresses. I practically choke when I discover the cheapest one is seven hundred dollars. The shoes that go with it are two hundred and fifty. Feeling lightheaded, I put it on and turn to stare at myself in the mirror. The crimson red contrasts nicely with my dark hair, and I know immediately that I would have chosen this dress no matter what.

Claire quickly cuts all the tags off and then puts my own clothes into a bag. Once my makeup is done, I feel like Julia Roberts in *Pretty Woman*. You know, if Julia was playing a single mom instead of a sex worker.

After my transformation, Claire takes me back out to the main floor where Ethan and the boys are waiting. My breath hitches in my throat at the sight of them. Handsome doesn't begin to cover it. I've never seen Ethan in a suit, as there's no reason for him to wear one in Alaska. He's breathtakingly gorgeous. Emotion clogs my throat as I remind myself that he's a cad. *A cad meant for a supermodel, not me.*

"Mr. Caplan," Claire says. "Would you like me to send your street clothes over to your house."

"Please," Ethan tells her as he pulls out his wallet and hands her a wad of cash. "Thanks so much, Claire. As always, you've outdone yourself." I'm guessing the money is a tip for her last-minute services, as he had no way of knowing which dress I was going to choose. Note to self, sell the diner and become a personal shopper. Although in Gamble, I'm guessing customers would be few and far between.

We're back in Ethan's car in only fourteen minutes and we all look like we're about to be presented to the queen. I'm so overwhelmed that speech evades me. My boys look amazing, and I feel like a princess. Ethan looks like he's ruler of his own country.

A dreamlike haze encompasses the evening and even though Ethan and I barely speak to each other, I don't let that ruin a meal that will go down in history as the best and most expensive food that's ever passed my lips.

Tomorrow, we go back to Gamble and the fairy tale ends. It makes my heart ache, but I'm grateful to have found out Ethan's true character before I was in too deep.

Chapter 40

Ethan

The trip home is long and devoid of any excitement. We got up at the crack of dawn to get to LAX on time, only to find out the flight would be delayed. The boys are grumpy and quiet, as are the grown-ups. The wall of ice between Moira and me is so thick, I don't even care to try to knock it down.

I spend the entire day going through the motions as an increasing sense of dread builds inside. I don't even have it in me to try to cheer the boys up, knowing that the moment we touch down in Gamble, Moira and I will have no reason to see each other again—other than at the wedding, of course.

Last night was hell. Moira looked incredible in that red dress. I have never wanted a woman as badly as I want her. It's not just because she's beautiful on the outside, either. She's selfless and caring and she'd do anything for someone she loves.

In addition to all the good things, she's also a bit of a wounded bird. And even though she's made it clear she doesn't want me, I can't help but want to do things to make her life better. Hence last night's extravagance. I knew after we left California, she'd never let me do something like that for her again.

She nearly freaked when she saw the cheapest steak on Maestro's menu was over fifty bucks. I thought she'd faint when she discovered the price didn't include any of the sides. She wanted to share her steak with the boys, but as it was only four ounces, that would only have gotten them all two bites.

The boys spent the entire meal talking about how much food they could buy in Gamble for the cost of our meal. Instead of being horrified by the indulgence, they were thrilled by it.

Every time Moira shifted in her chair next to me, my gaze would drift to her bare legs. Moira is more beautiful than a thousand Bridgette Hills, she just doesn't know it.

I feel horrible about how I played things with Bridgette, and it kept me up half the night. The other half was spent fantasizing that Moira would walk through my bedroom door so we could talk things out. I imagined that talking would end with her crawling into my bed so I could show her what she means to me.

But she didn't knock on my door, and the night passed without us fixing anything.

I haven't felt longing and angst like this since I was a teenager. But the truth is, I regret nothing. I put myself out there in the most honest way I could. I can't be responsible for how Moira feels. God knows if I could have changed things, the night would have ended much differently.

Digger has a hundred questions for us when he picks us up in Anchorage. The boys are happy to fill him in on every detail, but Moira keeps her answers to one word. Fine. Okay. Good. Nice. She might as well have spent the week at the Motel 6 in Burbank.

It's almost six in the evening when the lodge comes into view. Despite being hungry and tired, the kids perk up when they see Harper, Lily, and Liam standing on the dock waving while waiting for us to land.

The boys scramble out of the float plane the second Digger opens the door, then take off to tell their soon-to-be cousins everything about the trip. I wait until Moira is off to climb down, then help Digger get the bags out of the cargo hold.

When I join everyone else, Harper is quick to ask, "So? How was the trip?" Her expression says it all. Prisha must have filled her in on what happened when she saw us.

"Lovely," Moira says with a tight smile. "It was a vacation the boys will never forget."

Harper looks back and forth between us, then her gaze lands back on Moira. "Did you like LA?"

"It's a great place to visit, but I can see why you wanted out of there," Moira says with a forced laugh. She glances at me, and adds, "Ethan was an extremely gracious host. He definitely gave us a taste of what life would be like there." Her tone lacks warmth and I can't help but take her comment as a slight.

Digger and Harper exchange a concerned look, before Digger says, "Grandpa Jack has supper ready, so why don't we take a load off and go eat?"

As hungry as I am, I promised myself I was going to cut and run the second we got back. I can't stand another second of this tension. "Thanks, Digger, but I'm going to head back to the cabin. You know, make sure no one stole the sheets while I was gone." I try to keep my tone light, but my voice cracks with emotion.

"You sure?" Harper asks. She's staring at me so intently, I know she's going to call for details the second she has a chance.

"Yeah, I'm beat." As soon as I say that I remember that I'm Moira and the boys' ride home. "You wouldn't mind giving the gang a ride home, would you?" I ask Harper.

"Of course not." Her eyebrows are knit together in worry.

"Thanks. I appreciate it." Turning to Digger, I add, "And thanks for the ride back."

I risk a glance at Moira, whose expression is unreadable. She gives me a short nod. "Thank you for everything."

"You're welcome," I tell her as I grab my suitcase. "I'll go tell the boys I'm leaving." I'm glad the kids have run up ahead of us, as it gives me an excuse to do the same. I step off the dock and walk up the path to the lodge on wobbly legs. An important chapter of my life is ending, and the grief is nearly overwhelming. I didn't even feel this bad when Paige left.

When I finally catch up to the kids, they're on the back deck with Lily and Liam watching a video on Liam's tablet.

Wyatt motions for me to come over. "You gotta see this, Ethan. This guy drinks a whole glass of milk through his nose!"

Chuckling, I walk over and ruffle his hair, then watch the thirty second video. The kids are killing themselves laughing, shouting about how gross and cool it is. When it's over, I say, "I have to head back to my place, guys. I just wanted to thank you for being such wonderful guests this past week."

Holding my hand up, I offer each of them a high five

while they thank me for letting them stay at my "wicked house" and for showing them around.

Saying goodbye to the boys feels like a much bigger deal than it should. Sure, I'll see them around town while I'm here, but it won't be the same because I know they'll never be mine. We're not going to be the family I was hoping we'd be. The very thought makes my eyes water.

"See you for lunch tomorrow?" Wyatt asks.

"Ah, I don't know. I need to get some serious writing done on my book, so I might try to hunker down at the cabin for a few days."

"Okay." I can see in his eyes that he's worried something has changed. "Maybe we can stop by your cabin and say hi."

"Have your mom call me." Even as I say this, I know she never will.

The twins launch themselves at me en masse. "You're the coolest, Ethan," Colton says. Ash squeezes so tightly, it's clear he isn't oblivious to the gravity of what's happening here. Even though the kids can't put it into words, they know this goodbye is bigger than it seems.

As soon as I'm safely in my car, I let out a long sigh and close my eyes for a second. I wonder how long it's going to be before I feel even remotely happy about my future again.

Based on the amount of pain I'm feeling now, I'm guessing it's going to be a very long time.

Chapter 41

Moira

"What in the world happened while you were away?" Harper asks as soon as Ethan is out of earshot.

"We went to Disneyland, the beach, and a Dodgers game," I tell her, knowing full well I'm not addressing what she really wants to know.

"You seem tense," Digger interjects, with a concerned look on his face.

"It's been a long day. A busy week."

"Yeah, but …" he begins.

"I have a really bad headache," I announce. "I feel like I might throw up."

"Oh, dear," Harper says. "Why don't I drive you home? We can keep the boys overnight if you want."

Nothing like the threat of a little projectile vomiting to get some alone time. "I'm sure they'd love that, thank you."

I'm aware that both my brother and Harper are dying to ask more, but we walk up the path in silence

I make quick work of telling the boys I'm heading home. They cheer when they're offered a chance at another sleepover. After quick goodnight hugs, I make a beeline to the parking lot with Harper following close behind.

I toss my bags into the back before getting in the cab. I barely have my seatbelt on when Harper demands, "*What* happened?"

"I don't know what you mean." I say a silent prayer that she'll leave well enough alone.

No dice. "What's going on between you and Ethan? And before you say 'nothing,' I know you guys were dating before you left on your trip."

"Who told you that?"

"Ethan."

Crap. Fidgeting with the strap of my purse, I tell her, "It became painfully obvious that he and I lead very different lives."

"And …" she prods.

"And there's no way our two lifestyles mesh. End of story."

"That's *so* not the end of the story." Harper throws the truck into reverse to aim it in the direction of the road.

"It really is," I tell her. "Ethan is some rich bigwig Hollywood guy, and I'm just a small-town girl. I don't fit into his world."

Shifting into drive, she pulls out onto the main drag. "It seems to me that you're not trying."

That was a rude thing to say. "Excuse me?"

"Obviously, Ethan fits into your life here in Gamble enough that you were willing to date him."

"So?" I'd rather jump out of the truck and walk home than hear her answer.

Brushing back the blonde hair that's escaped her ponytail, she says, "He's the same guy here as he is in California."

"I beg to differ," I tell her sharply. "Here, he's a guy who comes into my diner in his shorts and T-shirt and spends the day writing. *Here*, he's normal."

"Because it's *your* life he's fitting into?" *I hate Harper right now.* "Did you even try to fit in there?"

"Why do I have to change who I am to fit into someplace as ridiculously pretentious as Beverly Hills?" I can feel the steam rising from my skin.

"It *is* ridiculously pretentious there, but that's not what I mean. I know for a fact that Ethan was beyond excited to share his world with you, and his world is not the fake people who live for highlights and facelifts."

An image of Bridgette Hill pops into my head, but I *really* don't want to get into that. "Ethan's life is a huge house that he barely spends any time in. He has a housekeeper, for God's sake, and …" I try to think of what else bothered me and can only come up with, "His pool lights keep the tempo of the music."

Harper laughs like that's the funniest thing she's ever heard. "You've got a chip on your shoulder as big as the one that Digger used to have."

"What do you mean by that?" My hand inches toward the door handle. We're only going twenty miles an hour. Surely it wouldn't hurt too badly to jump out of the truck before she can answer.

"Your brother hated me before he bothered to get to know me. And do you know why?" She doesn't wait for me to hazard a guess. "Because I was a movie star and in his pea brain all movie stars are fake, attention-seeking numbskulls."

"Most are. Take your ex-husband, for instance." I

know that was mean, but at the moment Harper is not one of my favorite people in the world.

"Brett *is* a total waste of skin," she agrees. "But I'm not. If Digger hadn't opened his mind and heart to me, we both would have suffered. We would have missed our chance at happiness."

"Look, Harper, I don't mean to be unkind …" *I really do though, I'm that mad.* "But Digger would have never made it in California. You guys are only working because you came here, and as far as I can figure, you came here because you didn't like life in California, either."

"I loved California," she says with a hiss. "I just hated being the center of the paparazzi's endless attention."

"So, if the paparazzi didn't follow you, you think Digger would happily live there with you?" She can't be serious.

"When he came to California to get me, he told me he'd live anywhere that I wanted to. And he would have, too, Moira. That's what real love is."

"If that's what you want to believe." I've known my brother for a lot longer than Harper has, and I know for a fact he would have hated every second of living in La La Land.

"What I believe is that your brother was willing to do something that went against his grain if that's what it took for me to be happy. Love is caring for something bigger than just yourself. It's compromise and growth."

I glare at her profile and practically yell, "I do care about something bigger than myself. I care about my kids and my job and my extended family. Look, Harper …" I'm not sure continuing my thought is the best way to go, but I'm so worked up right now that I can't seem to stop myself. "I'm sorry your husband cheated on you, but you've got to face it, your life was pretty cushy. I work my ass off at home and then I go into the diner and do the same thing. I don't go shopping all day and have lunch with my friends while the nanny raises my kids."

Harper slams on the brakes so hard, I have to put my hands out to keep from hitting my head on the dashboard. "Is that what you think of me? Because I'll have you know I worked damn hard, and just because my kids had a nanny doesn't mean I wasn't there for them every day of their lives."

"I guess …"

"You know what, Moira? You're playing martyr and it's not a good look on you. Get off the damn cross and see what's in front of your face. Ethan loves you for you. It's too bad you can't do the same for him."

"Wow, you're really bitchy when you want to be," I tell her.

"Takes one to know one."

We ride the rest of the way to my house in an angry silence, and when she comes to a stop, Harper stares out the front window, not so much as deigning to glance in my direction.

I open the door handle to get out. The last thing said between us is from Harper. "Grow up, Moira, and quit playing the victim. I know your life hasn't been easy, but here's a newsflash: no one's is."

I slam the door so hard I'm not sure it'll ever open.

Chapter 42

Ethan

My parents had so much fun together while I was gone, they decided to take off and explore parts of Canada. Happily, that means they aren't here to witness the sad state of their only son's life.

The next few weeks pass slowly. I get up, go for long runs (the entire time torn between hoping I see Moira and praying I don't), then return to the quiet of my cabin and do my best to forget the sad state of my personal life. Writing is secondary.

The evenings are excruciatingly long and lonely. I find myself sitting out on the deck, sipping beer and watching the sun go down over the lake. I wish I was reading the boys a chapter from *Captain Underpants*. I miss their laughter and their excitable energy. I miss everything about Moira, other than her insecurity that tore us apart.

I spend hours thinking through every detail of our time together in LA, wondering what I did that was wrong and wishing things had turned out the exact opposite of how they did.

I barely sleep and every meal I make is tasteless, even if it's got bacon on it. Nothing pleases me. Harper texts me a lot, hoping I'll come by for supper or just meet up to talk, but I'm pretending to be on such a roll with my writing that I have to keep going. *Lies, all lies.*

I'm currently standing in front of the fridge, trying to decide what to make for supper, when there's a knock at the door. My first thought is that maybe it's Moira, which causes my heart to pound wildly. Then I glance down, realizing I'm wearing ancient sweatpants and a stretched-out t-shirt.

Raking my hands through my hair, I hurry over to the door and pull it open, only to see Harper standing in front of me holding a brown paper bag. She breezes past me before I can invite her in. Setting the bag down on the kitchen counter, she says, "I figured you must need a real meal by now, since you've locked yourself up here, supposedly typing until your fingers bleed." She looks down at my hands and cocks an eyebrow. Then she looks at my computer.

Damn. My laptop isn't even open. "Thanks, that's very kind of you."

"More like kind of Digger and Jack. Spareribs, corn bread, mashed potatoes, salad, and a slice of wild blueberry pie."

I walk over to the fridge to grab a beer, all the while continuing to avoid eye contact. No one knows me as well as Harper, so hiding my pain from her is going to be damn near impossible. "Beer?"

"No, thanks. I'm getting married in a few days; I don't want to be bloated," she says, settling herself onto one of the stools.

"That's right, the big day is approaching," I say, cracking the can open and offering her a bright smile. "You excited?"

"I'd be a lot more excited if my best friend and my future sister-in-law weren't hell-bent on breaking each other's hearts." She gives me her best "mom glare."

"What makes you think that?" I ask, doing my best to look casual.

"Because you've been avoiding the world for weeks and Moira's walking around town with red, puffy eyes," Harper says. "So don't go telling me nothing happened and that you're totally fine."

Setting down the beer, I start pulling the food out of the bag, my stomach growling as the heavenly scents waft through the air. "Nothing did happen, and I *am* totally fine."

"That's what she said. But I'm not buying it, no matter what you two knuckleheads tell me."

I shrug. "This is America. You're free to be wrong if you want." I take the foil off the large plate and get out a fork and knife. "Would you like some?"

"I already ate," Harper says, irritation written all over her face. "You do know you'd be perfect together, right?"

"I don't think so," I say while settling myself on the stool next to hers. I pick up a rib and have a bite, letting the tangy barbecue sauce wash over my tongue. After I swallow, I add, "Look, I may have entertained thoughts of a future with Moira. I may have even tried to show her what a life with me would be like for her and the boys, but she made it exceedingly clear that she is not interested. Period. End of story. No more to say."

"How did she make that clear?"

"What do you mean how?" I ask, annoyed at her

persistence. "She used English. She spoke in full sentences and told me it was not going to happen."

"You don't need to get snippy with me. I'm trying to help."

"I don't need your help," I tell her, digging into the mashed potatoes. "Mmm, those are some creamy potatoes."

"Jack uses a stand mixer to fluff them up," Harper says, plucking the cornbread off my plate and breaking off a chunk. "I just don't understand what went wrong. You two were falling in love with each other."

I choke a little, then say, "How do you figure that?"

"You were *super* obvious. The kissing on the street and in the closet, the way you'd stare into each other's eyes and laugh and make sure you'd sit next to each other all the time," Harper says, listing things off on her fingers. "The way you raffled off your LeBron jersey for Wyatt's team so you could make sure they'd take a trip with you, and you could give them a tour of your life …"

Shrugging, I tell her, "I wanted to help the poor kid out. Besides, I didn't even like that jersey."

"Are you serious right now?" Harper asks, raising her voice. "You *love* LeBron. Love. Him. And you *loved* that stupid jersey."

"So, I got caught up in a moment of sympathy for a kid who doesn't have much. Big deal." Picking up another rib, I take a big bite, chewing furiously.

"Oh, my God, you two deserve each other. You're both a couple of stubborn asses."

"I'm not the stubborn one," I say with a full mouth. "She is." I swallow hard, then have a sip of beer to wash it down, pent-up anger bubbling up in my chest. "*She's* the one who decided we didn't have a future together. Not me. I tried, Harper. Believe me, I pulled out all the stops, showing her exactly how amazing their lives could be with me. But she doesn't want it and she doesn't want me, and there's *nothing* I can do about that. You want to lecture someone? Go find Moira Bishop. Her house is about ten blocks from here."

Harper glares at me for a long time. Finally, in a calm tone, she says, "So, you wanted to show her how she could fit into your life?"

"Not just her, the boys, too," I tell her, feeling defensive. "And they loved it there, by the way. The pool, the screening room, nice big bedrooms, *Disneyland* ..."

"You just assumed that she'd be cool leaving her entire life behind so you wouldn't have to be the one to make that kind of sacrifice?"

"Yeah, what a hardship it would be—a housekeeper, gardeners, money ..." I snap, then I take a deep breath and calm myself down. "But it doesn't matter. She already decided it wasn't going to work before I even broached the subject of a future together. She just shut down and put up a wall, like she's so damn sure I'd eventually leave her."

"It kind of makes sense based on how her life has gone so far."

"Like I told her, just because she's been let down, it doesn't mean I'm going to do that to her, too. But she doesn't believe it, and there's nothing I can do to change that, Harper. Nothing. You can't convince someone to love you. They either do or they don't."

"I know she loves you," Harper says. "I can tell. Digger can, too, and he knows her better than anyone. Before you guys left for California, he told me his sister had never been this happy, not even when she and Everett got married."

"Please stop. This is hard enough on me without you stirring it all up again. I'm going to stay here until your wedding, and then I'm going home. It's not how I want it, but it's reality, and the sooner I face it, the better off I'll be."

"You're not even going to try to talk to her again?" Harper leans forward and stabs me in the chest with her pointer finger. Hard.

Leaning out of her reach, I say, "I'm going to respect her decision, which is the right thing to do. As Moira pointed out, she's an adult. She knows her mind. If we had something worth fighting for, I'm sure she'd fight." Brandishing a sparerib in her direction, I add, "Now, I appreciate you bringing me supper and trying to help, but there's nothing you can do to change what's happened, so please just leave it alone."

Harper slowly stands up and gives me a kiss on the cheek. "You two are so perfectly suited, a blind person could see it."

"Tell that to Moira," I scoff.

"Oh, I did, and believe me when I tell you, she's being as big of a jackass as you are." Before I can figure out how to respond to that, she adds, "You're one of the good ones, Ethan. Don't you forget it."

A lot of good that does me. I've lost the only woman I've ever truly loved, and the sons I was starting to believe could be mine.

Chapter 43

Moira

It's been almost three weeks since we got back from California, but it feels more like a year. Summer holidays have officially ended, and the kids are back in school. There was a whirlwind of back-to-school shopping for shoes and clothes, as well as school supplies, which was a great distraction. The added bonus was the kids weren't begging to see Ethan or go out to the lodge every day.

I haven't been this torn up inside since my mother left us. The truth is, I love Ethan, and I don't know how to make myself stop. He was the man I was thinking of when I made my vision board, and he was offering me a life together. But I turned it down because I was too damn scared to try to find a compromise.

I know I won't fit in where he's from, but maybe there's a way to find a middle ground. I have no idea what that might look like, but I at least owe it to myself (and him, and the boys) to try, don't I?

The thing is, I have no idea how to tell him that since he's gone out of his way to avoid me for the past few weeks. I think I have to accept the fact that I blew it with him. It's over, and I'm definitely going to spend the rest of my life regretting it.

If that isn't enough, the things I said to Harper swirl around my brain. I didn't mean any of that stuff about her having a nanny or her life being so easy, and I wish I could take it all back. But the truth is, I'm also hurting from what she said. Calling me a martyr, telling me I didn't try.

After obsessing over it for weeks on end, I realize she's not entirely wrong. Yet, she still jumped to conclusions before she had all the facts. She didn't even give me a chance to explain before she decided *I'm* the bad guy.

Each day, I wake up with a tightening in my chest, knowing I have to fix things with Harper, and I'd better do it before the wedding. The problem is, I barely have the energy to get through all the things I have to do in a day, let alone go find her so we can have an emotional conversation.

Ed's biopsy results came back as positive for cancer, so he and Edna are in Anchorage for his first round of treatment, which means I'm truly on my own without any help with the boys at the moment. This means bringing them with me to the diner before school, so I can make sure they get on the bus in time. The bus drops them back here after school.

I look over at my boys, sitting at table six, looking worn from the back-to-school grind. They're supposed to be doing homework, but instead they're trying to see who can blow the paper off their straws farther.

I decide that even though I may not be able to fix things between Ethan and me, I definitely need to try to patch up my relationship with Harper.

By the time I have the boys loaded in the car to go out to the lodge, I'm a bundle of nerves. I hope Harper is willing to listen and to forgive me.

When we pull into the parking lot, the boys take off in search of Lily and Liam while I take a minute to give myself a pep talk. Internally, I do the whole "Give me an M! Give me an O! Give me an I ..." After spelling out my whole name, I'm ready to look for Harper. I don't have to search for long, either. She's in the front office, sitting behind the desk doing some paperwork.

I knock gently on the open door, and notice that when she looks up, her face falls a little.

"Is now a good time for me to apologize?" I hurry to ask.

She stands up from her chair and walks over with her arms outstretched. "I'm sorry. I never should have said any of that," she tells me as we hug.

"Me, too," I say, choking back a sob. "I didn't mean any of that. I know how much you love your kids and that you've always been a hands-on mom."

"And I never should have said that stuff about you being a martyr. You've been through so much. Of course, it's hard for you to trust someone again," she says, rubbing my back.

We finally let go of each other. Wiping the tears from my eyes, I say, "Thank God that's over. I've really missed you."

"Same! I've wanted to call you at least a thousand times a day, but I was just so scared you wouldn't talk to me."

"You're going to be my sister-in-law, which in my book is as good as being my sister. I'll never *not* talk to you, Harper," I tell her with a smile. "Being that we're going to be family, we have to forgive each other more quickly from now on."

"Deal. And I promise to try to stay out of your business from now on," Harper says with a firm nod.

"Thank you." I pause before forcing myself to admit the truth. "But, you may not have been totally wrong about things."

A flicker of hope sparks in her eyes. "Really?"

"Yeah. I pushed Ethan away. Hard. I just got so scared …" My voice trails off and tears fill my eyes again. "I convinced myself that he didn't love me, and honestly, now, I'm not sure he ever could. Not after what I put him through."

"I think you two can still work this out. I've never seen him this upset, and I've seen him through more than one big break-up. That has to mean something."

She's giving me hope that I might mean as much to him as he means to me. "I've made such a mess of everything."

"Messes can be cleaned up," she tells me with a smile.

I chew on my bottom lip, terrified at the thought of admitting to him that I was wrong.

"What if he doesn't want to hear it? What if it's too late?"

"Then you'll know. It's better than spending the rest of your life asking yourself 'what if?'"

That night, after I get the boys to bed, I dial Ethan's number. My heart pounds so hard, I can hear it in my eardrums. After six long rings, the call goes to voicemail. I close my eyes while I listen to him tell me to leave a message, then I hang up quickly.

I consider texting him, but then decide against it. When I see him at the wedding rehearsal, I'll know whether he might be willing to give me another shot.

The truth will be written in his eyes.

Chapter 44

Ethan

I wake up with the sun, my gut churning and my body aching like I've just climbed a mountain. Not only is today the wedding rehearsal, it's also my last weekend in Gamble. I've decided that I can't stay here any longer.

These past few weeks trying to avoid Moira have been pure hell. I'm making no progress on my novel, I don't sleep, and I'm wracked with guilt for abandoning the boys. I ache for what might have been, and I simply can't put myself through that.

I shouldn't have assumed Moira would want my life just because it was easier. Yes, she's been stressed out about money and not having any time. She's been overwhelmed by her house, and all of her responsibilities. But I could have used my money to make her life better *here*. She didn't need to move; I could have done that just as easily. Easier, really, as it's only me.

Having said that, her having completely shut me down

without even considering a future with me means she didn't care for me as much as I did for her. As much as I do. And for that reason, I have to leave.

I'll be on the Monday morning flight back with my parents, who came back late last night, in time for the festivities. So far, my dad hasn't pried into what happened with Moira and me. Miraculously, Prisha, Sheila, and my mother have all stayed silent as well. But somehow their silence feels judgy.

Prisha and Sheila got here two days ago and have been staying at the lodge to help Harper and Digger get ready. I've bowed out of as much of the pre-wedding stuff as I can, as I'm assuming Moira would be there. If there's one thing I don't want, it's to make things uncomfortable for the happy couple. I love Harper, but after everything she's been through, I'm not about to put a damper on her joy just because I'm miserable.

Moira tried to call me the other night, but I couldn't bring myself to answer. I'm guessing she wanted to call a truce for this weekend. She has nothing to worry about from me. I'll be polite in a detached-but-friendly way like I am with my clients. I'll focus on the kids and on Digger and Harper, and then it'll be over forever. I imagine that I'll eventually come back to Gamble to visit Harper, but I won't do that until I'm completely over Moira.

Tossing on a long-sleeve T-shirt and some sweats, I make my way downstairs to start the coffee, only to find my dad already has. He smiles over at me while he pours a mug for himself. "Coffee?"

"Please," I tell him, grabbing a mug from the cupboard and holding it out so he can fill it.

Without talking, we head out to the deck, as per what has become our routine. Autumn has come, bringing with it a chill in the early morning air. The sky is clear blue and the trees surrounding the lake are putting on a show of oranges, yellows, and reds.

"Is Mom still sleeping?" I ask.

He nods. "She's never slept better in her life. Must be the fresh air."

I smile, glad that my parents seem so happy these days. "This trip has been good for you guys."

"I agree. It's really put a spark back into our marriage," he says, having a sip of coffee. "Sometimes in life you have to shake things up and remind yourself that you're still alive."

"Makes sense," I tell him, wondering if he's subtly trying to tell me I need to shake things up, too. If he only knew …

Kicking his feet up so they're resting on the wooden support beam, he says, "I'm surprised you're coming back to LA before you finish your book."

"I need to face reality."

"Is that what you call it? It seems to me that you might be running from something."

Pausing with my mug up to my lips, I ask, "What's that supposed to mean?"

"It means maybe things got a little too real for you here and you can't handle it." He must see the anger written on my face because he adds, "I spoke with Harper last night."

"Oh, yeah? And I suppose she's blaming me for what happened?"

"She was very neutral in her comments. In fact, she barely said anything. She just said that things didn't work out between you and Moira. She's still hoping one of you will pull your head out of your ass and fix it."

"Well, I'm not the one who needs to do that," I tell him. "The truth is, when things got too real, Moira's the one who cut and ran. Not me." I brush off the memory of me making a date with Bridgette in front of Moira, which was very wrong.

Dad sighs and stares out at the lake for a bit. "Falling in love is the scariest thing you can do in life. It requires the biggest leap of faith there is."

"I was ready to leap, but she wasn't. There's nothing I can do about it now."

"Moira isn't Paige, son. I hope you can see that."

Rolling my eyes, I tell him, "Look, Dad, I know what you're trying to do. You're about to tell me that you only want to see me happy and that you've never seen me light up the way I do around Moira. You'll say I'd make a wonderful father for the boys and that this may be my best shot at happiness. But you're wasting your breath—"

"—I didn't say anything."

"But you were going to. Admit it."

He makes a tsking sound. "Not in those exact words, but … yeah, the sentiment was there."

"You're preaching to the choir, Dad. Moira's the one who turned me down. Not the other way around."

"And there's nothing you can do to change her mind?"

"Nope."

"Even if she's had second thoughts, and she's too scared to tell you?"

I think about the fact that she called, and I didn't pick up, but I'm not going to get into that with my dad. "The ball's in her court."

Dad sips his coffee again. "Well, in that case, I suppose it's best not to try again. You don't want to get your feelings hurt. Even if you'd regret it for the rest of your life."

Frustration bubbles up in my chest. "So as far as you're concerned, I'm a quitter? Again, Dad, you're talking to the wrong person. Moira's the one who quit, so I'm not about to get down on my knees and beg for forgiveness. I didn't do anything wrong."

"Good for you, son," he says, standing up and patting me on the shoulder. "At least you'll have your pride."

He slides the patio door open and steps inside. Just as he closes it, he adds, "That ought to keep you warm for the rest of your life."

Chapter 45

Moira

I wake up the morning of the rehearsal with my emotions all over the place. They stay on that roller coaster for my entire shift at the diner. I'm thrilled to have the opportunity to stand up with my brother as he pledges his life to the woman he loves, but I'm also filled with fear.

What if there's no way to fix things with Ethan? But come hell or high water, today I'm going to find out. By the time I crawl back into bed tonight, I'll know if there's still a chance for us, or not.

Getting in my truck to head home, I grab my phone and check my texts. There's nothing from Ethan. He would have seen that I called four days ago, and I was praying he'd decide to reach out.

The only text on my phone is from Digger.

Digger: *Hey, Sis, tomorrow's the day!*

Me: *It's going to be beautiful. I'm very happy for you.*

Digger: *Thank you. I just wanted to see if you're okay.*

Me: *Why wouldn't I be?*

Digger: *I know things didn't turn out the way you had hoped between you and Ethan. I don't want the rehearsal to be too hard for you.*

Me: *Don't wo*
rry about me. This weekend is all about you and Harper.

Digger: *If you need a shoulder to cry on after the ceremony, I'm all yours. See you at six.*

Lily and Liam are going to stand up for Digger and Harper, along with Ethan and me. Which means I'll have a lot of time near him in a very romantic setting. I can only pray that some of that optimism and happiness will flow through the two of us, if not this evening, tomorrow.

The school bus meets me just as I pull up in front of our house. After a quick hello hug for each of the boys, I remind them of our plans for the evening. "You can play for an hour while I make supper, but then we're going to have to eat quickly, shower and get dressed for the rehearsal, okay?"

They race off to play, giving me some quiet so I can think. I make quick work of throwing together a tuna casserole and some salad. After it's in the oven, I hurry upstairs to shower. Twenty minutes later, I'm dressed in a violet floral print dress that I bought at Target a couple of years ago. It's not stunning like the red dress Ethan bought me (which I'm saving for tomorrow), but I look all right in it. I stare at myself in the mirror and realize that I look more than all right. I look great.

One of the conclusions I've come to since Harper unloaded on me is that I really do have an inferiority complex. Somehow, over the years, I've decided that everybody leaves me because I'm not good enough. I've recently concluded that their fates had nothing to do with me. Accepting that as truth has opened me up to thinking that maybe I deserve more in life than I'd previously let myself believe.

This realization has allowed me to hope that things don't have to be over between me and Ethan. I know he flirted with that supermodel at the baseball game, but in hindsight, it's very possible he was doing that to get even with me for rejecting him. If that's so, I can't really blame him. I was awful to him the night before.

I hurry to plate up the food and call the kids to the table. We eat quickly and then I order them off to shower while I go back up to my bathroom to do my hair and makeup. When all is said and done, I feel like a queen. "You got this Moira. Go get your man."

"Come on, crew!" I call to the boys from the top of the stairs. "We need to get going."

As I walk down the stairs, my eyes settle on my living room, and I look at it through new eyes. This house is only my home because the people I love live here. At the beginning of the summer, I was ready to sell and move somewhere newer with less to take care of.

If I'm honest with myself, that place *could* be Ethan's house in California. A weird rush of energy jolts through me. Once again, Harper is right. I love Ethan, and if that means living in California, then why the heck wouldn't I do it? The kids already think it's the best place on Earth.

Once we arrive at the church, the boys run inside like

their pant legs are on fire. They're beyond excited to be part of their uncle's wedding.

Instead of following behind them, I sit in the car and think. I'm so nervous to see Ethan again, my stomach feels like it's become home to a swarm of butterflies.

How do I go about telling him that I've changed my mind about us? How do I apologize for all the horrible things I've said? And finally, what if he doesn't want me back?

I don't know how long I sit there, but I don't pop out of my trance until I hear a sharp knock on the window. It's Digger.

"Earth to Moira, come in, Moira. It's time to get inside."

I hurry to open the door and let him help me out. "Hey, groom," I tease. "Bet you never thought this day would happen."

"You know I didn't." He offers me his arm. "But life has a way of opening doors when you let it." He opens the church door with a flair to emphasize his point.

"I'm beginning to see that," I tell him.

Digger excuses himself so he can go talk to the preacher, leaving me standing alone at the back of the church. I inhale deeply in hopes of building my fortitude to face what's about to come. The door opens behind me, and when I turn, my gaze lands directly on Ethan. He stops in his tracks and looks at me and I see a world of pain in his eyes.

I offer a silent prayer. "Please, Gran, Dad, Mom, Everett, anyone who's ever loved me up there, please don't let Ethan walk out of my life …"

I don't have a chance to talk to him because Harper walks up the stairs leading from the basement and spots us.

"Hey, you." She hurries toward me and takes my hand in hers. "How are you doing?"

"Who cares how I'm doing? How are *you*?"

She inhales deeply before releasing it. "I'm better than I've ever been in my whole life." She reaches her other hand out to Ethan, who reluctantly allows himself to be drawn into our little circle. "If brides got to make a wish, mine would be that you two find the same happiness that I have with Digger."

Ethan clears his throat and instead of looking at me, he glances down at his feet. "Thanks, Harper, but I think we need to focus on the matter at hand."

Digger and the preacher appear in the vestibule. "Everyone ready?"

Harper nods. "Let's do this."

The preacher has a quick chat with my boys about how to properly serve as ushers, then he has them go up to sit in one of the pews near the front. He directs Digger and Ethan to the front of the church and tells Lily, Liam, Harper, and me to wait here until the music starts. The entire time, I feel like I'm holding back a wall of emotion that's ready to burst.

When the first strains of "Trumpet Voluntary" begin to play, Harper gestures for her kids to start walking up the aisle. Liam takes his sister's hand, and they start their slow march.

When we reach the altar, I stand behind Lily and Ethan goes to stand behind Liam and Digger. I look at Ethan and am surprised to see that he's not looking at the bride. He's watching me. Chills of something—Hope? Excitement? Dread?—run up my arms to the base of my neck as I stare back at him. It's impossible to read his expression.

I don't break our staring contest until the minister says,

"At this point I'll welcome everyone and talk a little about love and how sometimes in life you can't see the forest for the trees, and how often we're too busy seeing all the obstacles in our path to get a whole picture of what loving someone is all about."

He smiles at the happy couple. "You two met at a time when you both felt you had enough on your respective plates and thought you couldn't handle anything more. I think it's important for your friends and family to hear how love managed to reprioritize your lives for the better because you never know if there might be someone in the congregation who needs to hear that love really can conquer all."

I chance a look at Ethan again. He's still watching me. His eyes bore into me like he can see right through me. The truth of the minister's words, coupled with Ethan's intense gaze, is almost my undoing. All I had to do was let Ethan in. Instead, I found every reason under the sun to close the door on him. Tears start to pool in my eyes.

"Then we'll move on to you two reading the vows you wrote," the minister says. "Go ahead and practice them now, unless you want to surprise each other tomorrow."

"I'd like to practice," Harper says.

"Same here," Digger agrees.

My brother and his soon-to-be wife turn to each other and hold hands. Harper is the first to speak. "Digger, when I met you, I wasn't looking for love. My life was so chaotic and full, I honestly never expected to find love again. I'm not even sure I wanted it."

Girl, I feel ya, I think, but obviously don't say.

She continues, "Even though you didn't need any drama in your life, you were still so supportive, helpful, and great with my kids. I didn't so much as open the door to you, as you crawled under it, completely evading all the walls I'd put up."

Dear God, Harper knows exactly how I feel.

She pauses for a moment to compose herself. "Digger McKenzie, you are everything I could have ever hoped for in a husband. You're kind, patient, passionate, and you've welcomed me and my children into your life with open arms. That kind of acceptance—that kind of love—is a gift. I'm not sure I deserve it, but I happily accept it."

A choking cry escapes my mouth and everyone, including Harper and Digger, turns to look at me. I quickly wave them back to the matter at hand, but I don't as easily contain my emotions.

Harper promises, "I vow to honor you, cherish you, protect you, love you, and accept you, not only until the end of my life, but until the end of time."

Loud, gut-wrenching sobs explode out of me like a live canon. I manage to stop them long enough to say, "Please pretend I'm not here. I'm fine."

Digger raises his eyebrow. "It's a little hard with those choking sounds. You gonna be okay, Moira?"

Common courtesy requires that I say yes, and that I pull myself together instead of hijacking their rehearsal. But of course, that's not what I do. "NO!" I shout. *Shout.* "I'm not okay. I've totally screwed up everything and I don't know how to fix it."

The pastor looks at me with wide eyes. "Do you suppose we can help you work things out *after* we're finished with the rehearsal?"

"I'm sorry, but I think I have to deal with this now." I take a deep breath, then say, "I'm so sorry about this. I know I'm behaving horribly, but there's something I have to say."

Instead of continuing to talk to them, I walk over to

Ethan and stand in front of him. When I look up at him, I see complete shock at the spectacle that I've drawn him into.

"Ethan," I practically choke on his name. "I have been so unfair to you. All you've done since you've come into my life is to make my world better. You selflessly do things for me and the boys. You've freely offered your help, your time, your worldly possessions. You make me feel important and you make me laugh. And in return, I was awful to you. I know you made that date with that model right in front of me, and there's a chance that you actually do want to go out with her and that you're totally done with me. I get that. But I'm hinging everything on the hope that you only did that because you were hurt about how I acted when you tried to tell me you loved me."

Without letting him say anything, I continue, terrified that if I stop talking, he'll turn me down. "Ethan, I love you. I. LOVE. YOU." *That bore repeating.* "I don't care where I live so long as I'm with you. And I know this isn't the right place or time, but I have to know if maybe you might still love me too."

A dead silence fills the church. Swallowing hard, the only sound I hear is the pounding of my heartbeat in my ears. My knees feel weak, as I wait for Ethan to say something. Anything. Yes. No. Anything would be better than this horrible silence.

I stare into Ethan's eyes and watch as his look of shock is replaced by a giant smile. My heart soars as he says, "Wow, when you make up your mind, you really make up your mind."

I chuckle through my tears, my heart still thumping.

"First off, I never should have flirted with Bridgette like that. I'm sorry, and you were right, I only did it because I was upset." Rubbing his hand across the back of his neck, he says, "As stupid as it sounds, I was hoping it would make you jealous, and that if you felt jealous, you'd maybe realize you had feelings for me too. I promise I'll never do anything like that again."

"You never have to," I tell him. "Because now you know how much I love you, and I'll spend the rest of my days proving that love to you."

"You're everything to me, Moira. I've never felt so alive or had such a sense of purpose as I have since I met you and the boys. These last weeks, knowing I was going to miss out on a lifetime with you, have gutted me. I want to be with you forever. And if it means living here in Alaska, or California, or the moon for all I care, the answer is yes. Yes, I still love you. Yes, I want to be with you and the boys more than anything in this world."

He lowers his head and plants the mother of all kisses on me. It's not just a kiss, it's a promise for a life together. It's everything I've wanted for so long but was too afraid to hope for. It's all the beauty and truth and hope I put into my vision board come to life. It's the start of a new and perfect chapter in our lives. Shouts of excitement erupt from the small group as my boys rush the altar to wrap us in a football huddle of love.

Several minutes pass before the minister asks, "Are you planning on getting married right now or might we see to Harper and Digger first?"

I face the bride and groom. "I'm so sorry, I don't know what came over me."

Harper takes my hand in hers. "I do. You're in love and you couldn't suppress it for another minute."

Digger wraps his arm around my shoulder. "Your heart was in the right place. Your timing was a little off …"

"Better now than tomorrow, though," I tell him.

"Can we wrap this up?" the pastor asks. "I haven't had supper yet and I'm getting a little hangry."

"Of course," Ethan tells him, pulling me to his side.

"Sorry," I add.

I don't go back to Harper's side. Instead, I stand right next to Ethan for the rest of the rehearsal, gripping him like I'm afraid he's a figment of my imagination and is going to slip away.

And while I'm slightly mortified by my behavior, more than anything, I'm thrilled to have fully opened the door to love. My life is changing in ways that I never saw coming and I can't wait to see what comes next.

Chapter 46

Ethan-One Year Later

One Year Later

"Wyatt, don't forget your lunch!" I call as he yanks open the front door.

He spins on his heel and tippy toes toward me, his muddy runners leaving tracks on the hardwood.

We both glance at Moira, who is too busy shopping online for pink baby clothes to notice. "I'll come to you," I tell him.

Without looking up, she says, "I'm not cleaning that up, mister man. When you get home, you've got a job to do."

"How does she do that?" I whisper to Wyatt, handing him the lunch kit.

"Magic," he says, before sprinting out the door.

I watch from the front deck as he runs to the end of

our driveway, where Ash and Colton are already waiting for the bus. He makes it just in time. I wave to Mrs. Upton, the driver, and she hollers out the open door to me, "How's Moira feeling?"

"Grouchy!" I call, then say, "Just kidding. She's wonderful, as always."

Mrs. Upton laughs until she wheezes, then pulls the door shut and they're off for the day. I take a moment to enjoy the view of the lake from our new home and revel in my wonderful life.

Moira and I got married exactly one month after Harper and Digger. Once we made up our minds to spend the rest of our lives together, we couldn't wait. Ours was a tiny civil ceremony at town hall with only our closest friends and family. Moira felt that she already had one big over the top wedding, and what she really wanted was an intimate gathering.

After I moved in (having successfully completed my rental move-out inspection—no sheets were stolen), we decided a fresh start was in order, meaning a move rather than a long, drawn-out renovation.

This place came up on the market the same day we found out we were expecting, and Moira took it as a sign that this was the house for us. I suppose it didn't hurt that it's a seven-bedroom walk-out cabin with incredible views, a hot tub, and a huge kitchen.

We kept the house in LA and go back there on school holidays so we can see my parents and do all the fun California stuff. It's more than enough to satisfy my craving for good sushi, surfing, and sun.

My first book sold, and I'm already hard at work on the second one. I don't write at the diner anymore. Instead, I've turned one of the bedrooms into an office.

Moira hired Abigail to manage the restaurant, and she

hired two new servers, so she doesn't have to work all day every day. She pops in to do the books and check on things, but there's no pressure anymore.

Inhaling the fresh pine-scented air, I turn and pull the door open and go inside to find my wife. She's sitting on a chair in the kitchen with her feet propped up on another one. "Forty dollars for a onesie? I don't think so," she mumbles at the computer.

I walk over and drop a kiss on her forehead, then place my hand on her growing belly. "You know we can afford clothes, right?"

"Yeah, but that doesn't mean I'm going to open my wallet and let someone rob us blind," she answers, placing her hand on mine.

"You happy?" I ask her.

"So happy. You?"

"I had no idea this kind of joy was possible," I tell her honestly.

Just then, I feel a thump coming from inside her belly. A thrill shoots through me. "Was that?"

"Her first kick," Moira says, tearing up. "And you got to feel it, too."

Feeling myself get a little choked up, I whisper, "There's a real little human in there."

"Isn't it incredible?"

Nodding, I clear my throat, then crouch so I'm closer to the baby. "Hey you, get used to this voice because I'm your dad. I'm going to read you lots of stories and sing off-key to you and teach you how to surf and swim and catch fish."

The baby kicks again and Moira grins up at me. "I think she likes you already."

"The feeling's mutual."

Standing, I give Moira a kiss on the lips. "I'd better get to work if you're shopping for high-end baby clothes."

Laughing, Moira says, "Yes. Those books don't write themselves. Good luck with the commute!"

"Let's hope they cleared that collision on the I-10," I tell her, walking over to the counter to top up my coffee.

"But seriously, Gamble is so much better than Los Angeles, isn't it?" Moira asks.

"It is. For so many reasons. The most important of which is because this is where I found you and the boys."

"I love you, Mr. Caplan. Have a great morning."

"Love you, too, Mrs. Caplan. See you at lunch."

And just like that, we're going to have yet another perfect day...

Coming Soon: Hate, Rinse, Repeat
A GAMBLE ON LOVE MOM-COM, BOOK 3

Christmas is a time for hate...

Maisy Moore is not looking forward to the holiday season. As owner of the only hair salon in Gamble, Alaska, she'll be run off her feet helping her clients get dolled up for Christmas and New Years Eve parties. Parties she'll never be invited to.

But that's not the worst of it. As a single mom, she knows she still won't be able to give her seven-year-old son, Jack, the kind of magical Christmas his classmates get. Telling him how much she loves him will only get a kid that age so far. If only she could give him what he really wants—to know who his dad is.

The last thing Maisy needs is for NHL star Chase Evans to come waltzing back into town like he's God's gift to women. But that's exactly what Chase does.

After a taking a crosscheck from behind, Chase's season is over. Instead of scoring goals, he's recovering from shoulder surgery, and according to his mother, there's no better place to recover than home. Because let's face it, basking in the glow of local adoration won't be too bad. There are no fans quite like hometown fans.

The last thing Chase expects is to find Maisy Moore still single. He decides to see if maybe they could rekindle their brief romance that occurred the night of their ten-year high school reunion. But when he tries to talk to her, he discovers Maisy's feelings of lust have turned to loathing. And he's determined to find out why.

Will Maisy manage to keep the identity of her son a secret? Will there be a holiday miracle that will reunite two hard-headed lovers? Will the BOGO special on shampoo and conditioner be a hit?

Find out in the deliciously funny and ridiculously romantic final installment of the Love is a Gamble Mom-Com Series.

Pre-order Hate, Rinse, Repeat today!

About the Authors

WHITNEY DINEEN

USA Today Bestseller Whitney Dineen is a rock star in her own head. While delusional about her singing abilities, there's been a plethora of validation that she's a fairly decent author (AMAZING!!!). After winning many writing awards and selling nearly a kabillion books (math may not be her forte, either), she's decided to let the voices in her head say whatever they want (sorry, Mom). She also won a fourth-place ribbon in a fifth-grade swim meet in backstroke. So, there's that.

Whitney loves to play with her kids (a.k.a. dazzle them with her amazing flossing abilities), bake stuff, eat stuff, and write books for people who "get" her. She thinks french fries are the perfect food and Mrs. Roper is her spirit animal.

MELANIE SUMMERS

Melanie Summers lives on Vancouver Island in Canada with her husband, three kiddos, and two cuddly dogs. When she's not writing, she loves reading (obviously), snuggling up on the couch with her family for movie night (which would not be complete without lots of popcorn and milkshakes), and long walks on the beach near her house.

Melanie also loves shutting down restaurants with her girl-friends. Well, not literally shutting them down, like calling the health inspector or something. More like just staying until they turn the lights off.